# CASSANDRA VEGA
# Her Nightshade

*Copyright © 2025 by Cassandra Vega*

*All rights reserved. No part of this publication may be reproduced, stored or transmitted in any form or by any means, electronic, mechanical, photocopying, recording, scanning, or otherwise without written permission from the publisher. It is illegal to copy this book, post it to a website, or distribute it by any other means without permission.*

*This novel is entirely a work of fiction. The names, characters and incidents portrayed in it are the work of the author's imagination. Any resemblance to actual persons, living or dead, events or localities is entirely coincidental.*

*First edition*

*Cover art by Turning Pages Designs*

*This book was professionally typeset on Reedsy. Find out more at reedsy.com*

# Contents

| | | |
|---|---|---|
| *Please Note:* | | v |
| *Translations* | | vi |
| 1 | Ana | 1 |
| 2 | Charlie | 8 |
| 3 | Ana | 13 |
| 4 | Charlie | 22 |
| 5 | Ana | 28 |
| 6 | Charlie | 35 |
| 7 | Ana | 43 |
| 8 | Charlie | 52 |
| 9 | Ana | 59 |
| 10 | Charlie | 69 |
| 11 | Ana | 78 |
| 12 | Charlie | 90 |
| 13 | Ana | 97 |
| 14 | Charlie | 108 |
| 15 | Ana | 120 |
| 16 | Charlie | 132 |
| 17 | Ana | 140 |
| 18 | Charlie | 150 |
| 19 | Ana | 158 |
| 20 | Charlie | 172 |
| 21 | Ana | 180 |
| 22 | Charlie | 192 |

| | | |
|---|---|---|
| 23 | Ana | 210 |
| 24 | Charlie | 221 |
| 25 | Ana | 230 |
| 26 | Charlie | 242 |
| 27 | Ana | 253 |
| 28 | Charlie | 266 |
| 29 | Ana | 275 |
| 30 | Charlie | 287 |
| 31 | Epilogue | 291 |
| *Acknowledgments* | | 294 |
| *About the Author* | | 295 |

# Please Note:

This is a dark romance and contains heavy and sexually explicit topics. Please take a look at the list of trigger and content warnings on my website <u>authorcassandravega.com/ pages/trigger-warnings</u>.

**This book is not a manual for BDSM or any other sexual acts. Please do your own research and play responsibly.**

# Translations

- *diabla* — devil
- *un pedazo de mierda* — piece of shit
- *por favor* — please
- *Hola, pequeña. ¿Qué estás haciendo?* — Hi, sweetheart. What's going on?
- *sneaky cabrón* — sneaky bastard
- *Buenas noches, mama* — goodnight, mom
- *Dios mio* — oh my god
- *Mi diosa* — my goddess
- *Mierda* — shit
- *Hola, mija. ¿Que pasa?* — Hi, sweetie. What's up?
- *Te amo* — I love you
- *¿Qué estás haciendo* — What are you doing?
- *domesticado* — domesticated
- *De nada, mi diosa* — You're welcome, my goddess.
- *¿Hablas español?* — You speak Spanish?
- *Él era jodida perfección* — He was fucking perfection.
- *Mi vida/amor* — my love
- *Gracias, pequeña. Te amo* — thank you, sweetheart. I love you.
- *También te amo* — I love you too.
- *Entrégate a mí* — Give yourself to me.
- *mi buen chico* — my good boy

- *mi niña* — my little/sweet girl
- *¿Qué coño?* — what the fuck?
- *Fue asombroso. Mejor de lo que podría haber imaginado.* — It was amazing. Better than I could have imagined.
- *¿Perdón?* — Excuse me?
- *Lárgate!* — Go away!
- *¿Entiendes?* — Do you understand?
- *Es cierto* — that's right
- *¿Estás bien?* — Are you okay?
- *¿Qué tienes, estás bien?* — what's wrong, are you okay?
- *¡Hijo de puta!* — Son of a bitch!
- *Ay, mi amor, pobrecita* — oh, my love, poor thing

"It seems to me, that love could be labeled poison and we'd drink it anyways."

— Atticus

# 1

# Ana

I woke up in a cold sweat in my New York City apartment. Memories came flooding back, just as they always did in my dreams. We used to live in New York before Jake was elected president. Back when we were a happy little family. And then he ruined it all.

I had to stop dwelling on the affair—it had nearly broken me. Sleeping with that *diabla* Sarah, risking not just our family but Sloane's life in the process. She had manipulated him so thoroughly, and he'd been too fucking blind to see it. If Callan hadn't pieced it all together and exposed Leo's involvement, who knows what might have happened? Now Leo was rotting in jail, just like Sarah—exactly where they both deserved to be.

I spent nearly six months in Madrid with my mother, trying to escape the memories and the relentless media frenzy. I got dragged through the mud right alongside Jake, despite not having done a thing. As if being a better wife, some more subservient, compliant woman, would have prevented it. What a load of sexist bullshit. Blaming the victim, especially a woman, didn't surprise me. Society hadn't learned a thing, always taking one step forward and two steps back.

I had to pull myself out of the spiral, one I constantly found myself in. Instead of screaming my rage to the world and getting branded the angry feminist, I kept my mouth shut. I didn't speak ill of Jake to the public; I was taking the high road. Words always got twisted so I didn't bother. But behind closed doors, he was nothing more than *un pedazo de mierda*.

*Okay, I'm spiraling again. I need a breath of fresh air.*

I grabbed my bathrobe and draped it over my shoulders as I stepped out onto the terrace, watching the sunrise over Manhattan. I had been looking for a place in Brooklyn, but then ended up finding the most charming apartment in Greenwich Village, complete with a spare bedroom for when Sloane and Callan visited.

Sloane. I missed my daughter. We were so close, and living across the country from her was difficult. I made sure she was settled in Los Angeles for school, but I never really worried about her. She was such a strong, independent young woman, and Callan was a wonderful addition to her life. She promised to visit during school breaks, and I promised not to bug her too much, even though I was already planning multiple trips out there within the next few months.

But as much as I missed Sloane, I was enjoying my solitude. I hadn't lived alone in twenty years, and there was a sense of freedom in doing whatever I wanted, whenever I wanted. Especially not having to endure the scrutiny that came with being the First Lady.

Once people got word I was living in the city, I started getting invited to events, premieres, appearances; I even got invited to a fashion gala that very night. I wasn't sure if I'd go, but it was nice knowing the option was there if I wanted to.

And even though I was a *former* First Lady, I still needed some sort of protection. Miles, my trusty bodyguard for the past six months, was a man of few words. When he did speak, he was funny as hell. He towered over me at 6'4", with dark blonde hair and the face of a male model. He was referred to me by Callan, and he'd been by my side ever since the scandal broke. Miles had traveled with me all the way to Spain and back to New York, where he now lived in the apartment directly below mine. So even though I was living alone, I wasn't *really* alone, and I found some comfort in that fact.

My apartment was spacious and filled with natural light streaming through the living room and bedrooms. The decor was a mixture of vintage and modern elements, with minimalist furniture alongside mid-century pieces. Artwork from local BIPOC artists brought vibrant pops of color to the walls. It was a space that reflected me, where my personality flowed through every room.

After Sloane moved to Los Angeles, I became the caretaker of her houseplants, making me a new plant mom. They were now my only responsibility, aside from myself, and I was enjoying my new little hobby.

As I watered my Monstera Deliciosa, a knock at the door startled me. It could only be one person; no one else had the code to access my floor.

"Miles," I greeted him, opening the door to find him standing there with a hanger draped in fabric, the word 'Versace' labeled across the front.

"This came for you. A gift from Brad. He said it's for tonight," Miles stated, waiting for me to invite him in.

I sighed heavily. I'd mentioned the gala to my friend and

stylist, Brad, and now he was taking it upon himself to dress me. I told him I wasn't even sure if I was going, but he was persistent. *I guess now I have to.*

"Okay. Come in. You can hang it in the closet, *por favor*," I instructed, motioning towards my bedroom.

"Yes, ma'am," he replied, already heading straight there.

Even after six months of me telling him to call me Ana, Miles never strayed from "ma'am."

He returned a moment later, lingering by the front door as I went back to tending my plant.

"I think you should go, Ana. I know you said maybe. But you might have fun. It might be good for you," he said quietly before turning and leaving.

As the door shut behind him, I sat there in stunned silence. That was the most he had ever said to me in the span of one day. And he called me Ana. *Shit. Now I really have to go.*

\* \* \*

I sat in a black car, waiting in line with others to enter the gala. I was starting to get nervous; I still wasn't sure if I was ready to face the world again. As proud as I was of my strength, the last six months were hard. I was still piecing myself back together, and now I was being thrust into the spotlight again. *Why did I let anyone talk me into this? Am I ready?* I hated feeling so unsure of myself.

Thirty minutes later, there I was, sitting at a table full of celebrities, a glass of champagne in hand. Oscar winners, pop stars, rock stars—they were all around me, offering kind words and small talk, but I could see the pity in their eyes. It was overwhelming, and I was more than ready to leave.

## ANA

Miles stood by the wall, his gaze scanning the room before landing on me. We locked eyes and I gave him a small nod, signaling that I was almost ready to go.

Then someone sat down next to me. I recognized him instantly: Charlie Ashford. He started out in a British boy band and later branched out on his own. He must've been in his late twenties now, insanely handsome, with brown wavy hair styled deliberately messy, and eyes the color of emeralds. He was cool—*too* cool—and I had no idea what to say when he smiled at me, his sharp jawline momentarily distracting me.

"Ana Martin, wow," he said with a shy chuckle.

"Del Rosario now," I corrected. "But please, just call me Ana."

I wanted nothing to do with Jake's last name anymore. I should have never taken it in the first place. Sloane was even thinking about taking my surname when she married Callan in the springtime, but I encouraged her to do whatever felt right. I didn't want her to feel like she was giving up her identity by changing her last name.

Charlie raised his eyebrows with a surprised grin. "Sorry, Ana." His British accent was charming, and I felt embarrassingly typical for swooning at it.

I laughed nervously, shaking my head. Why was I so flustered around this attractive, younger man? My cheeks burned with embarrassment as we made eye contact, perhaps for a little too long. It was so unlike me to feel this way, and it left me wildly confused.

"I'm Charlie. Charlie Ashford," he said, extending his hand.

"I know," I replied with a polite laugh. "I think the whole world knows who you are."

He chuckled softly and bit his lower lip. My heart fluttered. *He's too young for you, Ana.*

"I think you're much more famous," he quipped, then his eyes widened a little. "Because, you know…you're the former First Lady."

Of course. Was that all I'd be known for now? At least no one ever mentioned the affair, and for that, I was grateful.

"I suppose so." I shrugged, unsure of what to talk about with him. What could we possibly have in common? He was a British rock star, and I was a former First Lady who was almost forty-one.

"So, um…" He leaned closer to talk over the music. "Do you live in New York, or are you just in town for the gala?"

*He's trying to make small talk. That's sweet.*

"I live here now," I said. "Only a few blocks away."

*Does he need to know that?*

His eyebrows shot up again with surprise, making him look even more charming. "Me too."

My heart raced. *Cut this out, Ana. You need to get out of here.*

"Hmm." I nodded, trying to get out of my head. My eyes scanned the table. I felt too uneasy under his gaze. It wasn't unwanted, but the way he made me feel was throwing me off balance.

"Can I get you another drink?" he asked, his eyes still fixed on me.

I glanced down at my half-empty champagne flute. "No, thank you. I was just about to leave," I said, sitting up straighter.

"Oh, well, hey neighbor," he said lightly. "Do you want to…I don't know, meet up for coffee? Or a drink?" He placed his arm on the table as if he was thinking of reaching out.

I glanced at the tattoo peeking out from under his shirt cuff. "Are you trying to ask me out?" I asked bluntly. If he was, I needed to shut it down quickly.

He chuckled nervously, looking down before locking eyes with me again. "Yeah. What do you say?"

I let out a surprised laugh. "Charlie, I'm at least ten years older than you."

His smile didn't fade as he shrugged. "I don't care. Do you?"

Why *did* I care? I had been so accepting of Sloane and Callan's relationship, and they were twenty years apart. So what was ten?

*I shouldn't do this. I should say no.* But what was the harm in one drink? *Maybe I could use a little fun. But perhaps I should make him work for it, if he really wants it.*

"Alright," I said, challenging him. "How about this: Figure out how to contact me, and I'll go for a drink with you."

His smile widened, his eyes lighting up with mischief.

"Challenge accepted. I'll see you soon for that drink, then."

## 2

# Charlie

I couldn't believe it—Ana Martin. Holy fucking shit. I knew she was beautiful, but seeing her up close was something else entirely. Her brown, shoulder-length hair was tucked behind one ear as she eyed a champagne flute on the table in front of her. The gold gown she wore plunged deeply, teasing just enough of her cleavage to make my heart race. Dark red lipstick painted her lips, and I instantly fell in love. I always fell in love too fast and for all the wrong reasons. I barely knew anything about her, other than the fact she was the former First Lady married to that arsehole we had to call president. The scandal was huge, and I couldn't help but feel for her. *I bet I could help her forget all about it.*

As she straightened her shoulders and scanned the room, her eyes locked with mine, and she looked surprised.

"Ana Martin, wow," I said with a chuckle, awe-struck and unsure of what else to say.

"Del Rosario now," she corrected me, a slight smile on her lips. "But please, just call me Ana."

*Ana.* The way her full lips said her name, paired with that little Spanish accent, made flutters swirl in my chest.

"Sorry, *Ana*," I apologized. "I'm Charlie. Charlie Ashford." *Jesus Christ, I've never been so speechless before.*

She laughed softly, highlighting her high cheekbones. "I know. I think the whole world knows who you are."

I couldn't stop staring. Her big, hazel eyes seemed to pierce right through me, and for a moment, I nearly forgot what she said as my heart pounded uncontrollably.

"I think you're much more famous," I responded. *Fuck, did I just say the wrong thing?* "Because, you know…you're a former First Lady," I added nervously. *Fuck, that's not all she is, you wanker.*

She shrugged, seeming a little offended. *Shit.* "I suppose so," she said, now looking away from me and at the table.

I needed to reel her back in. I needed to keep her talking. "So, um…" I leaned closer, hoping I wasn't invading her space, but the venue was so loud. "Do you live in New York, or are you just in town for the gala?"

"I live here now," she said. "Only a few blocks away."

*Fuck yes, she's close to me.* "Me too," I blurted out, unable to hold back my enthusiasm, sounding like an eager little puppy.

Her eyes widened just a little, but she only nodded, responding with a quiet, "Hmm." I was bothering her, I could feel it. But I couldn't tear my gaze away, and for the life of me, I couldn't stop talking.

"Can I get you another drink?"

She glanced down at her half-full champagne flute. "No, thank you. I was just about to leave," she replied, looking like she was ready to stand.

I panicked. If she was leaving, I had to see her again. "Oh, well, hey, neighbor…would you want to—" I stumbled, feeling the pressure. "I don't know, maybe meet up for coffee? Or a drink?"

I leaned my elbow on the table, feeling my heartbeat through my ears. All I could think about was how much I wanted to feel the softness of her tan skin.

Her eyebrows furrowed as she glanced down at my hand on the table, resting close to her arm. "Are you trying to ask me out?" she asked, an amused expression on her face as her gaze shifted back to mine.

I let out a nervous laugh, glancing down at the table, feeling a bit embarrassed. She was blunt, but I liked that. When I looked back up, her eyes were still playfully locked on mine, and my heart pounded like a jackhammer. "Yeah. What do you say?"

She immediately laughed, and I found myself joining in, unsure if she was laughing *at* me or *with* me. I didn't care—I just wanted her attention.

"Charlie, I'm at least ten years older than you," she said with a smirk.

I shrugged. I loved older women—they knew what they wanted, and I was more than happy to give it to them. "I don't care. Do you?"

Her eyes lingered on mine, the internal struggle clear on her face.

"Alright," she finally said, leaning in just a little. "How about this: Figure out how to contact me, and I'll go for a drink with you."

It felt like I'd just won the lottery. If she wanted to play this game, I was more than ready, and I was confident I'd win.

"Challenge accepted. I'll see you soon for that drink, then," I said with a grin.

# CHARLIE

She flashed me another one of her breathtaking smiles before standing, grabbing her purse, and walking away. I couldn't help but stare at her round ass, completely in awe—not just of her beauty, but the way she carried herself. There was something about her that left me wanting more...*needing* more.

I watched as she left the room without looking back. She had to know I was staring. *Fuck, I'm already in love.*

Without wasting a second, I pulled out my phone and called my assistant. He answered immediately.

"Reese. I need you to find out how to contact Ana Martin, or Ana Del Rosario. The former First Lady," I said as I stood and made my way towards the bar.

"Uhhh," he began, clearly puzzled. "Any particular reason why?" he asked curiously.

Reese was one of my best friends, so he never hesitated to question me, and I didn't mind.

"I just met her at the gala. Holy fuck, Reese. She's even more stunning in person. She told me if I could figure out how to contact her, she'd let me buy her a drink," I explained in one quick breath.

He laughed on the other end. "You know she's way out of your league, Charlie. She's fucking classy. *Too* classy for you," he teased.

I smiled as I ordered a whiskey, turning around to scan the room while I waited, still hoping she might come back and change her mind.

"Yeah, I know. That just makes me want her even more," I said.

"You poor fucker. Alright, I'll get her contact information," Reese replied with a laugh. "Hey, isn't her daughter dating

Callan Holt?"

*Oh, shit. Yes. Fuck yes.* Callan moved to the west coast and started helping with security whenever I had press or appearances out there.

"I'm calling him now," I said, then quickly hung up.

The night was still young, and with my luck, I'd be having that drink with her by tonight.

I scrolled through my contacts and dialed Callan.

# 3

# Ana

I couldn't shake the thought of Charlie the entire way home. Even as I slipped out of my Versace dress and into a pair of comfortable pajamas, the image of his green eyes locked on mine lingered, searing itself into my mind.

Then my phone started vibrating on the dresser. It had to be either my mother, Sloane, or one of the few friends I still had. But when I glanced at the screen, a local number I didn't recognize flashed. I stared at it, letting it buzz again and again. *I'm not answering for a stranger.* It went to voicemail and I grabbed it, heading to the living room to find something to binge-watch for the night.

Before I could even turn on the TV, the phone buzzed again—this time, a text. My stomach dropped the second I read it.

**Found you. Someone owes me a drink. My place or yours?**

*How did he get my number so fast?* I should've known—famous people always got what they wanted. And it wasn't lost on me that I was one of them.

Before I could even think about replying, the phone buzzed again. This time, it was Sloane calling.

*"Hola, pequeña. ¿Qué estás haciendo?"* I answered with a smile.

"So," she began without a greeting. "Guess who just called Callan, asking for your number?"

I rolled my eyes. That sneaky *cabrón*.

"Let me guess: Charlie Ashford?" I replied lightly.

She immediately laughed. "Mom. What did you do to him?"

I scoffed playfully. "I did nothing! He threw himself at me. He can't be much older than you. It was ridiculous," I said, laughing along.

"He's twenty-eight, Mom. Only twelve years younger than you. Totally in the appropriate age range to date," she said bluntly.

I tsked. "Says the girl who's engaged to a man twenty years older than her," I teased.

She laughed. "Don't break his heart, Mom. He's like, known for being a sensitive, hopeless romantic."

My smile faded. "I'm not doing anything with him. I'm not ready," I explained.

Sloane sighed. "I know, Mom. I'm just messing with you."

I relaxed a little. The thought of getting involved with anyone made me feel sick, but I couldn't stop thinking about Charlie. *This is not good.*

"So, is he some kind of playboy?" I asked cautiously.

She laughed, clearly having fun teasing me. "I don't know, but he's always with someone. Better scoop him up now before someone else does."

I rolled my eyes. "Alright, I'm heading to bed. I'm an old lady," I joked, trying to end the conversation. "Goodnight, baby."

## ANA

"*Buenas noches, mama,*" she said cheerfully, then hung up.

I stared at my phone, re-reading his text over and over, torn between what I should say, if I should say anything at all, and what I *really* wanted to say, which was that I wanted him deep inside of me, fucking me all night long. *No, stop it, Ana.*

**If we have a drink, I just need you to know that I'm not ready for anything serious. I'm just warning you now. Don't fall in love with me or anything.**

I hit send, and I hoped that I sounded playful like I intended.

**Too late. I'll send a car over for you.**

Heat rushed to my face. *No, don't do this, Ana.*

**No, I'll get myself there, but only if you promise to behave. What's your address?**

\* \* \*

*What the fuck am I doing? I must be going crazy. Perhaps not being touched by a man in over six months has turned me into a horny teenage girl. Dios mio, now I know how Sloane must've felt around Callan.*

I stood in front of the floor-length mirror, eyeing my reflection in my casual jeans, sweater, and makeup-free face apart from a subtle red lip. It was such a stark contrast to how glamorous I looked at the gala. If Charlie wasn't interested in me like this, then he wasn't worth my time.

I grabbed a long pea coat off the hanger and shrugged it over my arm, stopping myself as I headed for the front door. *This isn't a big deal, right?* I stood frozen in my living room, locked in a battle with myself.

I pulled my phone from my back pocket, staring at the screen, searching for the right words to tell Charlie I wasn't coming. Instead, I opened my contacts and dialed Miles. He answered instantly.

"I need a ride up to the Flatiron district. I'm meeting Charlie Ashford." I hung up before he could question me.

Ten minutes later, Miles stopped in front of an apartment building on 23rd Street. The city was still buzzing around us and I sat for a moment as I collected myself. I planned on telling Charlie that this wasn't a date, that I was only keeping my end of the deal. I would have a drink with him, and then I'd go home. Maybe. Or maybe I'd have sex with him, but I'd make it clear that I didn't want anything more than that.

After a moment, Miles eyed me through the reflection of the rear view mirror, but he didn't say a word.

"Don't worry if I'm in there for a while. In fact, why don't you head home? I'll let you know when I need a ride back."

*Pretty presumptuous of me.* But I saw the way Charlie stared at me. I bet if I told him to get on his knees and beg to fuck me, he would…

"You sure?" Miles asked, interrupting my thoughts.

"Yes," I said as I opened the door and quickly shut it behind me.

Miles' car didn't move, like he was waiting for me to go inside. I smiled, grateful he was doing his job right.

I pulled my phone from my pocket and texted Charlie.

**I'm here.**

I didn't have to wait long. A moment later, double doors swung open and out came Charlie. A smile already lit up his face, highlighting his dimpled cheeks, and his eyes sparkled like he had just won a prize. He wore a plain white T-shirt that showcased the numerous tattoos on his arms and biceps, with dark jeans and sneakers. Somehow, he was even more good-looking now than he was at the gala.

"Ana. I'm so glad you're here," he said warmly, reaching in to give me a hug.

His body was warm against mine, and I could feel the firmness of his toned muscles beneath my hands as I returned his hug. His touch ignited a fire within me, and my cheeks burned when I realized how excited I was.

"Come in, please," he said, releasing me and gesturing towards the door before opening it.

His good energy was infectious and I couldn't help but smile as I stepped inside. I waited as he closed the door behind us, then followed him up the stairs, noticing how he glanced back at me every few seconds.

"Did it take you long to get here?" he asked when we reached a tall, black door at the top of the stairs.

I realized I hadn't said a word since arriving.

"No, I live only six or seven blocks away," I replied, clutching the peacoat draped across my arm.

"Oh yeah?" His smile widened, and I couldn't help but wonder what was running through his mind.

But my thoughts shifted as he opened the door, revealing a beautiful loft with high, exposed beam ceilings adorned with hanging lights. A row of large windows bathed the space in the city's glow. The walls were an eclectic mix of framed artwork and vibrant paintings, with sculptures scattered in various sizes. Two black leather couches faced each other in the middle of the room, separated by a coffee table piled with books. A piano sat in the corner atop a patterned rug, and green plants lined the windows. Nothing matched, yet it all came together perfectly. I was absolutely in love with it.

"Welcome to my home. Let me take your coat," he offered,

extending his hand.

"Thank you," I murmured, my eyes still taking in his space.

His style was so eclectic and artistic. I found myself even more drawn to him. He wasn't just a famous name and face anymore; I was beginning to see his personality, and it was reeling me in.

"So, what can I get you to drink?" he asked, snapping me out of the trance his loft had put me in. "I've got pretty much everything," he added with a grin, resting his hands on the kitchen island.

"Red wine. Cabernet, please," I replied, still wandering through the space, admiring the exposed brick wall behind his industrial-style kitchen and the floor-to-ceiling bookshelf filled with hundreds of books.

"Perfect," he replied, and I could feel his eyes on me as he opened the bottle, watching me quietly as I continued to explore his space.

"How long have you lived here?" I asked, slipping my hands into my back pockets as I wandered further into the open loft.

He moved towards me slowly, handing me the glass of wine. As our eyes met, I noticed the faint sound of music in the background. His green eyes locked onto mine, and for a moment, the flutter in my chest distracted me as he began to answer.

"About a year," he answered with a smile, his eyes still fixed on mine, making me glance away. "Do you like it?" he asked softly.

When I looked back at him, I could see the subtle, almost hesitant need for my approval as he waited for my response.

"Yes, it's beautiful," I said, my voice warm with praise, and I noticed his posture relax.

His dimpled smile nearly knocked me off my feet. *Fuck, I'm smitten.* "Let me give you a tour," he said, effortlessly taking my hand. My heart sank and my body tensed, the unfamiliar sensation of a man's touch leaving me unexpectedly flustered. But when he glanced back and smiled at me, I forced myself to stay in the moment, even if it was fleeting—because it had to be. I kept repeating over and over in my mind, *this is only for tonight.*

He guided me through the rest of his spacious loft, showing off more art, books, and plants, until we finally ended up in his bedroom. My eyes were fixed on the large, king-sized bed in front of an exposed-brick wall, the room softly lit by a single lamp beside the bed. We lingered in front of the bed for a moment, his hand still gently holding mine. He looked over at me, and for a quiet instant, the heat between us seemed to ignite, the air filled with sexual tension.

"Let me show you the balcony. We can sit out there for a drink," he said softly, almost hesitantly, as if he didn't want to leave that moment.

I nodded, unsure if I wanted to move or not either.

But then, slowly, our feet carried us forward, and with his hand still gently guiding me, he pulled open the glass doors at the end of the loft. We stepped onto a small balcony, where a loveseat sat in the corner, a blanket draped casually over it. The cold air bit at my cheeks, but the warmth from Charlie's hand sent heat throughout me.

"Is it not too cold to sit outside?" I asked hesitantly as he guided me towards the loveseat.

He sat down, pulling me with him. "I can keep you warm." He grinned, draping his arm around my shoulders. I could feel the strength of his bicep resting against me. I let myself enjoy his touch for a moment before coming back to reality.

"Charlie…" I began, as if to protest, but I stopped as his smile faded.

"What?" he asked, his eyes slightly widening.

*Just give it to him straight, Ana.*

I hesitated; he already looked so sad and wounded. "I'm really attracted to you, but if you're looking for more than something physical, I can't give that to you."

His brows pulled together. "It doesn't have to be physical yet," he whispered, gently shaking his head.

"Then why did you ask me here?" I argued.

"Because I wanted to sit and talk with you over a drink, get to know each other better," he said softly, a hint of sadness in his voice.

Suddenly, I felt like an asshole.

"So, that's all you want, then?" he asked, and I became painfully aware of his arm still snug around me.

"For now, yes," I replied honestly.

He bit his lip, staring at me for a moment, as if waging a war within himself.

"We don't have to have sex, Charlie. We can chat for a bit, I can finish this drink, and then I'll be on my way," I added bluntly; the last thing I wanted was for him to feel pressured.

"No," he said, shaking his head. "Don't leave."

He gently took the wine glass from my hand, set it on the small table beside us, and locked eyes with me again, intensity in his gaze.

My heart raced and my focus shifted to his lips, now just inches from mine. He was breathing heavily as his eyes fixated on my mouth. Then, without hesitation, his lips pressed against mine and we moved together effortlessly. I tangled my hands in his hair, pulling him closer, and instinctively, my leg draped over his lap.

"Wait," he said, pulling away breathlessly, his hands now gripping my hips. "Let's take this inside."

# 4

# Charlie

I hadn't planned on having sex with Ana so soon. I knew she was hesitant about meeting, and I wanted to make sure she felt as comfortable as possible. Yet, I still craved being close to her. I thought a cuddle would help her relax, that maybe she'd open up more without having to look me directly in the eye; I knew I was staring too much. But maybe the cuddle was actually more for me than for her. I wanted her in my arms so badly.

But she was so determined to make it clear why she was there and it stung a little. I knew we were both attracted to each other; I could see it in the way she looked at me. But I wasn't the kind of guy looking for a one-night stand. I craved her attention in every possible way, and when she looked at me, I wanted nothing more than for her to stay. I feared that if we had sex, she'd leave and never talk to me again. But I couldn't pass up the chance. I had to try.

Now, as we made out on my bed, her ample ass grinding against my hard cock through my jeans, I forgot everything else. Her full lips parted, and her hazel eyes burned with desire as she tugged on my hair, pulling my head back. I was ready and willing to drop to my knees and feast on her, make her come until the sun came up. When she slipped her sweater over her head, my hands immediately found the hook of her bra. She tossed the lacy black bra to the floor, arching her back as she rested her hands on my thighs, revealing her beautiful, big tits right in front of me.

My mouth instinctively found her nipple and she let out a soft moan as I teased her with my tongue, our eyes still locked on each other. Her hips continued rolling over my cock, and the tension built to an almost unbearable point—she was easily the sexiest woman I ever laid eyes on, and with her tits in my mouth, I was ready to come right then and there.

I grabbed her waist and lifted my hips, rolling us over until she was on her back. She watched me with a smile as I tugged her jeans down over her thick, irresistible thighs. My hands glided over her soft skin, gently grazing her thighs up and down, while I trailed kisses along the way, slowly working my way back up. I couldn't help but grin as I saw the desire in her eyes, eagerly watching me. Then, she hooked her thumbs into her black, lacy underwear and slid them down, scooting back to sit upright against my pillows. My cock strained painfully against my clothing as I took in the sight of her completely nude body—her big tits softly bouncing as she laughed, the gentle rolls of her stomach so refreshingly natural and real—a reminder she wasn't a stick-thin woman that this industry constantly celebrated, but a woman with curves, full and stunning.

I smiled back, though I wasn't sure what she found so funny.

"What are you waiting for? Get naked for me," she said playfully, clearly enjoying herself.

I immediately stood up, yanking my shirt over my head while kicking off my shoes at the same time. My eyes never left her as I quickly pulled off my jeans, and I watched in awe as she slid her hand between her legs, gently circling her middle finger against her clit. Her eyes widened slightly as she took in my body, finally settling on the outline of my hard cock straining against my boxer briefs.

"Naked, I said," she ordered, her voice playful but demanding, snapping me out of my hesitation. It wasn't that I wasn't eager to fuck her—fuck, I was—but her gaze left me feeling unsure of myself for the first time in a while. She was so fucking beautiful, and now I was the one on display. I'd never gotten complaints before, but her opinion of me suddenly meant more than anything.

I slowly lowered my boxer briefs, letting my cock spring free, carefully watching her reaction. She bit her lip as she stared, clearly pleased. Her eyes met mine, full of desire, while her fingers continued to play with herself.

"Stroke yourself," she commanded, her voice low and breathless.

I instantly spat into my palm, wrapping my hand around my cock and stroking slowly, afraid I wouldn't last long. It was like watching the best fucking porn on the planet with her lying on my bed, touching herself.

Her finger moved faster as she watched me. "Do you want to fuck me?"

"Yes," I answered without hesitation. *"Please,"* I begged.

She giggled, clearly pleased with my desperation. "Tell me how badly you want to fuck me."

I felt precum gathering at the tip of my cock, throbbing with the need to be inside her.

"I'd do just about anything to fuck you," I breathed, my heart pounding with desire as I watched her.

Her eyebrows lifted slightly. "*Just* about anything?" she asked teasingly.

"Anything," I clarified, my voice strained. "I would do *anything* to be inside you. You're the most beautiful woman I've ever seen," I added, desperate but completely sincere.

She bit her lip with a smile. "You sweet boy," she said, her other hand now squeezing her tit, teasing me. "Beg."

I didn't even hesitate. I fucking loved this. "*Please*, Ana. *Please* let me fuck you."

She narrowed her eyes at me. "I'm not sure that's good enough, Charlie," she said with a disapproving tone, and my heart dropped, right before I dropped to my knees.

"Please, Ana," I continued. "I'll worship your body, I'll make sure you're completely satisfied. I swear I'm gonna die if I can't at least taste you." It may have seemed over the top, but I sincerely felt that way.

She smirked, clearly satisfied with my answer. "Okay. Why don't you come taste me, and if you can make me come, I'll let you fuck me."

*Fuck yes.* "Yes, ma'am," I blurted out, but she quickly corrected me.

"No. You'll call me *mi diosa*."

Her accent, the Spanish, and the way she looked down at me with such confidence—it was so fucking hot. I didn't know how I *wasn't* going to fall in love with her; it may have even been too late.

I got onto my knees on the bed in front of her, and I took in her body once again.

"Yes, *mi diosa*." I licked my lips. "Thank you," I said as I leaned down as she spread her legs wide for me. "Fuck. Thank you," I repeated, then hungrily pressed my lips to her soft slit, sliding my tongue in.

She moaned softly before gripping my hair with her hands, lifting her hips as I took in her mouthwatering cunt. I pulled her legs over my shoulders before I clutched onto her fleshy thighs, and I looked up to find her watching me intently, her soft moans growing louder.

"*Ay, dios mio,*" she breathed, then I slid a finger inside her as I started to flick her clit with the tip of my tongue. "Yes, baby. Like that," she praised, parting her lips as her breathing sped up.

I continued, determined and basking in her praise, slipping in another finger, furiously teasing her clit. I watched as her eyes rolled back, her face contorting in pure pleasure, and she pressed her thighs tight against my face, letting out the sexiest fucking moan I'd ever heard.

Even as her hips slowed, I kept going, desperate to see her come again and again—all because of me.

"Yes, baby. Keep going," she breathed, her voice trembling with pleasure as her fingers tangled in my hair.

And I did it again, making her come over and over, basking in the sound of her moans and the way her body trembled for me, completely lost in the pleasure I was giving her. I would have been satisfied making her come all night, but after I lost count, she pulled me up and pressed her lips hungrily against mine. She lay back, letting me take control, and I squeezed her tits as my mouth trailed down to her neck.

"Fuck me now," she ordered urgently.

I didn't hesitate; I aligned my body perfectly with hers as I thrust my cock inside of her drenched pussy, and it felt like I had taken a hit of the best fucking drug I ever had.

"Fuck! *Mi diosa*, you feel so fucking good," I breathed as I looked down at her full, parted lips. I caught a glimpse of her tits bouncing up and down, but I only wanted to stare into her eyes; I wanted to get lost inside of her, and more than anything, I wanted to make her crave seeing me again after this night was over.

I wanted to hold off for as long as I could, and I was determined to make her come at least one more time. I rolled us over, keeping our bodies connected, and positioned her on top of me. She didn't hesitate to move her hips, finding pleasure on my cock, and I gripped her hips hard as she picked up her speed.

"Baby, your cock fills me perfectly," she moaned as she pressed her palms to my chest, pushing her tits together, making them look even more glorious.

"You were made for me, my love," I blurted out, instantly realizing I'd given her a nickname that revealed more than I intended.

But she just smiled down at me, clearly enjoying the ride. "Come for me now, baby. I'm close," she breathed, her voice trembling.

Those words were all I needed to finally let go. As I watched her lips part and her eyes close in pleasure, I lost control, coming inside of her with an orgasm more intense than anything I'd ever felt before.

Her hips slowed, but I couldn't let go. The intensity of what just happened left me craving more, not just physically but for something deeper. I needed her to stay, because in that moment, I realized I wasn't just hooked on her body—I was addicted to *her*, and to everything she made me feel.

# 5

# Ana

Charlie exceeded my expectations, his desperation to please me obvious as he made sure I came again and again. It was more than I'd ever experienced in such a short amount of time. Jake had always been generous, but he was more focused on his own desires. He wasn't interested in the fantasies I craved. He preferred to take charge in the bedroom, and on the rare occasions when I did, he didn't seem to enjoy it much. After he was elected to office, something shifted in him. And clearly, he started seeking his pleasure elsewhere too.

I hadn't even caught my breath or pulled away from Charlie before he sat up, wrapping his arms around me tightly and kissing me passionately, taking me by surprise. I could see the shift in his expression, like he was lost in thought, right after we came together. A part of me was afraid to know what was going through his mind. He really did seem like the sensitive, hopeless romantic type, and I hoped he hadn't started feeling too strongly about me yet. As fun as this was, I knew I needed to pull away before I let myself like him even more—and I already liked him a lot. Too much, in fact.

We broke the kiss and I rested my hands on his muscular, tattooed arms. He was more built than I'd expected, with a defined six-pack and that sexy V-line leading straight to his very well-endowed cock. The man certainly knew what to do with it, and that mouth of his...

His gentle voice broke me out of thoughts. "Why don't I fill your glass of wine? Maybe we can put a movie on?"

I hesitated before I finally crawled off of him, searching for my clothes. "Oh, um..."

"You said you'd finish your glass of wine and we'd have a chat, didn't you?" he asked playfully.

I glanced over at him and couldn't help but smile. He sat there with wide, hopeful eyes and a smirk on his lips. My eyes drifted down to his semi-hard cock, still on full display, and he didn't seem to mind lounging around completely nude. I didn't either, but I didn't want to get too comfortable.

"I caught you on a technicality, didn't I?" he teased, his smirk widening as he watched me.

"It could be thrown out in court since we already had sex," I replied, matching his playful tone with a grin of my own, but then his face fell.

"I need to be honest, Ana," he began, crossing his legs and looking down at the ground before meeting my eyes again. "I need to see you again. I absolutely need to. We don't have to have sex, and we don't need to be in a relationship. I just think you're so fucking amazing, and I want to be around you in any way I can."

His expression was so sincere, so heartfelt. He had no reason to tell me any of this unless it was the truth.

I glanced down at my underwear in my hand, my heart torn.

If I kept seeing him, I knew I'd fall for him. But if I walked away now, I would always wonder what could have been. Could we even be just friends, or was that impossible at this point?

"Sorry, Ana. That's…that's a lot to put on you. Just forget I said that," he muttered, defeat clear in his voice.

I couldn't even begin to express how I was feeling, so I simply muttered, "Okay."

"Okay," he echoed, standing up and pulling on his boxer briefs. "So then, now what?"

I kept my eyes down, unable to look at him as I pulled my jeans over my hips. I made everything awkward, and it was clear I'd broken his heart. I warned him, though. But did that justify what I'd done?

"What if…" he trailed off, his voice soft as I glanced up to meet his sad eyes.

I stood there, unsure of what to do next. Just as I was about to turn away, to tell him that I needed to leave, he gently caught my hand. He turned it over in his, his thumb brushing softly over my knuckles. The simple touch surprised me, stopping me in place.

He didn't speak, but the way he touched me was enough. It was intimate, unexpected. I stared at our hands; I should've pulled away, kept moving. But instead, I stood there, letting the moment sink in, second-guessing everything. My thoughts raced, but I knew I couldn't give him more than I was ready for.

I cleared my throat, breaking the silence. "Maybe…maybe we could meet for coffee one day. Or lunch. Just as friends."

His eyes softened, and a small smile lifted at the corner of his lips. "Yeah," he said quietly, nodding. "Lunch sounds good."

The tension eased slightly and I felt like I could breathe

again. His hand lingered in mine for a moment longer before he slowly let go.

"As friends," I repeated, more to myself than him, as if convincing myself that I could handle it.

"Friends," he echoed, still holding onto that gentle smile that made it hard to walk away.

Twenty minutes later, I was back home. I slipped back into the pajamas I'd worn earlier and sank into my bed, my thoughts racing. Part of me was excited about this new "friendship" with Charlie, but another part was terrified of falling for him. There was something about him that I couldn't quite shake. I was used to attention, but his felt different. Was it the freedom to finally explore after a twenty-year marriage? Or was it simply him?

I turned off the lights, ready to finally rest, when my phone buzzed with a text. I knew it was Charlie. Sure enough, when I unlocked my phone, I was right.

**I can't stop thinking about you.**

I smiled, but it almost felt like too much. I kept brushing it off. Maybe I was just overthinking it. He was sweet, attentive, probably just caught up in the excitement of something new. *People always get like this in the beginning, right?* After everything I'd been through, didn't I deserve to enjoy that? I was still in control. If it got to be too much, I could always pull back. Besides, the intensity and excitement would wear off eventually. *It's just a friendship...for now.*

**You're sweet, Charlie. Get some rest.**

His texting bubbles popped up immediately.

**I'll try, but it's hard to sleep when all I can think about is you. Sweet dreams, mi diosa.**

**I'm sorry. That's too much, I know. Can't wait to see**

**you again.**

As much as his words should have worried me, they didn't. Because I couldn't wait to see him again either.

*Mierda.*

\*\*\*

I woke up late, allowing myself some much-needed rest. When I checked my phone to see if I'd missed anything, I was surprised by the disappointment that washed over me; Charlie hadn't texted me again.

*Maybe I should text him. No, why would I text him?* As much as I thought about him, I was certain he was doing exactly the same. Was he trying to give me space? Was he offended that I didn't text him back last night? Why was I overthinking everything so much? *Why do I care so much? Why am I letting his attention—or the lack of it—get to me?*

Before I could stop myself, I pulled up Instagram, already embarrassed at myself. I hadn't done this before, hadn't ridiculously stalked a guy's profile like some teenager, but something compelled me to check his today.

I instantly found him and, of course, he was already following me. His latest story was from several hours ago, a photo of a half-empty glass of wine in his loft. *My* glass, marked with my deep red lipstick.

And below it, in white letters, the words: **Still thinking about you.**

My heart skipped a beat. He hadn't mentioned me by name, but he didn't need to. I stared at the story for a moment, my heart pounding. It was subtle enough for his followers to wonder, but I knew it was for me. It was his way of reaching out without directly saying anything.

*Why didn't he just text me?* I locked my phone, trying to shake off the anxiety creeping in. *Why am I letting this consume me?*

I had always been independent, in control of how I felt, never needing someone else's attention to validate me. But now, with Charlie, it felt different. The intensity, the way he quietly hinted at me—it was pulling me in. And I wasn't sure if I wanted to give in or push away.

I dragged myself out of bed, determined to shake off whatever hold this had on me. A hot shower would help clear my head. I needed to focus on something else, *anything* else.

Just as I stepped into the bathroom, my phone started ringing. I glanced at the screen—Sloane.

"*Hola, mija. ¿Que pasa?*" I answered, hoping my voice didn't give away how anxious I felt.

"Okay, Mom, I just have one question." Her voice was playful, but I could already sense where this was going.

"Just one? That's not like you," I teased, pretending I wasn't panicking inside.

"Whose red lipstick is on that glass of wine in Charlie Ashford's story?"

My stomach dropped slightly. I hadn't even thought of Sloane being a little sleuth, trying to find clues about my, or his, night via social media. But she was smart. *Too* smart, like always.

"What are you talking about?" I asked casually.

She laughed. "Come on, Mom. The caption? The red lipstick that is the exact same shade you wear constantly? Right after he asked for your number?" Her voice was teasing, but she knew.

I sighed, half-amused. "Sloane, it's nothing. Don't read into it."

She scoffed. "So, are you telling me it's not yours? You're gonna lie to your only child?" She was still teasing, but I wanted nothing more than for this call to be over.

I laughed. "I'm telling you it's nothing."

She let out an exaggerated groan. "Fine. Keep your secrets," she said playfully. "But if this turns into something, I better be the first to know."

"Bye, Sloane. *Te amo*," I said, smiling as I hung up.

As soon as the call ended, I exhaled, relieved to be free of her questions. I wasn't ready to answer anything about Charlie. I wasn't even sure *how* I felt about him. His intensity, his texts, his sneaky story, the way he seemed to occupy my mind even when I tried to push him out—it was all too much.

I stepped onto the terrace with my coffee, letting the cool air wash over me, hoping it would clear my head. But just as I finally started to relax, my phone buzzed again, this time with a text. I glanced down—Charlie.

**Good morning. I can't stop thinking about you. I hope you slept well. When can I see you again?**

My heart fluttered, the tension building in my chest. Now he was directly pulling me back in, his words filled with the same intensity, the same need, that both thrilled and unsettled me.

I stared at the message, feeling that familiar tug. And as much as I wanted to resist, I wasn't ready to push him away.

# 6

# Charlie

I knew I was being too much. The constant texting, the Instagram story about her, the way I couldn't stop thinking about her, even when I tried to distract myself. But I couldn't help it. Something about Ana had gotten to me in a way no one else ever had.

I stared at my phone, waiting for a response that still hadn't come. She hadn't texted back since last night, and even though I tried to tell myself to play it cool, I knew I wasn't fooling anyone. I was fucking crazy about her. No, I was obsessed with her. There was no denying it now. The worst part was, I knew I was coming on too strong, but I didn't know how to stop. If I didn't push, if I didn't keep reminding her how much I wanted her, I was terrified she'd slip away. She could pull back and disappear if I wasn't careful, and the thought of losing her made my whole body fill with dread.

And then there was last night. *Fuck*.

I shifted in my seat, my body responding to the memory of her taking control. It wasn't just about what happened—it was about the fact that it finally happened. I always knew I wanted this. I thought about being dominated, needing someone else to take charge, and with Ana…fuck, it was better than I could have ever imagined. The way she moved, the way she commanded every moment. It wasn't just exciting—it felt like something I needed all along, like a missing puzzle piece that completed me.

Now that it had happened, I needed it more. I needed *her* more.

She made me feel something I hadn't felt before, and now that I had a taste of it, I didn't think I could stop. I didn't *want* to stop. I could still feel her hands on me, guiding me, her voice low and commanding.

*Fuck, I need her to do it again.*

I tapped my fingers against the edge of the kitchen counter where I now stood, the restless energy pulsing through me. I had been with other women, but none of them had given me what I wanted, what Ana gave me. She had me tangled in knots, and the worst part was that I loved it.

I sent her the text this morning, half-expecting no response. Maybe I'd gone too far with the Instagram story, with how forward I'd been. Who knows if she even saw it? But if I didn't push, what if she drifted away?

*Stop, Charlie.*

My phone buzzed and my heart nearly leapt out of my chest. I picked it up quickly, hoping it was her. And there it was—her name lighting up my screen.

**Good morning. You're sweet, Charlie. I hope you're doing well.**

*Finally.* A small reassurance that I hadn't pushed her away. I let out a breath I didn't realize I'd been holding.

But that simple text didn't calm the hunger inside me. I was teetering on the edge, wanting more—more of her, more of what we had last night, more of that control she had over me. I *needed* it so badly.

I stared at her message, trying to keep myself calm. She hadn't pulled away yet, but it wasn't enough to quiet the constant fear gnawing at me. The fear that she'd disappear like everyone else had.

Being famous is supposed to mean you're never alone, right? Surrounded by people, fans screaming your name, always in the spotlight. But it's not like that. Fame is lonely as fuck. You're constantly surrounded by people, but no one really knows you. Everyone wants something—attention, proximity, publicity. It's this constant game of wondering why they're there, what they want.

But Ana was different. She didn't need anything from me. She had her own life, her own reputation. Former First Lady. More well-known than I was. She wasn't in it for clout; she didn't need it. And that made it worse, because she could walk away at any time.

I ran a hand through my messy hair, trying to shake off the dread. Years of questioning everyone around me, wondering if they're here for who I am or what I can give…it had burned me enough to know. You start to lose track of who's real and who's playing a part.

But Ana…I knew she was real. I needed to hold on tighter because for once, I had something *real*.

I typed out another message, my fingers moving faster than my thoughts.

**I've been thinking about last night a lot. I'd love to see you again when you're ready.**

I stared at the message before hitting send, my heart

pounding frantically. *Okay, that's not too much,* I told myself, trying to calm my nerves. It wasn't as forward as before, but it still let her know I was thinking about her.

*Maybe she'll be more open to that. Maybe this way, she won't feel like I'm pushing too hard.*

After sending the message, I tossed my phone aside, trying to will myself not to stare at it, waiting for a reply. I had to calm down. The more I hovered over my phone, the worse it would be.

I paced around the loft, trying everything to distract myself—reading, cleaning, working out—but nothing worked. My mind kept drifting back to Ana. *Has she seen my message? Is she even thinking about me?*

Finally, after what felt like hours, my phone vibrated in my pocket. I grabbed it instantly, my heart racing as her name lit up the screen.

**Have you eaten?**

I stared at the message, a mix of relief and confusion settling in. It wasn't the response I expected, but it was better than nothing.

**No, not yet. Why?**

A moment later, she responded.

**I'm hungry...but maybe not just for food.**

I blinked, my heart pounding as I reread her words. There it was—suggestive, flirtatious, leaving me hanging onto every word. She was playing with me, keeping me hooked.

**What are you hungry for?**

I sent the message, my anticipation growing. She hadn't pulled away after all. If anything, she was pulling me in deeper.

**I saw something I liked last night. I didn't get to taste it, but I wanted to.**

My breath hitched as I read her words. *Oh, fuck.* My mind raced back to last night, and I knew exactly what she was talking about. I didn't even care that she didn't blow me—all I wanted was *her*. She was teasing me, and I was getting hard already.

I quickly typed back.

**Maybe you should come over and get a taste.**

I was fucking hooked.

I stared at the screen, hoping for her next response. My heart was still racing from her last message. But the minutes ticked by and nothing. My finger hovered over the phone, resisting the urge to send something else. *Why hasn't she responded yet?*

I couldn't take it anymore. Without thinking, I tapped the FaceTime button, the anticipation too much to handle. The screen rang once…twice…and then she picked up.

"Charlie?" Her voice was light, and her face appeared on the screen, looking slightly surprised.

"I couldn't wait any longer," I admitted, trying to play it off with a grin. "You can't send a message like that and then ghost me."

She laughed softly, her eyes sparkling. "I don't do this often. I was just thinking of what to say next."

"Well, I'm here now," I said, my voice low and gentle, trying not to scare her off. "You said you saw something you liked?"

Her lips curved into a teasing smile. "I did. And maybe next time, I'll take my time and taste it."

I swear my heart stopped beating. I leaned closer to the screen, as if I could close the distance between us. My cock was straining against my sweats. "I would love that, *mi diosa*."

Ana's eyes glinted with mischief and she tilted her head slightly, watching me with that same teasing smile.

"I have an idea…" she said softly, her voice dropping to a sultry tone, the same one from the night before that went straight to my cock.

I leaned in. "Yeah? What's that?"

She bit her lip, pausing for a moment as if deciding whether to say it, then her eyes locked on mine. "Why don't you show me what you do when you're thinking about me?"

I exhaled, breathless. "You want to watch me?"

Her lips curved into a slow, seductive smile. "I do. I want to see how much you want me, Charlie."

My entire body responded to her words, heat rushing through me. Without another thought, I leaned back slightly, positioning the phone so she could see me. "Gladly…if that's what *mi diosa* wants."

I slid my sweats and boxer briefs down, freeing my hard cock. My hand wrapped around it as I began to stroke myself, unable to tear my eyes away from the beautiful woman watching me with unmistakable desire.

"Take your shirt off," she demanded.

Without hesitation, I tugged my shirt off with one hand, eager to follow her command.

"Good boy," she praised, and the words nearly made me burst instantly. The way her lips moved, the way she watched me—it intensified everything. I could barely hold on.

"Fuck, *mi diosa*," I groaned, my breath ragged. "Just looking at you, hearing your voice…it's gonna make me burst." I kept my strokes slow, savoring every moment.

Her smile deepened. "I want you to come into your hand while you say my name," she commanded softly. "Then I want you to lick yourself clean."

The second her words hit me, my body gave in. My cum

shot out, covering my palm, and I followed her command, her name slipping from my lips in a low, guttural growl. I waited until the last drop came out before I brought my palm to my lips and licked it clean.

"How does it taste?" she asked, her voice low, and I could see the phone shaking slightly. I knew she was touching herself, lost in the moment.

"Not as good as you, *mi diosa,*" I breathed. "You're so fucking sweet—you're the only sustenance I'd ever need."

Her lips parted, and I watched as her eyes fluttered shut, gently rolling to the back of her head. The sight of her getting worked up got me hard all over again.

"You have no idea how much I want to worship you," I murmured, my voice deep with desire. "How badly I need you." I wanted to be the reason for her release, even if I wasn't touching her. "I'm yours, *mi diosa*. I can't stop thinking about how perfect you are, how much I want to please you."

That's when I heard her low moan, soft and breathless, and then she graced me with a view of her beautiful face, lost in pleasure. The sight of her was too much, and before I could stop myself, my hand was on my hard cock again, stroking slowly, unable to resist.

"Please, *mi diosa*, let me come again," I begged, my voice filled with desperation. "The sight of you coming gets me so fucking hard."

Her eyes fluttered open, lighting up at my words, and I knew I was at her mercy once again. "Yes, baby. Come for me."

That was all it took. My body obeyed instantly, the release crashing over me with her words echoing in my mind, pulling me under completely.

As the waves of pleasure subsided, I collapsed back, breathless, the intensity of the moment leaving me reeling. My body was exhausted, but my mind…my mind was spinning with only one thought: her being mine.

I stared at the screen, watching her catch her breath, the satisfied smile on her lips sending another jolt of need through me. I'd never been this deep before. This wasn't just desire—it was something else entirely. Obsession. I knew I was in too deep now to pull myself out.

Ana's voice, her control, her presence—it consumed me, and I didn't want it to end. I was hers, in every possible way, and there was no going back. Not now…not after this. *I'm not letting her go.*

# 7

# Ana

Thinking about Charlie and the night before had me turned on all morning. Every touch, every word echoed in my mind, driving me crazy. I wanted him *so* badly and I knew I was going to give in; there was no denying it. I already *was* giving in. His need brought something out in me, something I hadn't felt in years—perhaps something I'd *never* felt before.

It was clear I had him completely wrapped around my finger during our call. The way he hung onto every word, how easily he surrendered to my commands—it was thrilling but also a little frightening. I could feel his desire, heavy and consuming, and it was almost suffocating in its depth.

Yet beneath that rush was a flicker of doubt. How long could I keep this going without getting tangled up in his desire to please me? Or worse—without getting tangled up in *him*?

I was playing with fire and I knew it. But the thrill overshadowed everything else. Right now, all I could think about was how badly I wanted him.

I tried to push my thoughts about Charlie aside all day and focus on my responsibilities. I spent hours organizing a charity event for a local women and children's shelter, sifting through endless emails, and juggling multiple Zoom meetings for the various organizations I was involved in.

As the day wound down, my phone buzzed—Charlie.

**Let me cook you dinner tonight. At your place.**

I stared at the message, feeling torn. Part of me wanted to say yes, but I knew it wasn't fair to keep letting him in when I wasn't sure where things were going.

**Not tonight, Charlie. I'm just going to relax on my own.**

A minute later, his response came.

**You can still relax. I'll handle everything. Just let me do this for you.**

I sighed, my guilt surfacing. Was I leading him on? I kept him at arm's length, but I kept pulling him a little closer with each interaction.

**I don't think it's a good idea tonight. I just need some space.**

There was a pause before his next message came through.

**Okay, I get it. I won't push.**

The sound of defeat in his response made me pause. He wasn't fighting for it this time, and that left an unexpected void. I should've felt relieved, but instead, something inside me softened. He wasn't demanding, wasn't pushing any further, and that made me reconsider.

I sat there for a few minutes in silence. The thought of sitting alone all night suddenly felt heavier than before. *Maybe a quiet dinner with Charlie wouldn't be so bad after all.* Before I could

## ANA

overthink it, I picked up my phone and responded.

**You know what…dinner sounds nice.**

I hesitated, then added: **Come over in an hour.** I included my address and even gave him the code for the elevator.

*Ay, this is such a bad idea.* The thought of Charlie being here, in my space, was both exciting and scary. I could feel the anticipation building in my chest, and as much as I wanted to convince myself this was just a casual dinner, deep down I knew better. I knew what would eventually happen, and *dios mio*, I wanted it again so badly.

The way he made me feel…it was overwhelming, thrilling, and completely out of control. And as much as I tried to tell myself that keeping distance was the smart thing to do, I couldn't resist the pull any longer.

I tossed my phone onto the couch and stood up, pacing the living room. I absentmindedly straightened the pillows, tucked stray books into a neat pile, and wiped invisible smudges off the kitchen counter. *Why am I cleaning? The place is fine.*

And then doubt crept in once again. Was I making a huge mistake? Again? My mind raced, replaying every moment we shared. I wasn't ready for this. I started to get irritated—I hated that I was second-guessing myself like this. I hated that this all felt out of control.

I grabbed my phone, my thumb hovering over the screen. *Maybe I should tell him not to come.*

I hesitated, biting my lip as I started to type out the text. But before I could press send, there was a knock at the door, startling me; he was twenty minutes early.

I glanced at my reflection in the mirror, eyeing the subtle makeup I applied earlier, and the way my hair fell around my face in soft, natural waves. I nodded at myself, trying to calm the nerves twisting in my stomach. For some reason, this felt different, more nerve-wracking than any of our other encounters. Was it because he was coming into *my* space? Or because deep down, I already knew what was going to happen tonight?

I took a deep breath, trying to calm myself down. The second knock at the door seemed louder in the quiet of the apartment, and I couldn't ignore the excitement I felt. I was walking straight into this, and there was no turning back now.

I opened the door and found Charlie standing on the other side, holding a grocery bag in one hand and a beautiful, trailing plant in the other. His eyes lit up as soon as he saw me, a gentle smile spreading across his face.

"Hello, beautiful," he said, his voice soft and warm.

"Hi," I replied, stifling a little school-girl giggle that threatened to escape. I stepped back, motioning for him to come in.

He took in the surroundings as I closed the door behind us, his gaze roaming over the space as he walked in. But soon enough, his attention shifted back to me, his grin soft but knowing. "This place is very you."

I nearly responded with *you hardly know me*, but I stopped myself. The truth was, in some ways, it felt like he knew me all too well—more than I was comfortable admitting.

"So, what are you making me? And what's that?" I asked, glancing at the plant he had just set down on the coffee table in the middle of the living room.

"It's a string of hearts. I saw you eyeing my plant collection and figured I'd add to yours," he said sweetly.

Butterflies swarmed around in my belly and I couldn't help

but smile at his gesture. "Thank you," I said softly.

Charlie's grin widened, a glimmer of satisfaction in his eyes. "You're welcome," he replied. "And dinner is a surprise. Why don't you sit down and relax, and I'll take care of it?"

I could see the need for approval in his eyes, the quiet vulnerability beneath his confidence.

I didn't protest. I walked further into the living room and settled onto the couch, watching him confidently move through my kitchen cabinets like he belonged there. There was something about the way he carried himself—comfortable, but still seeking my approval in small, unspoken ways. The quiet domesticity of it all made the butterflies stir again, though I tried to push the feeling down. It felt like he belonged there with me, and that thought alone scared me.

"Any allergies I should know of?" he asked, pulling items from the bag while catching me watching him.

I shook my head. "Sloane's vegetarianism rubbed off on me, but otherwise, I'm good."

He paused, a look of surprise on his face. "I'm vegetarian as well."

I wasn't surprised. Charlie didn't seem like he could hurt a fly. He glanced at me for a moment longer before softly saying, "I didn't expect this, you know...finding things in common with you." His voice was calm, but there was a hint of something deeper there. "It's nice."

He smiled, but the way his eyes lingered on me made my heart skip a beat. I had to look away. He could be so intense, which felt so different from how he naturally submitted to me. It was like he carried two sides of himself—the vulnerability that let me take control, and this deep, simmering intensity that surfaced when I least expected it.

"So, I'm glad you answered my FaceTime earlier," he said as he continued on with prepping dinner, his boldness creeping back in.

I shouldn't have felt so giddy, so nervous about him mentioning what *I* had initiated in the first place.

"I'm sure you are," I replied teasingly, trying to mask the flutter of nerves with a playful tone. His eyes flicked to mine, a grin creeping up at the corner of his lips as he caught the shift in my tone.

"You have no idea," he murmured, his voice dropping just enough to send my heart racing, his English accent driving me insane.

I laughed softly, trying to keep things light, but the sexual tension between us was undeniable. He had a way of pushing just enough to keep me on edge. And now I couldn't help myself, once again. I needed to gain control back.

I stood, slowly walking over to where he stood at the counter. His eyes followed my every move, anticipation clear on his face. "You like when I take control, don't you?" I asked quietly, testing the waters.

A slow smile spread across his face. "You know I do," he replied, his tone laced with desire.

I bit my lip, feeling the tension between us grow. "I'm not hungry for dinner quite yet," I said, stepping closer. "I think I'd like a taste of what I mentioned earlier."

His eyes darkened, understanding immediately, his breath catching slightly as I closed the distance between us. The playful banter from moments ago faded, replaced with the heat that now filled the room.

"Why don't you stop what you're doing and give me your full attention," I said quietly yet firmly.

Charlie swallowed hard, his eyes glued to mine, waiting.

"Come here," I commanded softly, grabbing his hand and pulling him towards the living room.

I walked in front of the couch, then nudged him to sit. Slowly, I sank to my knees, my hands sliding down his thighs. "Stay still, and don't move unless I tell you to."

Charlie's breathing sped, his body tense with anticipation, but he stayed obedient, watching my every move, waiting for what was to come next.

I slid my hands up, feeling his hard cock straining against his jeans, desperate to be freed. Slowly, I ran my hand up and down the length, teasing him with each movement. I smiled as Charlie squirmed under my touch, trying to keep still as I commanded, but clearly struggling with the effort.

"Such a good listener, my sweet boy," I teased, inching my fingers closer to the zipper of his jeans.

Charlie only nodded as he bit his lower lip, his focus entirely on my eyes. When I unzipped his jeans, my fingers hooked into the waistband, pulling them down slowly. He lifted his hips, silently helping, eager but still obedient to my control.

My hands were back to the length of his cock, still covered by his boxer briefs. The wetness between my thighs begged for me to tear his clothes off and jump on his cock, but I was having too much fun teasing him.

"Your cock is so big. How does it fit so perfectly in my pussy?" I murmured, continuing my slow stroke.

He let out a low grunt. "You're perfect, *mi diosa*. Perfect for me in every way," he murmured back, his voice quiet and intense.

I chuckled, slipping my hand through the front slit of his boxer briefs, watching his reaction as my fingers brushed against the warm flesh of his cock. His brows pulled together and he bit his lip with a quiet, desperate need as I wrapped my fingers around him. He exhaled softly, his mouth parting, and I felt precum beading at the tip. I smiled as I began to stroke gently, pulling his cock out for a better look. I widened my eyes slightly as I opened my mouth and leaned down, licking his precum with the tip of my tongue. I pulled back and closed my mouth, letting my eyes flutter shut.

"Mmm. You're as tasty as you look," I said, slowly opening my eyes.

"Fuck," he breathed. "Please, *mi diosa*."

"What, baby?" I asked, leaning down further to press my lips against the length of his cock, letting my tongue swirl around as I did so.

"I need you, *mi diosa*. Please let me kiss you. Please let me taste you," he begged, watching me intently.

This power was thrilling and I wanted it to last all night. The control over him, the way his body responded to every touch, the way he begged—it gave me a rush that I had never felt before.

"I love when you beg, my sweet boy," I said quietly, then took one hand to his hair and pulled him toward me, pressing my lips hungrily against his.

I almost lost control as I began to stroke him quickly, feeling his hands explore my body, getting lost in the heat of the moment. But suddenly, I remembered what I was doing, and I pulled back just as quickly as I started. Charlie sat back, breathing heavily, moving his hands back beside him, eyes wide with hunger. He waited silently for my next move. It was then that I removed my hands from him and stood up, backing up a few steps.

"You can continue dinner now," I said with a teasing smile. The playful air hung between us and I could see the way his hunger shifted from desperation to something darker, but he obeyed, rising to his feet with his dimpled, charming grin.

He let out a low breath. "You have no idea what I'd do for you," he murmured. He stood up slowly and added, "But for now, I'll finish dinner, *mi diosa*." His eyes lingered on me, as if he was saying much more than his words could convey, before he covered himself back up and walked into the kitchen.

# 8

# Charlie

Ana was enjoying herself, and so was I. Every touch, every command, only pulled me deeper into this. She could edge me and tease me all night long if she wanted to, and I'd still beg for more. There was a thrill in giving up control, in letting her lead. I wasn't just playing along—I *wanted* it. I'd do anything she told me to do. I'd fucking chop my finger off if she desired, and I'd do it with a smile on my face.

I eyed her as I began slicing an heirloom tomato, but I couldn't keep my focus. I was desperate to watch her every move. She sat on the couch, phone in hand, a hint of a smile on her lips. The way she was so calm, so in control, drove me crazy. Just as I was about to look away, she glanced up, catching me staring.

"Are you sure you don't want help?" she asked sweetly, her Spanish accent like music to my ears.

I shook my head, trying to keep my cool. "No. You're supposed to be relaxing," I replied, focusing on the tomato but still stealing glances at her. "What do you do to relax?"

She smirked slightly, her gaze lingering on me. I could feel the tension rising again, and staying cool around her was a losing battle.

"I read, or listen to music, or just sit on my ass and watch twelve hours of TV," she answered with a laugh, her smile easy and natural.

I couldn't help but grin. "Twelve hours, huh? Sounds like you've got the art of relaxing down."

She leaned back, her gaze still on me, playful and relaxed. "I'm good at it," she teased. I could tell she was getting more comfortable around me and I was reveling in it.

At this rate, the caprese salad I planned on making was destined to be forgotten.

"What do you like to listen to?" I asked, wondering if she ever heard my music. *She must have, right?*

She gave me a knowing smile, pausing just long enough to keep me guessing. "A little of everything. I love oldies, Motown, alternative, anything female-driven. But I was obsessed with the Backstreet Boys when I was young. I don't know if you know anything about boy bands." Her eyes lit up with mischief, teasing me.

I laughed, shaking my head. "Boy bands, huh? I might know a little something about them."

Her laugh was addicting. I needed to hear more of it.

"You have some great songs, too," she said, her tone turning serious for a moment.

I raised an eyebrow, trying to keep things light despite the compliment. "Oh, so you *have* listened to my music?" I teased, grinning. "Which song is your favorite? Don't tell me you're just saying that to be nice."

She laughed, shaking her head. "I'm serious! And no, I'm not just being nice. I like your stuff…only when I'm not listening to the Backstreet Boys."

I chuckled. "So?" I asked, desperate for her validation. "What's your favorite of mine then?"

I could feel the anxiety in my chest as I waited for her answer. It wasn't just a casual question—I needed to know what she thought, if what I created meant something to her.

She met my gaze, her expression softening. "Your latest," she admitted, naming the title. "The ballad and the piano. It's…real, and sad. It's beautiful."

Her words hit like a warm wave, filling the void I hadn't realized was there. I was already planning on writing at least a dozen songs about her.

"So, you're a fan then, huh?" I teased, trying not to show how excited I actually was. Inside, my heart was pounding with pride.

She raised an eyebrow, smirking. "Maybe. But don't let it go to your head," she quipped, though I could see the hint of warmth in her eyes.

We settled into an easy conversation, talking about favorite places to travel and movies we liked, and I was finally getting around to making the caprese salad. At one point, we delved a little deeper.

"Is there something that's always stayed with you? Something that's shaped who you are now?" she asked, leaning her elbow on the couch and laying her head against it.

I took a deep breath, the old memories surfacing. "Yeah…my dad left when I was young. It changed everything for me. I've never been able to shake that fear of people walking away."

She was quiet for a moment, her eyes softening as she got up and walked towards the kitchen where I stood. "I'm so sorry,

Charlie. I can't imagine how hard that must've been…but I get why you'd feel that way. That kind of loss—it stays with you."

She reached out, her hand gently brushing mine. "But not everyone leaves. Some people stay, even when it's hard."

Her words echoed in my mind. The thought of her leaving… fuck that, I couldn't let that happen. She had become too important, too necessary. The more she cared, the deeper the hold she had on me. I didn't just need her anymore—I needed her and had to *keep* her. The idea of her walking away was unbearable. I wouldn't survive it, and I couldn't let it happen.

I knew it was obsessive and unhealthy—this need, this desperation—but it was too late to turn back. She had slipped under my skin, into my mind, and there was no escaping it now. The more I thought about it, the more I realized it didn't matter if this was healthy or not. I couldn't *not* want her. I couldn't stop this pull even if I tried. I was past the point of no return, and I didn't ever want to go back.

Before I could stop myself, I pulled her in, pressing my lips to hers with a desperate need. When I pulled back, my hands trembled, nervous about what I was about to say.

"I can't let you go, Ana," I whispered, my eyes searching hers. "You've become too important to me. I don't know how to stop this, and I don't want to. I need you in my life."

She hesitated, her brow furrowing slightly before she spoke. "Charlie…I care about you. I really do," she said softly, her hand resting on my arm.

I nodded, trying to believe her, but inside, the fear still took hold of me. She was trying to reassure me, but it didn't stop the panic rising in my chest. Then she pulled back, just slightly, like she needed space, like maybe everything I just said was too much for her.

"I'm sorry," I blurted out, my voice shaky. "I know I'm being too much. I'll stop. I don't want to push you away."

I could hear the desperation in my own words, but I couldn't take them back. I hated feeling like this, like I was overwhelming her, like I was losing control of myself.

I could feel her watching me, sensing my panic. Without a word, she leaned in and kissed me, and it was like she was telling me everything would be okay without saying a thing. I didn't hesitate. The second her lips touched mine, I leaned in, pulling her closer. I wanted to get lost in her, to forget everything else. This was all I needed—her, in this moment. The kiss deepened and I let myself drown in her.

She pulled away and took my hand, her fingers threading through mine. There was no hesitation as she gently tugged, leading me towards the bedroom.

And I could feel it—she was using this to avoid conversation. Maybe she didn't want to confront what I had confessed so deeply, or maybe she was scared of hurting me. But right now, none of that mattered to me. I'd take what she was willing to give, even if it was just this. I needed her too much to question it.

She had me on my back before I could even take in the surroundings of her room. It was quick and I didn't have time to keep overthinking as her body pressed against mine, her lips finding mine frantically. It felt like she needed this— like her control over me was a way to fight whatever she was feeling. I'd let her take the lead and use this moment to escape whatever fear she was avoiding because right now, I needed her just as much.

I sat up as she quickly hopped off of me, pulling her jeans and underwear down and eyeing my hard cock through my jeans. She pulled her shirt over her head, her bra completely filled with her gorgeous tits. I waited and watched, my breathing quick, ready for whatever she was going to give or take from me. I didn't have to wait long—she was back on her knees on the bed, her fingers pulling down my jeans and boxer briefs, carefully letting my aching cock spring free. Her hands were instantly stroking me, her lips desperately finding my cock. It was like something ignited in her, making her lose control as her warm mouth slid up and down my length. I was still letting her take the lead as I watched, the sight of her blowing me almost too much as her hazel eyes stared up at me with desire.

"I'm gonna come, *mi diosa*. Your mouth is too fucking good," I said breathlessly.

I could see the smile curl up on her lips as her head continued to bob up and down.

Her hands replaced her mouth for a moment. "Good, baby. Come for me. My good boy deserves to come in my mouth," she whispered, then her lips found my cock again.

With her approval, I let go and felt the pulse of my cock throb as a wave of pleasure shot down, my cum releasing into her mouth as we continued to lock eyes, the low hum in her throat making everything feel more intense.

She swallowed every drop of me before sitting up and crawling over me, kissing me hard with the taste of myself on her lips. She pulled away before she sat up and aligned her perfect pussy with my face, then lowered her hips and instantly began grinding against my open mouth. My tongue swirled deep in her cunt as her hips swayed back and forth, our eyes locked, our connection fucking magical. She lowered her upper half and grabbed my hands, pinning them beside my head, leaving me completely at her will. Her full tits bounced perfectly in my view as I flicked the tip of my tongue against her clit, igniting soft moans from her lips.

"Yes, baby. Just like that," she praised, and I rapidly continued, watching her mouth widen and her breaths hitching.

"Fuck yes, Charlie!" she moaned loudly, and my cock instantly twitched from hearing my name on her lips as she came on my mouth.

I wanted to watch her come over and over again, but before I knew it, she lifted her hips and leaned down, capturing my lips in a passionate kiss, her hands lightly tugging my hair. Her body pressed against mine, soft and demanding. My hands gripped her plump hips tightly as I lifted my own, instinctively searching for her warmth, desperate for more. Without hesitation, she slid onto me, my cock filling her completely. She sat up, her hips grinding against mine as she chased her pleasure. Her eyes locked with mine, intense and full of need, pulling me deeper into the moment.

And it was then that I desperately wanted to tell her that I loved her. But I couldn't say it. If I did, I knew she'd pull back, she'd end this, and I'd ruin everything between us. She wasn't ready for that. The second those words came out, I'd lose her. So I kept quiet, even though it hurt, knowing that holding it in was the only way to keep her close.

# 9

# Ana

Charlie was quiet after we came together. I knew something was on his mind and I wasn't sure if I wanted to hear it, because I was certain I knew what it was. I'd seen that look in his eyes so many times before, and it broke my heart while mending it at the same time. I couldn't keep reeling him in like this. I was too scared to admit my own feelings, because I was in *deep*. I needed him and that terrified me, because I had never felt this way before. That wasn't me. I was proud to be self-sufficient, proud to need only myself for happiness. I didn't need anyone to complete me. But now, with Charlie, it was different. He had broken through those walls and the idea of needing someone else—needing *him*—was shaking everything I thought I knew about myself.

Every time I felt out of control with him, I took the lead sexually, as if it could help me gain the upper hand. But now, I was starting to see it for what it was—I was only digging myself into a deeper hole. Each time I tried to control the situation, I only lost more of myself to him.

"What are you thinking?" he asked, pulling me out of my spiraling thoughts.

We lay together on my bed, his arms around me, and I cuddled closer, wanting to feel the warmth of him. We stayed like that for a moment before I sat up on my elbow, leaving my other arm draped around his chest. "I'm thinking that I'm starving. You never finished making our meal," I joked, trying to make things light.

He smiled, though it didn't reach his eyes. "Guess I got a little distracted," he said playfully, but the disappointment in his voice was undeniable.

I could feel it, the heaviness creeping back in. I was in denial about how far I had let this go, how much of him I was pulling in without fully giving myself back. I was continuing to hurt him whether I meant to or not.

I swallowed, trying to keep my tone light. "Maybe you should…maybe you should go. Get some rest. We can finish dinner another time." The words felt forced but I couldn't ignore the unspoken tension between us anymore.

He blinked, clearly taken aback, his hand frozen on my waist. "You want me to leave?"

I sighed, sitting up. "It's not that I *want* you to leave, Charlie. I just…" I trailed off, unsure of what I wanted to say. I tried searching for the right words but found myself caught between what I felt and how I was too scared to admit it.

He sat up beside me, his eyes narrowing slightly in confusion. "Just *what*?"

I glanced at him, my heart heavy with guilt. "I don't want to keep doing this if I'm just…hurting you."

His face shifted, the playful spark in his eyes fading. "Hurting me?" he repeated, his voice low. "Ana, it hurts me to be away from you."

I looked down, avoiding his gaze, wringing my hands together. I didn't know how to respond to that.

"I don't want to hurt you, Charlie. I just…" My voice trailed off again, my emotions tugging my heart in opposite directions.

He sighed, his hand still resting around my waist but lighter now, almost like he was afraid of touching me. "Then don't push me away. You keep saying you're afraid of hurting me, but this hurts more than anything you could do."

I stiffened, the defensiveness rising in my chest. "I'm not pushing you away," I shot back, pulling away from his touch. I stood up, crossing my arms. "I'm trying to figure things out, Charlie. I keep asking for space and you keep nudging yourself back in, making it impossible for me to think straight."

His eyes widened with a mix of frustration and fear. "I'm nudging myself in because I don't want to lose you," he said, his voice breaking slightly. He got up and stepped towards me, his desperation heightening. "Ana, I'm scared that if I give you too much space, you'll disappear…that you'll decide I'm not worth it."

I froze, his words hitting me harder than I expected. "I'm not going anywhere, but I need to breathe, Charlie. You can't just cling to me like this; we've literally only known each other for a few days."

He gripped my hand. "I know, but it doesn't feel like just a few days to me. It feels like…" His voice cracked again, and the vulnerability in his tone caught me off guard. "I don't care how long it's been, Ana. I can't help it—I *need* you."

I shook my head, stepping back slightly, trying to put some space between us. "Charlie, you're suffocating me. I don't even know what this is yet, and you're acting like it's already too late, like you're going to lose me if you don't hold on tighter."

He stepped forward, refusing to let me create that distance. "Because that's how it feels! I don't know how to slow down, Ana. I don't know how to just…let you go without feeling like I'm losing something important." His voice was strained and he ran his hand through his hair, the frustration clear on his face.

I looked away, guilt and confusion swirling inside me. "It's not fair to put that kind of pressure on me. I can't be the thing that holds you together. You have to stand on your own, Charlie."

"I *know* that," he said quickly, his eyes wide and pleading. "I'm trying, but it's hard. Being with you is the only thing that makes sense to me right now." He took my face in his hands, his touch both gentle and desperate. "Just tell me you'll stay, that you'll give this a chance. Please."

I swallowed hard, his words sinking into me, twisting around my own uncertainty. "I can't promise you anything right now. It's too much, too fast, and I need room to figure out how I feel. You can't keep pushing me like this."

His forehead rested against mine, tears welling in his eyes as he whispered, "I'm not trying to push you. I'm just scared; I'm scared that you'll realize you don't need me at all."

I closed my eyes, his vulnerability breaking through my defenses. "That's not fair to either of us."

"I know," he said softly. "But I'm not going to give up, Ana. Even if you need space, I'm still going to be here. Waiting. Wanting you."

His lips hovered near mine, and before I could think of what to say, they crashed into mine again—this time more urgent, more desperate. The tension from our argument ignited something between us and my hands instinctively grabbed his waist, pulling him closer.

We stumbled backwards, my back hitting the wall as the kiss deepened, all of our anger and frustration dissolving into passionate, heated desire. His hands slid from my waist to my hips, gripping me tightly.

I broke away for a second, panting. "Charlie, this isn't going to fix anything…"

"I know," he whispered, but his mouth was back on mine before I could protest further.

I let myself fall into him again, surrendering to the pull I couldn't resist. I had laid everything bare and he wasn't going to back down. Maybe that's exactly what I needed—or maybe it was dangerously toxic. But I pushed it aside, because somehow, I wanted him more than ever.

\* \* \*

I lay beside Charlie in the faint morning light, his tattooed, muscular body relaxed in sleep next to me. It was as if my words from the night before had never been spoken. After our heated exchange, we ended up having wild, passionate sex. Without needing to say a word, he stayed the night, and now in the quiet aftermath, the reality of it all settled around me.

Charlie wasn't going to let me push him away. He wasn't going to leave. Even if I shoved him out the door, screaming at him to stay away, I knew he'd break it down and force his way back in. And why did that excite me? Why wasn't I more terrified? Instead of running, I was drawn to it—to *him*. This rockstar, this icon, this man who could have anyone in the world, was desperately throwing himself at me and refusing to let go. And it wasn't scaring me off. It was pulling me in deeper.

I refused to continue to think of what was happening between me and Charlie. All I knew was that I wanted to live in the moment. And right now, I wanted him—*badly*. No matter how many times I had him, the itch never seemed to be satisfied.

As I gulped down a glass of water in the kitchen, the memory of his body against mine sent a rush of heat through me, goosebumps prickling my skin at the thought of what he did to me. And of what I did to him.

I casually walked back into the bedroom, wanting to steal another glimpse of him before he woke up, but when I stepped through the doorway, I found him already awake, staring down at a phone in his hand. *My* phone.

My heart dropped as I froze in place, the casual ease of the morning suddenly evaporating. He looked up at me with wide eyes as if he'd been caught.

"*¿Qué estás haciendo?* What are you doing?" I demanded, marching up to the bed and snatching my phone out of his hand.

He didn't say anything at first, his lips parting like he was trying to come up with an excuse, but my attention shifted to the vibrating phone in my hand. Sloane's name flashed across the screen.

I felt the tension grow between us, my heart racing. "Why are you going through my phone, Charlie?"

"It was going off. It woke me up. I thought it was mine," he said, a sincerity in his eyes that made me believe him.

## ANA

Tension immediately released from my shoulders as I sighed, glancing down at my phone before turning to walk out of the room. *"Hola*, baby," I answered, my voice softening as I stepped into the hallway.

"Hey, I tried calling you yesterday," Sloane's voice came through with a mixture of concern and curiosity. "Are you okay? I haven't heard much from you lately."

I leaned against the wall, my eyes drifting back towards the bedroom where Charlie still sat. "Yeah, I'm good. Just...a little distracted."

He instantly flashed his charming, dimpled smile at me as he listened in on the conversation. I had to look away, biting back the smile that crept onto my lips. It was infuriating how easily he could disarm me.

"Distracted, huh?" Sloane teased through the phone. "Any particular reason why?"

I sighed heavily as I walked further away from Charlie, needing privacy. "Charlie Ashford will not leave me alone," I said quietly and playfully.

Sloane gasped on the other end. "No way, Mom," she said with a laugh. "Tell me everything," she demanded, and it was the only time I ever felt uncomfortable with how open we were with each other.

"I...I don't know, baby. I'm not sure what this is yet. It's intense. *He's* intense," I admitted, making my way towards the terrace, needing some air.

"I told you, Mom. He's a little crazy," she said, her voice still casual despite her words.

"What? You said he was sensitive...a hopeless romantic?" My heart started to race; was Charlie actually known for being "crazy?" And why did that surprise me? Didn't I already know that?

Sloane let out a soft chuckle. "Well, yeah. He's both. That's why everyone says he's a little crazy when he's with someone."

For some reason, the thought of him being with anyone else made my chest flutter with jealousy. I wasn't a jealous person—at least, I never had been. But all of these new feelings Charlie was stirring up inside of me left me feeling like I was a whole different person.

And then it hit me—this feeling Charlie had for me, this intense obsession, wasn't something he reserved only for me. It wasn't unique. He'd been like this with others before, and I hated how much that upset me. The thought of not being the only one who made him feel this way gnawed at me, sparking an ugly jealousy I never expected to feel.

"You there, Mom?" Sloane's voice snapped me back to reality.

"Yeah. I have to go, baby. I'll call you in a bit," I said, my voice clipped and breathless from the jealousy biting at my chest.

I ended the call and stormed back into the room. Charlie looked up and smiled as I entered, but I couldn't shake the unsettling feeling of not being special, of just being another one of his obsessions.

"What's wrong?" he asked, his eyes widening as his smile faded.

I paused, staring at him, the words swirling in my mind. "Have you ever felt this way about someone else?" I blurted out, my heart racing. "Or am I just the latest in a long line of people you've been obsessed with?"

His face instantly fell, hurt flickering across his features before determination took over. "Ana, no. You've got it wrong," he said, his voice rising as he got up and took a step towards me. "I've never been like this with anyone else. Not even close."

I held my ground, arms crossed, my heart pounding. "You've *never* done this before?" I asked with accusation.

"No," he growled, his voice firm and unwavering. "Not like this. Not like I am with you." His eyes locked onto mine, full of desperation. "What I feel for you—it's not some fleeting obsession. This is fucking real, Ana. You're different. I don't just want you…I *need* you. I've never needed anyone like this."

I paused and I couldn't look away. He was adamant, almost to the point of being frightening in his conviction. And I hated the relief that washed over me, my jealousy turning into something else—something darker, triumphant. It felt wrong to crave this kind of validation, yet I couldn't deny how deeply I needed it. His obsession wasn't scaring me anymore, and that fact alone began to frighten me.

His eyes searched mine, his breathing heavy, and then quietly, he said, "I love you, Ana."

I froze, my heart thudding in my chest. His voice softened almost to a whisper, his desperation turning vulnerable. "I was afraid to say it before. I was afraid I'd scare you away. But I can't hold it back anymore. I'm *in love* with you."

The words hung in the air between us and I felt like I couldn't breathe. He stepped closer, his hand reaching for mine. "I don't just need you, Ana. I love you. Completely. And I've never felt like this about anyone."

I stared at him, every part of me reeling from his confession. I didn't know if I was ready to hear those words, but something about the way he said them made it impossible to turn away or argue.

His green eyes softened as he looked at me, sensing my hesitation. "You don't have to say it back," he said quietly. "I don't need to hear you say you love me. I just need you to know how I feel…to know that I'm entirely devoted to you, more than anything, no matter what."

I exhaled slowly, relieved that he wasn't pushing for something I couldn't give. He stepped closer, his hand squeezing mine gently. "I'll wait for you, Ana. However long it takes. I just want you to know that I'm not going anywhere."

It was impossible to deny the comfort his words brought, the reassurance I didn't know I needed. "Thank you," I whispered.

And even though I couldn't say it back, I already knew—I loved him too. The realization hit me like a slow burn, warming my chest and settling in deeper than I expected. I wasn't ready to admit it aloud, not yet, but it was there…and it was undeniable and terrifying.

# 10

# Charlie

I could feel Ana's shield slowly start to crack. I didn't expect to tell her that I loved her, especially after our argument about her needing space. But when she stormed into the room, accusing me of feeling this way for others, something inside me snapped. I couldn't hold it back anymore. It wasn't about pushing or pulling—it was about telling her the truth.

When she looked at me with that mixture of frustration and uncertainty, I realized I couldn't keep pretending I was okay with the distance. At least, the emotional distance. I loved her and I needed her to know, even if she wasn't ready to say it back.

I saw the flicker in her eyes when I said it—the way her defenses wavered, just for a moment. And in that moment, I knew she felt something too, even if she wouldn't admit it yet.

Thank God for Sloane and whatever the fuck she told Ana because it felt like we were finally moving forward. For the first time, it didn't feel like Ana was about to bolt at any second. There was a shift, something subtle, but I could feel it in the way she looked at me—less guarded, like she was starting to let me in, piece by piece.

She didn't ask me to leave again after that. As if I would anyway.

I made dinner up to her by offering to cook brunch. I wasn't a gourmet chef but I wanted her to see that I could cook, that I could take care of her in those little ways. I wanted to impress her. I *needed* to impress her. It felt like I was always trying to prove myself, constantly wanting her to see that I was more than just some rockstar. I wanted to show her that this wasn't just about sex; I wanted her to see who I really was. I wanted her to know I was serious about her—about *us*.

Offering to cook also gave me the perfect excuse to get her out of the apartment when I needed to pick up groceries. I wanted to see what it would be like for us to be somewhere other than the safe confines of the apartment, to feel her by my side in public, maybe sneak in a hand hold or two. It was something small, but it felt significant.

Being well-known in New York City had its perks—most New Yorkers didn't give a shit about famous people. They'd let you blend into the background. But there was always that chance we'd run into a group of tourists who'd hound you, or secretly snap pictures.

The thought of being caught with Ana thrilled me. Maybe it was reckless, but part of me wanted to be seen with her. A big part of me. I wanted to show the world she was *mine*.

We bundled ourselves up against the cold January chill as we stepped out of her building. Ana didn't need much convincing to go out with me, but she insisted on her bodyguard, Miles, trailing behind us. It was hard not to notice the guy, but I didn't mind, just as long as he kept his distance. What mattered was having this time with her, without the constant reminder of the walls she kept up. If she was going to open up, I didn't want anyone getting in the way of that.

I was a little disappointed to find that the small market was only around the corner, but it was something. It was a chance to be out with her, even for just a short walk. We stayed close enough that our arms brushed, and I took the opportunity to place my hand gently on her back as we wandered through the produce section, a small basket hanging off my forearm. She would steal glances at me and smile as I talked her ear off, my constant need for her attention running rampant. I couldn't help it—every time she looked at me, I felt like I had to say something and to keep her focus on me.

After we rang up, I realized I wasn't ready to head back yet. I wanted more time outside with her—more opportunity to be seen. I remembered a local coffee shop nearby, a small, private spot where we could be alone but still out in the world. It was perfect.

"Hey," I said, glancing over at her as we stepped out of the store. "There's this coffee shop a few blocks over. It's quiet there. How about we grab something warm and sit for a bit?"

Her eyes flickered with curiosity, and after a brief pause, she looked back at Miles. His face was stoic and unreadable. I could tell she was weighing whether to indulge me or not, but then she glanced back at me and nodded with a smile. "Sure."

It was a small word but hearing it felt like a victory. We started walking again and I felt that familiar thrill of just being outside with her. Then I noticed someone out of the corner of my eye; someone was holding their phone up, pointed right at us. My stomach dropped and I quickly looked away, hoping Ana didn't catch it. I didn't want this to end yet. This moment was too rare, too good, and the last thing I wanted was for her to retreat because of some random person snapping photos.

Then I felt it—possessive, protective, like a switch had flipped inside me. The sight of that phone aimed at us, at *her*, stirred something in me. My heart raced, and the need to shield her from the intrusion overwhelmed me.

Without thinking, I shifted closer to her, my hand resting firmly on her back. I wanted to keep her close, to make sure no one ruined this moment. She was mine right now and I wasn't about to let some stranger take that away from us.

She glanced up at me, a confused and slightly surprised smile on her face, as if she'd sensed the shift. She raised her eyebrows but she didn't pull away. Instead, her curious smile lingered.

"What are you doing?" she asked softly, her tone teasing but still unsure. "I wasn't planning on running," she added with a soft laugh.

I chuckled. "Good. I'd hate to have to chase after you."

"I don't know, I'd say you're pretty good at chasing after me now." Her smile widened as she looked up at me.

I laughed, though a part of me knew how true that was. "Yeah well, you make it worth the chase," I shot back, leaning in a little closer.

And then, fucking Miles called out her name, stopping her in her tracks as she quickly turned around. His eyes pointed to a group now gathering, phones up, stopping to take pictures of us. I saw her eyes follow, narrowing in frustration as she muttered under her breath. "Let's go. We'll have coffee at home."

Just like that, the moment we had shattered, and I felt the same surge of protectiveness rush through me again. I hated that something as simple as this had to be interrupted and taken away from us. I nodded, following her lead as we quickly headed down the street, her pace picking up, Miles close behind.

But as annoyed as I was, my plan worked. We were caught. Our pictures would be out in the world and now everyone would know she was *mine*. As much as I hated the intrusion, there was a twisted satisfaction in knowing that we couldn't hide anymore. The world would see us together—see her with *me*.

I glanced over at Ana as we hurried along, feeling a small smile forming on my lips. She had no idea how much I wanted this, how much I craved the validation of being seen with her, making it official in a way neither of us had quite admitted yet.

\* \* \*

I completely fucked up our omelettes. I tried to turn the omelette over, but as soon as I did, it fell apart in the pan. It was scrambled eggs now more than anything. I cursed under my breath, staring at the mess I made. I was too distracted, my eyes constantly drifting towards Ana as she scattered around the apartment, making calls, sending emails as she sat on the floor in front of the couch, completely restless. I couldn't stop watching her and couldn't focus on anything else. Every time she brushed her hair back or shifted positions, my attention was gone.

The ruined omelette was just the consequence of being completely consumed by her.

"Scrambled eggs are ready," I announced playfully, bringing

the mess of a brunch to the dining table, trying to make light of it. I set the plates down with a grin, hoping the disaster in the pan would be forgiven.

Ana glanced up from her phone, eyebrows raised, and then smirked when she saw the scrambled eggs instead of the omelettes I promised. "Well, at least you tried, my sweet boy," she teased, standing up and heading over to the table.

The words hit me like lightning, igniting something deep inside. I hadn't expected her to call me that outside of anything sexual. My chest tightened and I swallowed hard, trying to play it cool. She said it so casually, yet it carried so much weight for me. *Too* much. My cock began to harden and I had to walk away. This was such a nice, domesticated moment, and the last thing I wanted was to turn it into something sexual.

I gathered myself as I poured coffee for each of us, then made my way back to the table where she sat, waiting expectantly for me.

"I didn't realize you were so *domesticado*," she teased playfully. "Thank you," she added, her gaze softening as she looked down at her plate.

She was so sweet at that moment and it hit me—how disarming she could be. One minute she had me completely wound up, and the next, she was soft and unassuming, making me fall for her all over again.

*"De nada, mi diosa,"* I said just as playfully as I sat down across from her.

Her eyebrows lifted, a look of impressed surprise crossing her face. I lived for that look. *"¿Hablas español?"*

I shook my head, smiling. "No. But I'm a great student. I'd love for you to teach me," I replied, leaning in slightly.

Her smirk grew, her eyes gleaming with that spark I craved. "We'll see," she said teasingly. The way she looked at me in that moment, half intrigued, half amused—I'd do anything to keep earning that.

We sat in silence for a moment as we ate when Ana's phone began vibrating on the coffee table. She glanced back at it, the screen lighting up, and then looked at me hesitantly.

"You can take it," I said with a nod, secretly delighted that she considered me before answering.

She went to fetch her phone, but when she saw who was calling, her face fell. She picked up the phone, her voice soft as she answered. "Hey."

I watched as her eyes darted around the room and she began to slowly pace, listening intently. My stomach twisted with an unfamiliar sense of jealousy. Someone was taking up her attention and it wasn't me.

"Okay. Just keep quiet about it. We don't need to say anything," she said quietly.

Then it hit me—it was about the pictures. Excitement bubbled up inside me, but I kept it contained. She was too serious, too focused on keeping this contained for me to show how much I reveled in it.

"Yes," she went on, suddenly glancing up at me with a spark in her eye. "We are."

*We are* what?

My curiosity spiked, but before I could piece it together, her tone shifted. "Not every detail in my personal life needs to be shared with you, Marissa."

I love seeing her feistiness come through and I could see her defenses kicking in. She was standing her ground, that edge to her voice coming out, and I felt a strange sense of pride at her protectiveness. But still, I was desperate to know what she was defending so fiercely and why I was starting to feel territorial all over again.

She sighed, turning her back to me. "Okay. Bye." With a quick toss, she threw her phone onto the couch and faced me again, her expression a mix of frustration and resignation.

"Those pictures are all over the internet. My publicist went crazy," she said, putting a hand to her hip.

I nodded, trying to keep my expression neutral, but inside, that flicker of excitement returned. *All over the internet.* It was hard not to feel some kind of satisfaction. "I figured it wouldn't take long," I said, leaning back slightly. "How bad is it?"

She sighed again, crossing her arms. "It's everywhere. People are already speculating things…you know how it is."

I tried to stay calm though my mind was racing with the thought of us being out there, visible to the world. "Well," I said, giving her a small grin. "That just means we're official now, right?"

Her eyes flickered and I couldn't tell if she was more annoyed or relieved. Probably both.

"Charlie, you don't know what this means. It's serious," Ana snapped, her voice full of frustration. "I just dealt with that stupid fucking scandal with my stupid fucking ex-husband six months ago, and now I'm being thrown into the spotlight all over again."

I could see her anger surfacing and the exhaustion in her eyes. This wasn't just about the pictures. It was about everything she'd been through, everything she was trying to move past.

I stood up and stepped closer, keeping my voice soft. "Ana,

I get that. I know this is the last thing you wanted right now, especially after what happened. But you're not in this alone."

She looked up at me, a flash of skepticism crossing her face, but I kept going. "I know you're tired of the spotlight, of dealing with everyone's opinions, but I'm here. And this time, you're not dealing with it by yourself."

She stood there for a moment, her frustration still simmering. But slowly, I could see her defenses start to crack.

I should have felt guilty because, in a way, I caused this. I wanted to claim her as mine, to show the world we weren't some secret. But looking at her now, that desire to have her known as mine was stronger than any guilt I felt.

# 11

# Ana

Three days. That's all it took for the world to know that Charlie and I were together. There wasn't any official confirmation, but you could tell—you could see it in the photos, in the way we walked together, closely and intimately. The way his hand rested on my back, the way we leaned into each other, almost unconsciously. It was all there, plain as day, for anyone looking closely enough.

I wasn't sure how I felt about it. Part of me wanted to crawl back into my safe, private bubble, but the other part...the other part *liked* it. I liked being seen with him even if I wasn't ready to admit that yet. He was so goddamn handsome, and we looked *so good* together. You couldn't even tell there was a twelve-year age difference, not that it mattered. None of it mattered anymore.

I realized that I didn't care if he was too much, if he was overwhelming. The truth was, it was beyond my control now. The way he looked at me, the way he held onto me, I was drawn to it, to *him*. And now I realized I didn't want to let go. I was finally giving in, no longer resisting. I craved his unwavering obsession with me, the way he reassured me over and over again that he was in love with me. It wasn't just about the way he touched me or the way he looked at me like I was his entire world. It was the way he made me feel seen and wanted. His devotion was intoxicating, and no matter how complicated it made things, I couldn't resist it.

But even with those pictures out, I didn't want to leave the bubble we created in my apartment. He hadn't left since he arrived days ago; he had someone deliver clothes and everything else he needed. I didn't bother telling him he could leave, that he could go get what he wanted and come back, because I knew he'd refuse. He clung to me for dear life, and deep down, I liked it. The way he stayed, refusing to be anywhere else, filled me with a strange sense of comfort.

When Sloane called to say she and Callan would be in town for the weekend, panic set in. The bubble I had built with Charlie felt fragile, ready to burst. I hadn't prepared for anyone, *especially* my daughter, to witness what was happening between us. I raised her to be self-sufficient, to rely on no one for happiness, to stand strong on her own. And here I was, wrapped up in someone else, the complete opposite of everything I taught her. The thought of Sloane seeing me like this…it terrified me in so many ways.

When the news first broke, Sloane had called, teasing me in that way only she could.

"So, Mom." She laughed. "I thought I'd be the first to know if this turned into something!"

I brushed it off at the time, but now, with their visit looming, reality was sinking in. How was I supposed to explain this… whatever *this* was?

Charlie didn't seem excited when he learned about their

visit, even though he didn't say anything outright. His face fell just a bit, the usual easygoing attitude slipping away for a moment. I could tell he wasn't thrilled about the idea of us having company and the thought worried me. Was he trying to keep me only to himself? Did he want me to block out the rest of the world for him? The questions raced in my mind and I couldn't shake the nagging feeling that maybe this was more than just discomfort about my daughter's visit, about meeting her for the first time. Was he trying to pull me further into this bubble we had created, away from everyone else?

As much as I craved his obsession, the thought of him isolating us left a pit in my stomach. I had to figure out how to balance this, how to keep a hold of my own life, without losing myself entirely in him.

And then I thought of something, a way to keep control of this situation. I would use my hold over him. The way he needed my attention and approval—I'd use it to my advantage. He was always desperate to prove himself, to make sure I was happy, and now I'd turn that desperation into leverage.

I told him, carefully, as if I were revealing a vulnerable truth. "I'm afraid of losing my daughter's respect if she knew how much I needed you." The words came out soft, but I knew exactly what I was doing. I could see the way his face softened, his protectiveness flaring up instantly.

He wanted to reassure me, to prove that he could be what I needed. And I knew I had him.

It didn't feel good manipulating him. The guilt of it sat heavy in my chest, but I needed to know that I still had control, some semblance of power in all this chaos. I needed to remind myself that I had a say in this, even though I knew better.

He was already so wrapped up in me, so eager to please, that

## ANA

it almost felt too easy to pull the strings. But still, I hated that I was doing it. I hated that I was using his need for my attention to steer things in my favor. And I hated that I had to do it in the first place. It was alarming, but as always, I pushed that aside.

I told myself it was necessary, that it was the only way to keep things from spiraling. I needed to make sure I didn't lose myself entirely in him. It wasn't just about controlling *him*—it was about controlling *myself*. It was about staying true to who I was, even as I felt myself slipping deeper into this strange, intoxicating world.

\* \* \*

Charlie stood behind me in the kitchen, his hands wrapped around my waist as I prepared snacks for everyone. He seemed to savor every second of our closeness, like he was storing up all the affection he could before Sloane and Callan showed up.

I smiled when I heard the rapid tapping on the front door. As nervous as I was about having Charlie here during their visit, the excitement of seeing my daughter outweighed it. When Charlie slipped his hands from around me and stepped back, it almost felt like we'd been caught.

"I promise I'll be good, *mi diosa*," he said with a playful smile, like the secret we shared was an exciting game to him. And if I was honest, it thrilled me too; no one knew just how deep our connection ran, and that secrecy only heightened the excitement.

"I know you will be," I teased, giving him a quick kiss. I knew it was just enough to reassure him.

I made my way to the door, my heart full as I saw Callan and

Sloane standing there. Sloane's eyes gleamed with excitement and Callan seemed content, his arm wrapped around her waist.

"Mom," Sloane greeted, flashing me a knowing smile before glancing past my shoulder, no doubt searching for Charlie.

"Hi, baby," I said, widening my arms and melting into her embrace as she stepped forward.

After Sloane let go, I turned to Callan, hugging him warmly. A part of me wondered if Charlie would be jealous. I pushed the thought aside, because if that happened to be true, that would be an even bigger problem than I was ready to handle.

As I pulled away, I noticed Sloane already making her way over to Charlie, greeting him easily. Callan closed the door behind them as I followed, my heart already racing. I hated not knowing how this interaction would go.

"So nice to finally meet you, Sloane," Charlie said, his dimpled grin sending familiar flutters through me. "I've heard a lot about you." He glanced at me briefly, his gaze lingering just a moment before turning back to her.

"And I've heard plenty about you, Charlie," Sloane teased, reaching for Callan's hand.

Callan, setting their bags down, gave Charlie a friendly tap on the shoulder. "Good to see you, man."

Charlie, as if on instinct, searched for my hand as I moved to stand beside him. And without thinking, I did the same, feeling his presence like a tether. My fingers wrapped around his, gripping tightly, and the familiar comfort settled over me. I couldn't deny how much I needed that closeness too, especially in this moment.

I caught the briefest flicker of a smile on Charlie's face as he squeezed my hand. For a second, I worried it might be too much, but Sloane seemed unfazed as she and Callan walked further into the living room.

"More plants, Mom? You're worse than me now," Sloane teased, eyeing the new plant Charlie brought me.

I laughed, shrugging lightly. "Blame Charlie. He got me that one," I said, glancing at him with a playful smile.

Charlie chuckled softly, giving me a sideways glance. "What can I say? Gift giving is my love language," he said, but his smile quickly faded, as if he'd said something wrong.

But I didn't mind. In fact, I only wanted more of him—more of these little moments where he revealed pieces of himself so openly, despite my nervousness of this visit.

"Yeah? What's yours then, Mom?" Sloane asked, her eyebrows raised, completely unfazed by the question.

Before I could answer, Charlie beat me to it, his voice low and sure. "Physical touch," he said, his gaze still on me, a playful smile lingering on his lips as he bit down on his bottom one slightly.

My breath hitched for a moment. I glanced at Sloane, wondering if she noticed the true meaning behind his words.

"Gross," Sloane said sarcastically as she turned and made her way towards the terrace. "What's for dinner?"

Callan leaned casually against the couch with his arms crossed, his gaze following Sloane before shifting back to Charlie and me. He watched us observantly, though I barely noticed as Charlie's hand slid down my arm.

He leaned in closer, his voice dropping to a low murmur. "Speaking of physical touch…" he whispered, his lips brushing just near my ear, sending goosebumps over my flesh. His thumb traced small patterns on my skin, the meaning behind his words clear.

A flush crept up my neck, but before I could respond, I felt Callan's eyes still on us. I glanced up, catching the slight tension in his jaw. He definitely heard that. *So what?* His expression stayed neutral but the concern was there, unspoken but obvious to me.

Charlie didn't seem to notice or care that Callan had picked up on the subtle, sexual exchange. He just kept his gaze on me, a slow smile forming as his fingers lingered.

Then I wondered if he was silently staking his claim, as if he would have to do that in front of Callan, my daughter's fiance. Did his jealousy run that deep?

Callan, quiet but clearly uneasy, pushed off the couch and glanced towards the terrace. "I'll go see what Sloane's up to," he said casually, but the tension in his voice gave him away.

I didn't know what it was, but I knew Callan was thinking something, and he was going to let me know what it was, whether I wanted to hear it or not.

\* \* \*

Dinner had gone smoothly, the conversation flowing easily enough between the four of us. But even as we ate, I couldn't shake the tension from Callan from earlier. He had been quieter than usual, his focus drifting between Charlie and me, like he was working something out in his head.

After dinner we sat on the terrace, mingling amongst ourselves. When Sloane excused herself to take a phone call and Charlie went to grab something from the kitchen, Callan glanced at me. His demeanor had shifted from relaxed to something more serious, his arms crossed, as if he was guarding himself for what he was about to say.

"Ana," he started, keeping his voice low. "There's something I've been meaning to tell you…about Charlie."

My heart skipped a beat, but I tried to remain calm. "What do you mean?"

He hesitated, glancing towards the kitchen to make sure Charlie wasn't nearby. "Look, I didn't want to say anything before, but I've heard some things about him. Stuff that's… unsettling."

I furrowed my brow, feeling my stomach drop. "What do you mean?"

He sighed, lowering his voice even more. "Back when he dated someone a few years ago, that one actress, I heard he got…possessive. Really fucking intense. People talked about how he wouldn't let her go anywhere without him, how he was always checking up on her." His eyes darkened, concern clear on his face. "And when she broke up with him…apparently, he didn't take it well. Tried to hurt himself. Some people said it was a cry for attention, others said it was serious. But…I thought you should know."

I swallowed hard, my chest tightening. "Why didn't you tell me this earlier?"

Callan shook his head. "After Sloane told me about his history, I looked into it. I wasn't sure if it was true. People talk, you know? But seeing him today, I don't know, Ana. He seems…"

"Intense?" I finished for him, my voice quiet.

Callan nodded. "I get that you care about him, but I've seen this before. I've seen guys like this get worse. Just…be careful. I don't want you getting hurt."

I nodded, a strange feeling creeping over me. The red flags were there, screaming at me to run. But I ignored them, clutching red flags of my own.

\*\*\*

When Sloane and Callan settled into the guest room later, I couldn't shake the conversation with Callan from my mind. His words kept echoing in my head, and no matter how hard I tried to ignore them, the weight of it all kept pressing down on me. I knew I couldn't let it go.

Charlie must've sensed it too. He'd been watching me closely all evening, probably waiting for me to say something. Finally, when it was just the two of us in my room, he broke the silence.

"Ana, what's going on? You've been quiet…more quiet than usual." He pulled his shirt off over his head and I caught myself staring.

I swallowed, my heart racing. "Callan said something earlier…"

He froze, already defensive. "What did he say?"

I hesitated but I couldn't keep it in any longer. "He was concerned after he heard some…stuff. He said you were possessive with your ex. That you wouldn't let her have any space. And when she broke up with you…you tried to hurt yourself."

Charlie's face went pale and I knew right then that it was true. He didn't even try to deny it. He sat at the edge of the bed and shook his head. He ran a hand through his hair, clearly frustrated. "That was a long time ago, Ana. I was in a really bad place."

I shook my head, feeling the anger rise inside me. "You told me you were never like this with anyone else. You said it was different with me. That I was the only one you've ever been—"

## ANA

His eyes flickered with confusion and hurt. "It *is* different with you. It wasn't like that with her."

I scoffed, jealousy rising within me again. "I don't know what to believe anymore. I keep hearing that you've been crazy about these other women. And now suddenly I'm the only one you're like this with?" I hated every word coming out of my mouth but I couldn't stop them.

Charlie stood up and stepped towards me, his voice low. "No, Ana, you don't understand. It's not the same. What I feel for you…it's deeper. Endless. I never felt this way with her."

I shook my head, my heart pounding in my chest. "But you were still like that with her, Charlie. You said I was the only one. You *lied*."

Charlie's jaw clenched, his eyes pleading with me to understand. "I *didn't* lie. It's different with you, Ana—"

"Stop," I interrupted. Tears stung the back of my eyes but I blinked them away. As much as I hated it, I was jealous—jealous that he'd been this way with someone else, and even *I* knew how crazy that sounded. I knew how toxic this thinking was, but it was there, gnawing at me.

"Ana, please," Charlie's voice softened, stepping closer. "I don't want you to feel like this. What I feel for you is…it's so much more. It scares me sometimes, how much I need you."

I wrapped my arms around myself, trying to create some distance. "I know it's not right to even think this way," I admitted, my voice shaky. "But I can't help it. You told me I was the only one and now I don't know if I can believe anything you say."

Everything I was saying felt so juvenile, so immature, but it was as if something else entirely took over me.

Charlie's face fell and I saw the hurt in his eyes. "Ana, I didn't want to tell you because I didn't want to lose you. She's been the furthest thing from my mind. Insignificant. What I feel for you…it's so fucking different. It's…it feels all-consuming."

His words wrapped around me like a spell, intoxicating and magnetic, and I couldn't pull away. Something inside me shifted—something dark and possessive. *If he can be this way, why can't I?* I felt myself giving in. It was too late to turn back now. Because I loved him in a way that was not only deep—it was dangerous.

I didn't just want him—I wanted to own him too. The thought was unsettling but thrilling.

"Maybe it's not just you," I said, my voice dropping. "Maybe it's not just you that's obsessive, Charlie. Maybe…I am too."

Charlie's eyes widened slightly, obviously caught off guard by the shift in my tone, and I saw the spark of excitement in his eyes. He was enjoying this. No, he was *loving* it.

"Ana…" His voice trembled slightly.

I pressed my body against his, my fingers tracing up his chest slowly. His breathing sped, his heart pounding beneath my touch as I leaned in to whisper against his ear. "You think I don't feel the same? That I don't think about how much I *want* you to need me, to crave me the way you do?"

Charlie let out a low, shaky breath, his hands instinctively pulling me closer. "Ana…fuck."

"I want you to think about me constantly," I continued, a rush of power surging through me. "I want you so obsessed with me that it drives you crazy. It drives you *mad*. Because I feel it too, Charlie. I don't want you to ever leave. I want you right here, with me. Always."

A low groan escaped his lips, his eyes darkening with lust as I spoke. "Fuck, *mi diosa*…I love this. I didn't know you felt this way."

I smiled, but I felt something dark, just like the pull I felt inside. "You didn't think you were the only one who could be this way, did you?"

His eyes lit up with excitement, his breath growing heavier. "I love it," he whispered, his voice thick with need. "I love it, Ana. I love *you*. It's deeper than love. I want you to own me, possess me in every way."

I reached up, gently cupping his face. "I'll make sure of it, Charlie. I've never felt this way either. I've never been so desperate for someone before. So…so in love."

His grip tightened on my hips desperately. "Fuck, *mi diosa*. You don't know how much I needed to hear that."

There was a deep ache in my chest, and I needed him more than ever. "You belong to me now. Just like I belong to you."

Charlie groaned again, his hard cock pressing firmly against my body. "Yes," he breathed, his lips brushing mine. "I'm yours, Ana. Completely. I love you, *mi diosa*."

I could feel the heat between us, the way he responded to every word, every touch. It wasn't just about his obsession anymore. Because now…it was mutual.

# 12

# Charlie

I was on my back looking up at Ana as I tasted her sweet cunt in my mouth, swirling her clit with my tongue.

I knew I couldn't live without her. I'd always known this since the day we met, but now…something snapped inside me. Whatever control I had left, whatever restraint I'd been holding onto, it was completely gone. She was my life.

Ana, *mi diosa*, was everything I thought she was and more. That dark, possessive side of her…I didn't see it coming, but now that she had shown me, I became even more in love with her. She *wanted* me in the same twisted, consuming way that I needed her. She told me, *confessed it*, and it was all I could think about.

I never craved anyone like this. It's like my body, my mind, my entire soul was wired to her now. The way she looked at me when she said she loved me, that I belonged to her—it's all I'd been waiting for. Every second of every day, she was in my head, and now that I knew she felt it too, I didn't want to hold back. I *couldn't*.

She was my obsession and I couldn't control it. I didn't *want* to control it. I needed her and I knew she needed me in the same dangerous way.

"Yes, baby. I'm coming, I'm—" She moaned loudly in the open room, coming more times than I could count, and I smiled knowing that people would hear. I didn't care that it was her daughter and Callan, the fucking traitor who tried to pin my goddess against me.

"Please come on my face again, *mi diosa*," I said as my hands gripped her thighs after she lifted her hips slightly, sitting back on my chest.

She smiled down at me, catching her breath. Her tits rose up and down in sync with her chest, but she shook her head and scooted further down my body, making her way to my aching cock.

"No. Now I want you to come deep inside of me and claim my body. Fuck me so hard that you'll be weeping as you come because of how good I feel." Her voice was low and demanding as I focused on her perfect lips.

*Oh my God.* I licked my lips and grabbed her hips, syncing my cock perfectly with her pussy. "Yes, *mi diosa*." Relief flooded my body as I thrust into her, my mind overwhelmed with how much I loved her.

And I *did* weep as I came deep inside of her, because I knew that I would finally never be alone again.

\*\*\*

I jolted awake from a panicked nightmare as the faint morning light barely crept into the bedroom. In the dream, Ana had left me, and I was standing at the top of my building, screaming to the world that I didn't want to live without her. I leapt to my death—and that's when I woke up.

In the real world, if Ana ever tried to leave me, that's exactly what I'd do. I knew myself better than anyone—I was a lost fucking cause. I'd been in love before, but it was nothing compared to what I felt for Ana now.

And Callan had the nerve to try and take that away from me.

Anger seethed deep in my core. How the fuck would he know anything about my past? We'd talked a few times, sure, but we weren't friends. We were barely acquaintances. Yet here he was, talking to Ana like he knew everything about me. So what if what he said was true? I knew I had my issues. But he had no right to tell her. That was supposed to come from me.

But in a twisted way, it worked out. Her jealousy surfaced again and that's what I needed, because it showed me she cared. It proved that she loved me.

I carefully slunk out of bed and grabbed a pair of pajama pants from the pile atop Ana's dresser. It had become a temporary home for many of my clothes, at least until I bought us a bigger dresser. I couldn't even remember the last time I was home; it must've been the night I came over to cook dinner for Ana. So much had changed since then.

As I stepped carefully on the cold hardwood floor towards the kitchen, I could hear a faint noise, like the muffled sound of the TV. I rounded the corner into the living room and found Sloane curled up in the corner of the couch, knees pulled up to her chest under a blanket. Her eyes were fixed on her phone, but when I stopped, she glanced up, her gaze briefly flicking over my shirtless chest before meeting my eyes.

"Oh, hey," she said casually, quickly looking away. "What

are you doing up so early?"

I crossed my arms, suddenly feeling a little too exposed. "Couldn't sleep. I could ask you the same," I said, not moving from where I stood.

She shrugged. "Callan and I got into a little argument. I think you know why." Her eyes dropped to the floor, the sadness in them unmistakable.

*Oh, fuck. He told her too.* I sighed, my gaze falling to my feet. "I love your mum, Sloane. I know I can be a lot, but I'd never do anything to hurt her. I was young and reckless in my previous relationships. I've grown since then." I knew most of it was a lie, except for the part about never hurting Ana. That was true.

Sloane let out a heavy sigh and I glanced back at her, waiting for her to speak. "My mom is extremely independent. She's very self-reliant, keeps to herself. But I've never seen her this way before. She's...she clearly adores you." Her voice was calm but laced with concern. "I don't believe our past defines us, but I really hope you're good to her, Charlie."

I could see so much of Ana in her—fiery, passionate, and blunt. I knew I had to win her over, make her understand how much I truly cared for her mum.

I took a deep breath, trying to find the right words. "Sloane, I understand why you're worried. My past doesn't look great, and I get that you'd be protective of your mum. But I need you to know that she's everything to me. I've never felt like this about anyone."

I uncrossed my arms, forcing myself to meet her gaze, even though I could feel the fire growing within me. "Your mum's strong and independent and I love that about her. I don't want to change her."

My voice lowered and I felt my heart begin to race. "I know I can be a bit much sometimes, but I would never hurt her. I couldn't. She's the center of my world, Sloane. I'd do anything for her." I couldn't stop fucking talking.

Sloane's expression grew more concerned, but I kept going, my words flowing faster now, fueled by the deep need I felt. "I can't imagine a life without her. I want to be with her, always. I don't know what I'd do if she wasn't in my life…"

I trailed off, realizing I said too much. My jaw clenched as I forced myself to reel it back in. "What I'm trying to say is, I love her. More than anything. And I'm not going anywhere."

Sloane studied me for a moment. I could see the wheels turning in her mind, trying to piece together what I had just said. The silence stretched between us and my panic grew.

Finally, she let out a soft sigh, her eyes meeting mine with a mix of caution and something softer—maybe hope. "I believe you care about her, Charlie. I can see that. And I want to believe that you'll be good to her." She shifted on the couch, pulling the blanket tighter around her shoulders. "I'm just… I'm protective of my mom. She's my best friend. Seeing her this way with you is new for me. I just don't want her to get hurt, you know?"

Her voice was gentle but I could still sense the protective daughter in her still lingering. "But if you really love her like you say you do, then I'm glad she's found someone who sees her for who she is. Just…" She trailed off, pausing for a moment. "Just don't forget that she's always been fine on her own. I hope you keep her happiness in mind. It's all I care about."

Her words hit harder than I expected. *She's been just fine on her own. Keep her happiness in mind.* The way she said it, so

## CHARLIE

sure of herself, like she knew Ana better than anyone else. I clenched my jaw, forcing myself to stay calm, but inside, it felt like a slow burn. *Of course she's independent.* I knew that. I'd seen it firsthand. But the way Sloane said it, like Ana didn't need anyone, as if she didn't need *me*—it got under my skin.

No one really knew Ana like I did. They saw the version of her they wanted to see: the strong, self-reliant woman who didn't need anyone to complete her. But they didn't see her the way I did. The way she softened when it was just the two of us. The way she let down her guard, let me into parts of her life no one else could touch.

They didn't understand how much she needed me. How much she craved someone who saw past the walls she put up. Someone who said, only hours ago, that she wanted me to claim her body, that she was obsessed with me…that she wanted to be all mine.

Sloane could talk about her mum's independence all she wanted, but it didn't change the fact that Ana and I were connected in a way no one else could ever understand. She wasn't just "fine on her own." She was mine. And that was something no one else could claim.

I gave Sloane a small smile, keeping my tone light. "Your mum's happiness is all I care about as well. I'm glad we're on the same page."

Sloane only nodded and returned the smile back. Before I could hear any more of her shit, I turned around and walked into the kitchen, starting breakfast for everyone. The aroma of eggs and toast filled the apartment, and I knew *mi diosa* would be awake soon.

I set the table carefully, making sure everything was just right for when she woke. This was our world, and I intended to keep it that way. Just the two of us.

# 13

# Ana

My heart dropped when I woke up alone. I was so used to Charlie trailing kisses over my body, gently waking me up before sliding down to please me with his mouth. I had only been awake for one minute without him and I already missed him.

I was continually surprising myself with how I felt about him. In the light of the day, my confession from last night felt like a dream. All of the anger I felt about Charlie with another woman took me to another wavelength, another dimension, and now I was stuck in it. I was stuck in a world where I needed an English rockstar, twelve years my junior, who I was absolutely in love with. What scared me was that I was happy in this world, and I knew I never wanted to leave.

As I got up to grab a robe, the bedroom door gently opened, and there stood Charlie, shirtless, his pajama bottoms hanging low on his hips. My heart dropped at the sight of him, still not used to having such a gorgeous man in my bedroom. Jake had been attractive, but Charlie? *Él era jodida perfección.*

"*Mi diosa,*" Charlie murmured, his voice low and deep as

he walked towards me, wrapping his arms snugly around my waist. "Breakfast is ready."

I licked my lips before hungrily pressing my mouth to his and he didn't hesitate to pull my body close. I felt a certain power whenever his cock instantly hardened for me, aching for my touch. I was starting to lose control with Charlie, both emotionally and sexually. I didn't want to tease him, I didn't want to wait for his cock to be inside me—I wanted him, and I needed it immediately.

I pulled down the waistband of his pants before breaking our kiss and sliding down to my knees, letting his cock spring free and into my grip. I parted my lips, staring up into Charlie's green eyes—wide, wild, and filled with desire—waiting for me to please him. The look he gave me was one I'd never tire of, a look of complete awe and longing.

"I love you, Charlie," I breathed, then let my lips slide around his cock, watching as his brows furrowed together.

It was the first time explicitly telling him I loved him, and his eyes blazed with pride and awe as he heard the words aloud.

"Fuck, *mi diosa*. I love you," he moaned, gently taking my head in his hands and guiding me up and down his length, his eyes still locked on mine.

I exhaled a triumphant laugh before reaching down between my legs and rubbing my needy, wet clit.

"You need me, don't you, Ana? You need me like the air we breathe?" he asked with uncertainty between hitched breaths, his chest rapidly rising and falling.

I pulled my mouth from his cock and brought my hands to his length, stroking quickly as I spoke the words. "Yes, baby. I need you. I'm desperate for you, Charlie."

And I believed it. It was hard to admit, but I wasn't holding back anymore.

After I said the words, Charlie groaned loudly, as if my declaration turned him on even more.

"I'm consumed by you, *mi vida*," I continued, my strokes rapid and frantic. "I'm drowning in you and I never want to come up for air."

His eyes fluttered shut as he exhaled. "I'm gonna come, *mi diosa*. Please, I need to fuck you," he said with shaky breath.

I smiled, rising to my feet as I slowed my speed on his length.

"You're so sweet, baby. Tell me how much you love me as you fuck me, and then come all over my body to claim me," I whispered in his ear before letting him go, then dropped onto my back on the bed.

His eyes widened as he took his cock in his hand and knelt on the bed, parting my legs wide, his gaze falling between my thighs.

"*Mi diosa*," he breathed, licking his lips as he hovered above me. "I would burn the fucking world for you. I would kill for you, I would die for you," he murmured before thrusting himself deep inside of me.

His hips pounded against mine, his eyes locked on me, the fire between us growing with every second. His expression suddenly went from desperate to something darker.

"I love you so fucking much it physically hurts, *mi diosa*. If you asked me to, I'd bleed for you. I'd pour out every drop of my life just to show you how much I love you."

My breathing quickened, fear tugging at my chest, but desire overshadowed it all as he reached down, thumbing my clit, his eyes searching my face with an intense focus. My vision blurred as my pussy began to seize, pleasure bubbling in my core, and a cry escaped my lips as tears spilled down the sides of my cheeks. Charlie's low grunts echoed under mine as he pulled out and his warm cum shot out all over my body, claiming me as I commanded.

Even as the fear in my chest built, the power I felt surged through me like a wildfire. Our love was a dangerous thing, a beautiful chaos that would inevitably end in destruction. Someone was bound to get hurt—maybe both of us. The real question that haunted my mind was whether either of us would make it out alive.

\* \* \*

Charlie and I showered together, the silence between us thick as he washed me gently and carefully. I hadn't meant for this to become so intense, but now that I was in it, I couldn't trace where it all began. Our love kept spiraling, growing more consuming with every moment. How high would we climb before it inevitably crashed into dangerous territory?

With how strongly I felt, I was terrified to know what he was thinking. I couldn't imagine the intensity of his mind.

We walked into the kitchen, his hand lingering at the small of my back as we stepped into the quiet room. The smell of eggs and toast filled the air, but something about the atmosphere felt...off. Sloane sat at the table, her eyes glued to her phone, and Callan stood by the counter as he glanced up at us from his phone.

I smiled, trying to brush off the strange energy that seemed to hit us the moment we walked in. "Morning," I said lightly, glancing at Sloane and Callan, both of them unusually quiet.

"Morning, Mom," Sloane muttered, her eyes flicking towards Charlie and then quickly back to her phone. I couldn't help but notice the way her posture stiffened, how Callan would barely acknowledge us.

Charlie, calm on the surface but clearly more tense than usual, slid a plate in front of me. "For you," he said quietly with a small smile.

I took my seat, but my mind was already spinning, trying to piece together why the room felt so stiff. Maybe they were upset with each other? Sloane and Callan weren't arguing last night, but something must have happened. Something wasn't right.

Or…had they heard us last night and this morning? The thought shot through my mind like a bolt of lightning. I swallowed hard, the heat creeping up my cheeks. Charlie and I hadn't exactly been quiet and now I wondered if they heard *everything*.

I glanced at Sloane, trying to read her expression. Was she avoiding eye contact because she knew? She wasn't exactly shy talking about sex, but maybe actually *hearing* her own mother was another thing altogether. The thought made me shift uncomfortably in my seat, my palms sweaty under the table.

Charlie sat beside me, his hand finding its place on my knee under the table, but my focus was elsewhere. Callan still hadn't said much, and Sloane was unusually quiet, her eyes still fixated on her phone.

"Everything looks great," I said, trying to break the silence, but the awkwardness lingered.

"Sorry if it's a bit cold. Got a little distracted this morning," Charlie teased, his hand tightening slightly on my knee.

My cheeks flushed and I glanced at Sloane who bit her lip slightly, a small smile lingering on her lips. "I bet," she muttered.

I bit my lip, uneasy. *Dios mio, they* did *hear.*

"How did you guys sleep?" I asked, hoping to shift the mood.

Sloane shrugged, her voice flat. "Fine."

Callan was quiet for a moment, his eyes shifting between me and Charlie. "Yeah, I slept fine," he finally said, his tone too casual.

The thought that they might've heard everything from last night only made the tension worse. I tried to shake it off, focusing on the breakfast in front of me.

Maybe it wasn't just what they'd heard. Maybe something had happened between them, something I wasn't part of. But that possibility didn't ease my embarrassment at all.

I glanced around the room and it felt like something was about to snap. I was about to press them further when Sloane broke the silence, her voice now light and casual. "So, Mom," she said, glancing at me with a sly smile. "It didn't sound like you got much sleep last night?"

My cheeks immediately burned. Charlie's hand tensed slightly on my knee and Callan glanced away with a subtle eye roll.

"*Ay,*" I muttered, burying my face in my hands, unable to stop the embarrassed laugh that escaped me. "You heard us."

Sloane grinned and the tension in the room finally eased as she shrugged. "I think the whole building heard you," she teased. "But hey, it's your space. Do what you gotta do."

I let out a relieved laugh, though I could still feel the lingering embarrassment. "Sloane…"

Charlie chuckled beside me, the tension lifting from his body as well. "Sorry about that," he said, though his tone was unapologetic as he flashed me a wink.

Sloane waved it off. "Maybe you guys should like, I don't know...soundproof your room."

The room lightened, the awkwardness dissolving into something more familiar, but I couldn't shake the feeling that there was more to this. Still, I let it go. Whatever tension had been building, Sloane seemed to smooth it over.

"I was thinking," Sloane began as we cleaned up from breakfast, her voice low despite it being just the two of us in the kitchen. "We should go check out that new boutique thrift store that just opened down the street. Just the two of us."

I nodded, smiling as I opened the dishwasher. "Sure, baby. That would be fun." But as soon as I said it, a small tug of worry crept in, wondering what Charlie would do without me for a few hours. We had spent nearly every waking moment together this past week, and he made it clear that he never wanted to leave my side. But of course, we'd have to do things separately sometimes. It would be too suffocating if he were with me constantly...*right*? My head told me yes, but my heart said that I wanted him to follow me around like a little puppy. *Perhaps I could even get him a leash...*

"So, you and Charlie..." Sloane said, pulling me back from my thoughts. Her tone was serious with a subtle hint of concern. "I didn't realize how serious this was."

A flustered smile tugged at my lips and I shrugged, shaking my head slightly. "It's just...intense, and I don't know where it's headed. I'm not even sure I'm ready for something serious," I said softly, still not ready to admit my feelings out loud to anyone else yet.

Sloane let out a gentle laugh. "I think it's too late for that, Mom. Charlie's totally crazy about you. This morning, he even told me he loved you, and…it was a lot." Her tone was teasing, but she was cautious, watching my reaction.

*Wait—this morning? Was that why it felt so tense earlier? When did this happen?*

Sloane answered my unspoken question. "We had a chat early this morning before you woke up," she said, probably sensing my confusion.

"*Ay, dios mío,*" I muttered, pausing mid-motion. I'd explicitly told Charlie I wasn't ready for others to know about us. And yet, he'd gone and confessed it anyway.

"What?" Sloane asked, picking up on my irritation.

"Sorry to interrupt." Charlie was suddenly walking into the kitchen, carrying a stack of plates. His gaze locked with mine for a moment, a hint of uncertainty in his eyes, but he moved on, heading towards the sink.

"I'll go get ready," Sloane said quickly and disappeared down the hall.

I crossed my arms as Charlie rinsed a plate, casting a sidelong glance over his shoulder. His jaw was clenched and his shoulders looked tense.

"You're not ready for anything serious? You're unsure where this is headed?" he muttered, his voice clipped with anger, his eyes now fixed on the sink.

I inhaled sharply, caught off guard. "You were eavesdropping?"

"Yeah. Glad I did, too. Good to know I'm still being strung along here, even after you said you loved me. Or was that just a lie? Has everything you've said to me been a lie?" He slammed the plate down, turning off the faucet abruptly, his chest heaving as he finally faced me.

My heart plummeted and tears pricked the corners of my

## ANA

eyes. "No, Charlie. I *do* love you. But I asked you to keep this between us for now, and you didn't. I'm not ready for everyone to know yet."

"Why not? Are you embarrassed to be with me?" His stance mirrored mine, his expression a storm of hurt and frustration.

I took a steadying breath, searching for the right words. "No! It's because...because I'm not *supposed* to need anyone, Charlie. I'm not supposed to be so deeply in love like this, especially so fast, and it feels...it feels so out of control, and I'm scared." A single tear slipped down my cheek as I held his gaze.

The hard lines of his face softened, his breathing evening out as he looked at me with quiet understanding.

"I'm never going to hurt you, *mi diosa*. You're safe with me, even if this feels like we're jumping out of a moving vehicle," he whispered, taking a step closer. His voice softened, carrying a steadiness that clashed with the intensity in his eyes. "I know that feeling because that's exactly what this is like for me too."

He took another step and I could feel the heat radiating from him as he continued. "I'm never going to leave, and my feelings for you...they're never going to fade. This feeling...it's the biggest rush and the scariest thing I've ever known." He paused, taking my hands. "I just need to know you feel it too, that you're in this with me, and that you won't walk away just because it scares you."

I shook my head. "I already told you—I'm yours, Charlie. Just because I'm scared, it doesn't mean I'm going anywhere." My voice softened as I added, "But I need you to respect my boundaries. I need to feel like I can trust you."

He nodded earnestly. "You can trust me, I promise." A sudden hint of regret crossed his face. "I'm sorry. I know my impulsiveness and passion get the best of me sometimes. But I'll work on it. I'll try harder, *mi diosa*."

He gently cupped my face in his hands, his lips brushing softly against mine, igniting that familiar heat low in my belly. But before I got swept into another round of our intense lovemaking, I broke the kiss, resting my hands on his solid biceps.

"Sloane and I are having a little outing today. Just the two of us. Will you be alright?" I asked cautiously.

A hint of hesitation crossed his face as he stepped back. "Are you sure that's a good idea? With all the media chaos we've been dealing with lately?"

A sudden doubt crept in but I shook my head, trying to project confidence. "We'll be fine. Miles will trail behind us."

Charlie's jaw clenched, his green eyes darkening with frustration. "Why can't *I* protect you? You don't need Miles anymore," he muttered bitterly.

I let out a soft laugh to ease the tension. "This is Miles' job, baby. I know you're more than capable of keeping me safe."

Charlie's gaze flicked toward the hallway and mine followed, catching sight of Callan casually passing by the kitchen.

"*He's* not going, is he?" Charlie asked with irritation as he glanced back at me.

"No, just me and Sloane. You can stay here if you'd like," I offered gently.

He sighed, his stance softening. "No, I should head home for a bit. My plants could use some watering," he added with a playful smirk, the tension finally easing.

An idea sparked and I looked at him with a smile. "Why don't we all meet at your place for dinner? I'd love for them to see your beautiful home."

Charlie's dimples popped as he put his hands around my waist, his hips closing in on mine.

"I have to wait until dinner to see you?" he murmured, his charming grin making me melt as his hard cock pressed insistently against my stomach, teasing me.

Another idea popped into my head. I leaned closer, my voice dropping to a whisper, conscious of Callan just outside the kitchen.

"Share your location with me," I demanded softly, teasingly. "And update me every thirty minutes with a selfie. Make them dirty." I traced a finger along his jaw, feeling his breath quicken. "Tell me all the filthy things you want me to do to you. If you're good," I whispered, my lips brushing his ear. "I'll choose one of them to make happen tonight."

"Fuck. Yes, *mi diosa*," he murmured, his grip on my hips tightening as desire flickered in his eyes. "Please…let me fuck you before you go."

"No," I replied instantly, holding my ground despite the ache pooling low in my belly. "You need to show me you're a good boy first." I stepped back, a rush of regret already stirring inside me as I felt the wetness between my legs for him.

Charlie swallowed hard but he nodded. "Can I jerk off to you?"

I bit my lip, feeling that familiar thrill. He was handing me the reins, willingly surrendering, and I was thriving in the power of it. "No. All of your cum belongs to me."

He groaned but took my hand. "Every ounce of me is for you, *mi diosa*."

# 14

# Charlie

Being apart from Ana was pure agony. My chest ached with a raw, relentless need, a visceral emptiness that only her presence could fill. The distance was more than I could bear; my entire body felt her absence like a wound that wouldn't heal.

I hated sharing her attention, even with her daughter. We only had this one week together and already Sloane was slipping in, carving out pieces of our precious time. I knew I'd never fully understand the bond between a mother and daughter—especially one as close as theirs—but it didn't stop the simmer of resentment. Every moment Ana spent with someone else felt like something stolen from us.

And here I was, alone on my bed, sending Ana shirtless selfies, dick pics, and videos of me stroking myself, all while staring at my phone, waiting for her replies. With each message I sent, she'd respond just enough to keep me hooked, leaving me hanging onto every word. Hours had passed and all I'd gotten were a few tantalizing replies, but they were enough to feed the fire within me. Who knew that a simple "good boy" or "I love you" could satisfy my obsession so completely?

I ordered in dinner since I spent most of my alone time obsessing over my goddess, indulging in thoughts of her while touching myself, edging myself just close enough to save it all for her. Ana and Sloane were due to arrive any minute with Callan joining us later, much to my annoyance. I still hadn't forgiven him for running his mouth to Ana, and it was becoming my quiet mission to dig up anything on him that could shake things up between him and Sloane. If he wanted to interfere, I'd make sure he regretted it.

Just as I was unpacking Thai food, Ana texted to say she arrived.

I headed down the stairs, my excitement deflating slightly when I saw Callan standing beside Sloane, just behind Ana.

"Hi. Come in," I greeted them with a wide grin, my gaze locked on the most beautiful woman in the world.

Slipping my hand around her waist, I leaned in, brushing a soft kiss against her lips before pulling back and taking her hand to lead her upstairs. Behind us, I could hear Sloane and Callan following.

"I thought Callan was joining us later?" I murmured close to her ear.

"He finished his errands early," she whispered back.

I felt my mood shift, a subtle irritation creeping in. I'd been looking forward to a chance to win Sloane over without Callan's watchful, disapproving stare.

"Wow!" Sloane exclaimed as she took in the loft, her eyes wide with admiration. "This place is amazing, Charlie."

I smiled, giving Ana's hand a gentle squeeze before glancing at Callan. His gaze roamed the room, hands in his pockets, as if he were inspecting the place for something to call me out on.

"Thanks, Sloane. I ordered Thai—hope everyone's hungry," I said, leading them into the kitchen where I began setting out plates.

Ana was already settling in, draping her coat over a chair, while Sloane wandered over to the records stacked on a shelf by the wall. Meanwhile, Callan kept scanning the space.

"Oh my God, do you really have *every* Beatles album on vinyl?" Sloane asked excitedly. "They're Callan's favorite. Right, Cal?"

Callan's gaze met mine and he offered a polite smile. "Good taste, man."

I returned a forced smile. "Yeah, you too, mate."

As dinner continued, Sloane and Ana took over most of the conversation, laughter filling the loft. I sat back, listening as Ana's laughter came easily, her relaxed demeanor lighting up the room. It felt good seeing her like this—easygoing, in her element with her daughter. Right next to me.

But if I had to sit through the night with Callan, I figured I might as well try to win him over—or at least keep things civil. "So, the Beatles, huh? Any other favorites?" I asked, keeping my tone light.

He shrugged, settling his elbows on the table. "A bit of everything. Rap, hip hop. Classic rock. Metal. Not much for current pop stuff though," he said, eyes steady on mine, as if my music wasn't worth his time.

"Yeah, me neither," I joked, even though the urge to roll my eyes was hard to shake.

He gave a brief laugh, then turned his attention back to Sloane and Ana. But something in me itched to push back, to make it clear I wasn't just some pushover.

# CHARLIE

"You and Jake were pretty close, right? Are you still? I mean, even after what he did to Ana...to his family?"

His eyes snapped back to mine, a flicker of anger in his expression. "Nah, man. Fuck that. We don't speak anymore." His jaw clenched and for a moment, the room seemed to still around us. But then Ana and Sloane laughed, blissfully unaware of our conversation.

"I guess it would be difficult, hm?" I murmured, keeping my tone neutral, almost sympathetic. "I mean, with Sarah being your ex...then everything she did. With him. *To* him." I let my gaze linger on him, challenging him.

Callan narrowed his eyes. "Sarah's a fucking nutcase. So is Jake for doing that shit."

"Right," I agreed sarcastically, giving a slight nod. "It was all on them."

He didn't respond, but I thought he might stand up or cause a scene. I quickly decided to shift, keeping my tone casual, almost friendly. "Can I get you a drink? Got some whiskey that's just begging to be poured." I offered him a faint smile, as if I were simply trying to be a good host, but even *I* knew he was sober. I just wanted to continue to jab, remind him of all his weaknesses.

His face hardened, barely masking his irritation. "No. I don't drink."

"Oh, sorry," I replied, feigning surprise. I let a small smirk tug at my lips as I rose from my chair and made my way to the liquor cabinet, casting him a brief glance over my shoulder, a quiet taunt lingering in the air.

"Ana, love, can I get you a drink?" I called out, catching her attention with a warm smile, then turned to Sloane. "Sorry, Sloane. I'd offer, but...a little too young for that, yeah?" My eyes flicked briefly to Callan, letting a hint of judgment settle there, even though I didn't give a fuck.

"Cabernet, please," Ana replied with a nod, but then glanced over at Callan. "Actually, no, it's okay."

Callan shook his head. "No, go ahead, Ana. It doesn't bother me."

I flashed a quick smile. "Perfect. One cabernet coming up." I poured the glass, savoring the hint of tension that hung between us, then poured a whiskey for myself.

"Callan and I wanted to wander around for a bit," Sloane said, standing up and casting a quick glance at Callan before turning her attention to me and Ana. "Did you guys want to join us?"

I caught the way Callan's shoulders tightened and it was so fucking satisfying to see him on edge like that.

"No, baby, that's okay," Ana replied, standing up as well and reaching for her plate. "You two enjoy your time. We'll meet back at home later."

I took a casual swig of my drink, watching as they said their goodbyes. Sloane gave me a cheerful wave as she headed for the door. "Thanks for dinner, Charlie! We'll see you later?"

I nodded, raising my glass with a slight smirk. "Absolutely."

\* \* \*

I found myself sprawled on the bed, my hands gripping Ana's soft, irresistible thighs as she straddled me, her ass filling my view. She held my hard cock in her grip, stroking me slowly, teasingly, before backing up to align herself just above my mouth.

"Eat my pussy, baby," she commanded, rolling her hips with

a slow, steady rhythm.

I moaned, diving in without hesitation, my tongue sliding over her slick cunt, savoring every reaction as she shivered above me.

"Oh, fuck, yes," she purred, her voice filled with pleasure. "You know exactly how to please me, baby. Such a good boy."

Her hand tightened around me, strokes growing faster. I felt a warm line of spit slipping down my length, adding to the pulsing heat building between us. I moaned, the sound vibrating through her as I flicked my tongue over her clit, my hands spreading and squeezing her ass, holding her steady above me. It took everything in me to keep my own release in check; I couldn't let *mi diosa* down.

Ana's breaths came faster, her moans spilling out as her hips rocked above me. "Yes!" she cried, her voice catching as she began to ride my face harder, chasing her release. "Fuck, baby. I'm coming," she gasped, her pleasure cresting.

I slowed my tongue, letting her savor every second of her climax as her hips slowed, trembling above me. But I wasn't done; I lifted my head, trailing my tongue along her ass, tasting every part of her. She gasped, but her hips began to move again, as if neither of us could pull away, drawn into each other all over again.

"*Dios mío*, yes," she moaned deeply, her voice reverberating through me. Suddenly, I felt her warm mouth over my cock, her head moving quickly as she took me deeper, and something inside me snapped. I lifted my hips, matching her rhythm, my body responding instinctively as I buried my tongue in her ass, my hands gripping her thighs. She moaned against me, her thighs tensing around my face as another orgasm ripped through her, her body shaking in my hands.

I held back, barely hanging on, desperate for her permission to let go but needing to give her more, to bring her back to that edge again. She pulled her mouth from me, breathless, glancing over her shoulder with that devious smile that undid me every time. She swung her leg over, shifting to face me, her beautiful, big tits taking over my view as she lowered herself onto her knees. My gaze trailed over her perfect, beautiful body.

Her skin glistened and I took in every detail—the softness of her thighs, the stretch marks that traced her inner thighs and curved along her soft belly, the strength in her that drove me wild. She was all I wanted, all I needed, and as she moved closer, I felt an overwhelming urge to worship her. She was powerful, radiant, a goddess in every sense, and I was completely at her mercy, desperate to lose myself in her over and over.

"Lift your knees," she ordered, snapping me out of my reverie. I did as she said, setting my feet flat on the bed, anticipation thrumming through me.

Ana's hand wrapped around my cock, her strokes steady and confident. She laid on her belly flat against the bed, lowering her head as her tongue flicked over my skin, trailing down, inch by inch, until I felt the warmth of her mouth over my balls, her tongue tracing down to my ass. My breath hitched, a fantasy I held in my mind suddenly unfolding.

A wave of pleasure rolled through me as her tongue pressed against my ass, swirling in a way that made my grip on the sheets tighten, the anticipation building with every passing second. My chest rose and fell quickly, my body responding to her every move.

"You like that, baby?" she murmured, a smile in her voice as she looked up, her hazel eyes meeting mine with a knowing glint.

"Yes, *mi diosa*. I love it," I answered, the words an unabashed declaration.

She chuckled softly, pushing deeper, her moan vibrating through me as our eyes stayed locked. Every nerve in my body was tuned to her touch, and I knew with absolute certainty that I was hers, held together only by her command, ready to fall apart the second she allowed it.

"I...I can't hold off...much longer, *mi diosa*," I managed to murmur breathlessly.

"Yes, you can, baby," she whispered, pulling her mouth away just as a disappointed moan slipped from me, the ache of wanting her filling every inch of my body.

She smirked, her middle finger slipping between her lips, her eyes on me filled with that pride that sent a jolt through me. I knew what was coming. *Finally.*

She gently pressed her finger to my ass, her other hand wrapped around me, stroking slowly. Her gaze fixed on mine was playful and commanding.

"I really want to fuck your ass, *mi amor*. But until then..." She slowly eased her finger inside and I closed my eyes, the pleasure crashing through me in waves, almost too overwhelming.

"Oh, fuck," I gasped, my fists clenching the sheets as her finger moved with a rhythm that almost made me burst immediately.

"Mmmm," she moaned, her hum dripping with satisfaction. "Such a tight ass, baby. I can't wait to fill you up and pound you," she whispered, inching her finger deeper. "I'll fuck you hard, stroking you until you come all over yourself, and then you'll help me lick it clean." Her finger picked up speed, thrusting faster, each movement sending a fresh wave of pleasure through me.

"I can't fucking wait, *mi diosa,*" I gasped. "Please, I need you to fuck me…fuck, I'm so close!"

She chuckled and I couldn't help but smile, knowing she was relishing every second of this, taking her time, making me work for every bit of release.

"Alright, baby," she purred. "You've been such a good boy. You've earned it. Now come in my mouth."

Her lips wrapped around me, her warm tongue swirling as she took me in completely, and I let go, the pent-up desire spilling from deep within me. My moans grew wild and desperate as she took every wave of pleasure, her own moans vibrating against me, only intensifying the release.

She swallowed, slowly withdrawing her finger as I looked down at her, her eyes filled with triumph and satisfaction. I lay there, basking in the warmth of her gaze.

"I love you so much, Ana. You're my fucking dream," I breathed, releasing my grip on the sheets as I sat up, craving nothing more than to pull her close.

"I love you, Charlie," she replied with a soft smile, lifting herself to her knees between my legs.

"Then marry me," I blurted out, my heart suddenly hammering. The words slipped out before I could stop them, fueled by a longing so fierce it drowned out reason.

Her smile faltered as sadness crossed her face. "Charlie…" she murmured, shaking her head. "I just told you I'm not ready to tell the world about us yet."

"The world doesn't have to know," I replied, my voice filled with need. "It's just us. I need you in every way, Ana…

completely." I could hear the desperation in my voice, and somewhere, I knew I was pushing too hard. I knew she wasn't ready. But that didn't make the need any less real.

She blinked, her expression softening as she shook her head. "Please don't push this, Charlie. Not now. Isn't it enough that I love you? That I've already told you how much I need you…how I own you, and you own *me*?"

I shook my head, the frustration bubbling up before I could stop it. "But is it really enough, Ana? You say you love me, that you need me…but then why can't we make this real? Why does it have to stay in the shadows? I want all of you, and I'm tired of hiding it, pretending like I'm not completely yours."

Her eyes flickered with a mix of sadness and defensiveness, but I couldn't stop.

"You're everything to me. I want to be more than some… secret you're afraid to share. What's the point of loving someone if the rest of the world doesn't even know?"

She sighed, meeting my gaze with a new resolve as she let me sit there stewing for a minute. "Alright, Charlie…if you want more, then let's make it official." Her voice was steady, her determined eyes locked on mine. "Let's go out in public together again. No more hiding."

The words stunned me for a moment, excitement quickly sparking. "Wait, really?"

She nodded. "If it's what you need, then yes. But you need to know it's not just about us once we do. There'll be cameras, questions…people dissecting everything."

A grin broke across my face, my heart racing at the thought. "Then let's do it," I said, unable to keep the excitement from my voice. "No more hiding. Just…you and me."

She nodded but I caught the faint hesitation in her eyes,

the way her gaze drifted for a moment, like she was already bracing herself. "It'll be you and me," she murmured, her voice softening as if to remind herself. "But...everything changes once we're out there, Charlie."

I leaned in, taking her hand and pressing it to my chest where my heart was beating wildly. "All I want is for us to be real—out in the open, together. I'm not worried about the rest."

She gave me a small smile but I could see the weight of her thoughts still there. "I know. I know you're ready. I just...need a moment to let it sink in." She took a deep breath. "Because once we do this, there's no taking it back."

I squeezed her hand, unwavering. "I don't want to take it back, Ana. I've been waiting for this."

She nodded again, her fingers tightening around mine. "Then...let's do it," she said, as if trying to push through that last thread of uncertainty.

I wrapped her in my arms, her hesitation only fueling my resolve. "We'll face it together," I whispered.

She pulled back slightly, her eyes searching mine, her voice soft but serious. "Are you sure you're ready to deal with everything that comes with this? People will question us—the age difference, our lives, everything."

I didn't hesitate. "Let them question it. Let them talk. I don't care, Ana."

She looked down, biting her lip, and I could see the concern still flickering in her gaze. "People can be cruel, you know. I'll need you every step of the way. I've dealt with scrutiny before and it almost broke me."

I tightened my grip on her. "I know it won't be easy. But you mean more to me than anything they could say or do. Let them try. We'll show them that nothing they do can touch what we have."

She exhaled, nodding slowly as if she was letting my words sink in, her eyes glistening with a mix of fear and resolve. She held my gaze for a moment, then leaned into me, surrendering to the moment as if releasing the last of her doubts. Her head found its place against my chest and her shoulders softened. I held her tight, feeling a mix of exhilaration and defiance, finding the thrill of stepping into something unknown.

And though a pang of guilt tugged at my chest, whispering of my own selfishness, I smothered it without mercy. Because soon, the world would know she was mine—a truth that no amount of judgment or scrutiny could tarnish.

# 15

# Ana

Maybe it was the wine loosening my grip on caution, or maybe I'd abandoned reason long before tonight, somewhere around the time Charlie claimed us, deciding for both of us that we belonged together, bound by something neither of us would let go.

His marriage proposal was absurd, yet a strange thrill shot through me at the thought. His obsession with me wasn't some passing impulse; it was fierce, consuming, a desire to bind us in a way meant to be unbreakable. But I knew better than most that marriages could crumble, their promises left hollow. We didn't need that. I knew, with a certainty that ran deeper than anything I'd felt with Jake, that I loved Charlie in a way that went beyond vows or titles. It was a love that felt more real, more consuming, than anything that came before.

And even though I told Charlie to respect my boundaries only hours before, here I was, watching them crumble with every word, every touch. He broke down every wall, shattered every reservation I tried to cling to. I hated the way he unraveled me so completely but, *mierda*, I loved it too.

## ANA

I knew we had to go through with it before I changed my mind. I'd never been the impulsive type, but Charlie pulled qualities from me I barely recognized, qualities I wasn't proud of. But I was ignoring that, pushing away the warning signs as usual.

Sloane wanted to go to lunch before she and Callan flew back to LA that evening. We had missed them the night before, getting back to my apartment far later than they had, and I found myself wanting just a little more time with her before she left.

We chose a quiet spot in the West Village for lunch. I knew what could happen if we were all seen together in public but Sloane insisted. And Charlie—he was thrilled at the idea, of course. He was less thrilled, however, about Miles tagging along, hovering in the background, keeping a close watch from the shadows.

We settled into a cozy corner booth, surrounded by an abundance of vegetarian options that suited all four of us. Charlie had his arm casually draped over my shoulder as we chatted and thankfully, the tension that had lingered the past few days seemed to ease.

On the sidewalk afterwards, Sloane hugged me tightly, her voice soft in my ear. "I'm really happy for you, Mom," she whispered, the black car idling nearby, ready to take her and Callan to the airport.

"*Gracias, pequeña. Te amo,*" I whispered back.

"*También te amo,*" she replied with a warm smile as she pulled away.

"See you later, Sloane," Charlie said, offering her a quick hug. "It was a pleasure meeting you."

Callan reached out, placing a stern hand on Charlie's

shoulder. "Charlie." He turned to me, pulling me in for a warmer embrace. "Be careful, Ana," he murmured softly, his voice low in my ear.

As he pulled back, I forced a small, uneasy smile, unsettled by his quiet warning, especially with Charlie only inches away. I could sense the shift in Charlie beside me, his arm sliding around my waist as his possessiveness took hold, pulling me firmly to his side. "Safe travels," he said, voice light, almost sarcastic.

Sloane, blissfully unaware, waved happily to Charlie and me as Callan slid in the seat beside her. We waved back, watching their car pull away, and then Charlie slipped his hand into mine, his dimpled smile sending a swarm of butterflies through me.

"Shall we?" he asked lightly.

I nodded, bracing myself for whatever he had planned. I didn't want to know. If it was some grand gesture, I wouldn't put it past him to officially out us to the world in his own dramatic way. But instead, we found ourselves on the subway, heading towards Midtown.

"Where are we going?" I asked, slightly excited by the unfamiliarity of the subway, always having kept myself hidden from such public places in the past.

He wrapped his arm around me, pulling me close, as his other hand held the railing above us. "Central Park. I know, it's freezing," he said with a grin. "But it's big enough that sometimes it feels like you're in your own little world."

I exhaled a small laugh, surprised by the sweetness of his choice. "So, your idea of outing us to the world is a secluded stroll in Central Park?" I teased, pressing my hand to his chest.

"No," he replied, shaking his head with a laugh. "This is." He

## ANA

leaned down and pressed his lips to mine, the bustling noise of the train fading as his warmth washed over me. His kiss was deep, unhurried yet intense, as though claiming me in this crowded, public place. His arm tightened around me as our lips moved in perfect sync and the world melted away, leaving only the heat of his touch. I leaned deeper into him, letting his kiss say everything words couldn't. When he finally pulled back, I gasped for air, the excitement buzzing through me, knowing without a doubt that was the best kiss I ever had.

"You think that might've done the trick?" he asked, his voice a low, teasing whisper.

I laughed, biting my lip to hide my smile. "I think so." Almost too afraid to glance around the train, I scanned the crowd and caught sight of a few discreetly raised phones, snapping back down once I noticed them. Charlie followed my gaze, his laughter spilling out, rich and carefree. He leaned in close, his eyes glinting with mischief. "Oh, I *know* so."

I silenced my phone as soon as we got home. *Home.* My apartment was now *our* home. When the calls began pouring in from everyone—Marissa, Jake, others from my team, even distant family members—I hit *do not disturb* and put my phone face down on the dining table.

It was starting to sink in: we just made out on a crowded train for everyone to see. I knew that we'd be splashed across gossip magazines, online headlines, and every corner of social media. But the thought of it, the idea of claiming Charlie as mine so openly, and knowing he wanted to do the same, was exhilarating.

As I sank into the couch, the room wrapped in a comfortable silence, Charlie sat beside me with his phone in hand, a mischievous spark lighting up his eyes. I was about to ask what he was up to when he tilted the screen towards me, showing a photo he'd taken earlier, just the two of us, as a drafted post on Instagram.

It was candid, the kind of photo that felt private, like a glimpse into a moment meant to stay between us. My head was tilted towards his, our smiles subtle, his hand resting lightly on my knee.

"You're posting that?" I asked hesitantly.

We had already stirred up enough drama for one day, but Charlie seemed to want more.

"Yep," he said with a triumphant smile, then hit "share." It had been posted for the world to see.

My heart stuttered as I leaned closer, reading the caption he'd written beneath the photo:

**Some things are too real to hide.**

It was simple, but it spoke volumes.

I stared at him, caught between shock, annoyance, and exhilaration. He didn't say anything; he reached for my hand, letting his fingers intertwine with mine, his thumb brushing over my skin.

I couldn't stop myself—I swung my leg over his lap, pressing my lips to his with a desperate urgency. I could feel that darkness twisting inside me. Charlie had become like oxygen, like some essential, primal thing I couldn't live without. It wasn't just wanting him near me—I needed him with a hunger that clawed at me, insatiable and relentless. He'd broken down every wall, every layer of my careful composure until all that was left was this raw, vulnerable version of me—someone who craved him and this reckless, all-consuming passion, no matter the cost.

The boundaries between us were gone, erased so completely

that I didn't know where I ended and he began. And I didn't want them back. I wanted his chaos, his obsession, his recklessness. I wanted to lose myself in him, to be consumed completely, even if it meant becoming someone I didn't recognize. There was no return from this, no piece of myself he hadn't already claimed.

Something shifted in him as his fingers pressed into my skin, his breath quickening. His kiss grew deeper, darker, filled with an urgency that surprised me, something more intense than anything I'd felt from him before. Excitement and a whisper of fear pulsed through me as he pulled back, his eyes wild and almost fevered.

"Ana," he murmured. "I don't think you understand…I can't put into words what you mean to me. Sometimes it feels like nothing I say could ever be enough." He ran his hand through his hair, looking away for a moment before his gaze returned, fierce and desperate. "I need you to know…to feel how much you own me."

He pulled something from his pocket and I realized it was a pocket knife. He held it out, opening it, his eyes searching mine. My breathing sped, my heart pounding with a sudden, instinctual fear. But then his expression softened. "I'd never hurt you, Ana. This…this isn't about pain. It's about you, and me. Something words can't touch."

Something dark, but thrilling, built inside me. I hesitated, glancing down at the blade, feeling its weight in my hand as he placed it there, his fingers lingering against mine. "What do you want me to do?" I asked quietly.

"Mark me," he whispered, his voice barely audible. "Leave something of yourself with me, something I'll carry always. And let me do the same to you."

My heart pounded at his request—this was something that went beyond possession, beyond anything I imagined wanting. And yet, as I looked at him, I realized that I did want this, more deeply and fiercely than I ever expected.

I brought the sharp blade to his chest, my hand steadily drawing a shallow line, watching as blood blossomed against his skin. The sight was so intimate, our connection laid bare, visible in a way that felt both haunting and thrilling.

I looked into his eyes, feeling the last trace of my hesitations vanish, replaced by something so powerful as it was consuming. There was no return from this—only him, only us, bound in a way that defied all sense and reason. And as he brought the blade to my skin, his eyes dark, I realized I wanted this as much as he did. We were two halves of the same, each claiming and being claimed, our love sealed in a vow of blood and desire that neither of us could ever let go.

\* \* \*

We decided to venture out the next evening, craving a moment of normalcy amid everything that felt so intense between us. The morning and afternoon were spent lazily entwined in bed or curled up on the couch, our conversations drifting from lighthearted banter to quiet, intimate confessions, finally peeling back layers of each other in a way that felt long overdue.

As the sky began to darken, we got dressed, our laughter mingling with the noise of the city as we headed out. It was exciting walking through the streets together, his arm draped protectively over my shoulders, as if we were just any other couple. But even here, out in the open, I could feel the weight of our secrets, binding us in a way that made each step feel like a silent declaration.

Charlie suggested a quiet place tucked away in the East Village, a place he swore was private and unnoticed. But as we walked down the street, fingers intertwined, it became clear that "unnoticed" was no longer an option for us.

The flash of cameras began before we even reached the restaurant, quick bursts of white that blinded me momentarily. Voices called our names, more faces than I could count, more lenses than I could imagine. My heart raced and for a split second, I almost pulled my hand from Charlie's, the urge to disappear pressing hard against my chest. But his fingers tightened around mine, reminding me that this was a choice we both made.

As we finally made it inside and away from the chaos, I let out a shaky sigh. It was surreal, a reminder that what we shared was no longer just ours. Headlines had already spread across every outlet imaginable: *First Lady No More! Ana Del Rosario Seen in Public With Younger Rockstar. Age Gap Romance or Midlife Crisis?* and *Ana Del Rosario's Scandalous New Love Affair.*

Charlie seemed unfazed, grinning at me as if we had just strolled through the park. And as uneasy as I felt about the intrusion, there was also a strange, dark excitement coursing through me. The world was seeing a part of me they'd never known, a side I hadn't even known myself. They'd talk, speculate, criticize...but none of it mattered, really. I had to keep reminding myself that. Because the only reality that felt tangible was this: Charlie, his hand still in mine, his quiet smile that told me he understood every bit of what I was feeling.

"I love you. Quite the wild start to our night, huh?" he said lightly, pulling me out of my tangled, racing thoughts.

I wanted to take in every detail, to let the moment settle over me—the way his messy brown hair waved over his head, the faint stubble tracing his jaw, and those mesmerizing green eyes, fixed on me with a tenderness that felt like it belonged only to me.

"I love you too. Wild is an understatement," I replied, leaning closer to him. "I've never experienced anything like this…at least not so unexpectedly."

He laughed softly, squeezing my hand. "It's been going on for about…ten years for me," he admitted, his eyes holding a mix of humor and sadness. "Not here quite as much, but in other places I've traveled to…it's intense."

A pang tugged at my heart as I realized how little I knew of his life, the questions I hadn't thought to ask while I was swept up in our passion. *What else had he been through that I hadn't seen?*

"Are you close with your family?" I asked gently. "I haven't heard you talk about them much."

His gaze flickered away, a shadow of sadness crossing his face before he met my eyes again. "No. My dad left when I was young, as I told you, and I never had much of a relationship with him. My mum…" He hesitated, swallowing. "She passed away about ten years ago, right when the band took off. I'm an only child, so it's just been me ever since."

The vulnerability in his eyes was heartbreaking, and I put my other hand atop of our already clasped hands. "I'm so sorry, baby. That sounds so hard. You've had to go through all of this—fame, life…all by yourself."

He smiled faintly but the hurt lingered in his gaze. "It was rough. Sometimes it still is," he admitted quietly. "But then you came along. And now…it doesn't feel so hard."

His words sent a warmth through my chest. I gave his hand a gentle squeeze, a silent promise to be there for him, to help fill the spaces left by everything he lost.

We finished dinner with easy conversation, sharing glances across the table as we made flirtatious banter. By the time we returned to my apartment, there was an ease between us that felt deeper, like every conversation brought us even closer together.

"We're out of wine," I said over my shoulder as I glanced in the liquor cabinet. Charlie had suggested we take a bath together and relax with a glass of wine, and that was an offer I couldn't turn down.

"I've started the bath already—why don't you get in and relax and I'll run down to the market and grab a bottle?" he suggested.

"Okay, baby. Thank you," I said with a smile.

He gave me his dimpled grin and was out the door before I knew it. The apartment was quiet, filled only with the faint sound of the running water. I headed to the bedroom to grab an extra towel and stopped when I noticed Charlie's phone vibrating, the screen lighting up on the nightstand. I glanced over, surprised he left it behind, but curiosity pulled me in.

The message preview showed a text from an unsaved number. Unable to resist, I tapped on the screen and was prompted to put in a password. *I shouldn't do this.* I decided to try just once, tapping in my birthday, and sure enough, the screen unlocked. I smiled, but as I tapped on the thread, my heart began racing as I read:

**Left the penthouse, Monarch Tower. Black SUV. Only**

**one guard today.**

My stomach dropped. Monarch Tower, just outside D.C.—that was where Jake lived. *Is someone tracking him?*

**Returned to Monarch. Elevator straight to top floor. Stayed in for the rest of the afternoon.**

The updates went on, each one more chilling than the last, detailing Jake's movements.

The latest message, from just now, was the worst of all:

**Alone today. No additional security. Prime time to send a message whenever you're ready.**

I felt a surge of dread. These weren't just observations. Whoever was messaging Charlie was not only watching Jake but hinting at something worse.

Just then, the door opened and I quickly placed the phone back on the nightstand, my heart pounding as I tried to make sense of what I just uncovered.

I walked out to the living room as the door closed behind him. Charlie set down the bottle of wine, flashing me a soft smile. But fear suddenly rose from my chest and I found it hard to even return his gaze, knowing what I just read.

I took a slow, steadying breath. *You have to ask. There's no way around it.*

"Charlie," I began, struggling to keep my voice calm. "I saw some…messages on your phone."

His smile faltered, a flash of confusion crossing his face.

"My phone?" He looked over towards the bedroom and I saw a momentary flicker of realization as if he remembered what I must have seen.

"Yes," I replied, unable to stop now. "From someone… someone tracking Jake's every move."

His expression hardened, but he tried to cover it with a

casual shrug. His smile seemed forced as he walked towards me and slipped his hand into mine. "You're misunderstanding this, Ana," he said softly, as if trying to soothe me. "I just wanted to make sure he couldn't hurt you again. I would never do anything reckless."

I shook my head. "But this isn't just harmless, Charlie. You have someone following him, waiting for the right moment? For what? That's not protecting me—that's *stalking* him for no reason. It has to stop."

Frustration passed over his face before he masked it with a look of hurt. "Ana, I can't let him walk away from everything he's done to you."

I shook my head, refusing to back down. "If you care about me, then stop watching him. Let him go. Jake is out of my life, Charlie. I don't need you or anyone else keeping tabs on him."

His expression softened, sighing as he shook his head. "If that's what you want…" he said reluctantly. "I'll call it off. No more watching him. I promise."

I studied his face, searching for the sincerity in his words. I wanted to believe him but I could still sense his anger, lingering between us like a storm cloud waiting to break. Still, I nodded, choosing to trust him.

"Thank you," I murmured, feeling both relief and an odd sense of dread. He pulled me into his arms, but as I rested my head against his chest, I couldn't shake the feeling that this was far from over.

# 16

# Charlie

What I felt for Ana was beyond logic. It stripped away any hesitation, leaving only a fierce need to make her happy, no matter the cost. I wanted what was best for her, even if she didn't fully understand what that was yet. Just like when I asked her to mark me and let me mark her. She hadn't realized how deeply she wanted that, *needed* that. But when she felt our love physically, the devotion etched onto us both, she understood. I needed more of that—to find new ways to show her the depth of what we shared.

Hiring someone to watch Jake had been disturbingly easy. Money shut people up and made them do whatever you needed for a couple hundred thousand—a steep cost for stalking the former President. I wasn't certain where this would lead or what my intentions were. I just knew I wanted him to hurt, to know the fear and pain he caused Ana. Part of me wanted to scare him, to see him suffer in any way I could. Ending his life—that was still a decision I hadn't fully weighed. I'd never done anything like this before, but then again, I'd never felt this way about anyone before. I'd do *anything* for her, even if it meant taking down the former President for all that he did to her. But I knew Sloane would probably be devastated if something happened to him, and her pain would trickle down to Ana.

For now, I'd have to set aside my focus on Jake and find another way that could bring Ana the justice she deserved without leaving devastation in its wake.

The only thing keeping me from dwelling on Jake was channeling my energy into the songs I was writing for Ana. I wanted to surprise her, crafting each lyric and chord with her in mind. As we sat quietly together—her absorbed in work on her laptop, me scribbling notes and arranging melodies—she had no idea that each line was tailored just for her. Songs were timeless, and even after Ana and I were gone, the world would know of my devotion to her. My songs would capture the way she smelled, the way she tasted, every way I loved and adored her.

I'd reveal them to her the day before our one-month anniversary. I wanted to take her somewhere special. The timing was perfect for us to have a little getaway—my next tour didn't start for a couple of months. Though I hadn't told her about it yet, it was already planned: she'd be coming with me. There was no other option. Without her, I'd cancel the whole fucking thing.

But I had to tell her sooner or later. The evening was quiet, just the two of us wrapped in the comfort of our shared space. As we sat on the couch, I had a feeling that now was the time to bring it up.

I cleared my throat, trying to catch her attention. "I wanted to talk to you about something. My tour's coming up soon...in a couple of months." I tried to keep my tone light, but her expression shifted, her eyes narrowing slightly.

"You have a tour in a couple months? And you're just telling me now?" She set her laptop on the coffee table and crossed her arms as she sat back.

My heart sank. She was angry.

"I wanted to tell you, I just…I guess I thought it'd be easier when it was closer," I replied, leaning closer to her. "But I was hoping you'd come with me. Actually, I *need* you to come with me."

She sighed, her hands falling to her lap, her gaze following. "You'll be busy. Even if I'm with you, it's not like we'll have much time together." Her voice softened, and I took her hands with mine. "I don't want to feel like I'm in the way, or just there in the background while everything else comes first."

The faint jealousy in her words made me pause. It stirred a flicker of satisfaction mixed with the need to reassure her. "Ana," I said gently. "You won't be in the background. I'd be there with you every chance I get. I won't do this without you."

She hesitated, searching my face, her eyes darkened with something I recognized as the same intensity that burned in me. "But will you have time for me?"

I nodded. "I'll make time. This tour would mean nothing if you're not there."

She nodded slowly, but I could see the doubt lingering in her gaze. I sensed her own need to have me close, to hold onto what we had as tightly as I did. And if she needed a reminder of how much I needed her, I'd make sure she saw it.

\* \* \*

A few days later, the invitations for Grammy pre-parties arrived, a reminder of yet another event I couldn't imagine facing alone. I'd been nominated for a Grammy again, this time for Album of the Year, and although it was exciting, the nerves hit me every time I thought about it. But my mind was focused on something else: the perfect way to reveal the songs I wrote for Ana. What better opportunity than a night dedicated to celebrating music?

Ana was curled up on the couch, her attention wrapped in her laptop, and I moved beside her, settling in close.

"There's something I need to talk to you about," I said, meeting her curious gaze.

Her eyebrows lifted, a look of hesitation on her face, as if she was bracing for more unexpected news. It wasn't that I didn't want to tell her, I was just so wrapped up in our bubble that I honestly forgot.

"I have to attend a Grammy pre-party tomorrow. My album's nominated for Album of the Year." I paused, watching her reaction.

She smiled, her face lighting up with pride. "Charlie, that's incredible. I'm so happy for you!"

I nodded, but my excitement mixed with an urgency I couldn't hide. "I need you to come with me, Ana. I can't go a whole night, a whole weekend, without you. You've got to be there with me. Besides," I added, reaching for her hand. "It'll be the perfect opportunity to show you something I've been working on."

She tilted her head, her hazel eyes intrigued, and I knew she wasn't going to argue. "And what's that?"

I hesitated, wanting it to be a surprise, but I couldn't keep it from her any longer. "I've been writing songs for you,"

I admitted. "And I want you to hear them, to understand everything I'm putting out there. But you've got to be there. It's not an option."

She smiled, a hint of surprise and warmth in her eyes. "Charlie, I...of course I'll be there. That sounds amazing."

It was all coming together perfectly, and I knew this night would show her that everything I did was for her.

\* \* \*

The next morning, Ana and I headed to the airport for our first flight together to Los Angeles. We were flying first-class, held discreetly in a private lounge and whisked through a secluded entrance without drawing any attention. I was almost disappointed—I liked the attention we drew together, the world being reminded that she was mine.

"We need to get together with Callan and Sloane while we're in L.A.," Ana said, resting her head on my shoulder as we soared 11,000 meters in the air.

The last thing I wanted was to see Callan or to share any part of her attention. But I only nodded, resting my hand on her thigh. "Sounds like a plan."

We landed at LAX with only a few hours to spare before the party. I didn't want Ana to see how nervous I was. Always craving her approval, I couldn't help but wonder if the songs would be good enough for her. She was a fan of my music, but that didn't mean she'd love everything I've written.

After we checked into our guest cottage at the Chateau Marmont in West Hollywood, we were instantly bombarded with stylists and makeup artists. I barely had a moment to appreciate *mi diosa* in our own secluded retreat in the garden area of the hotel.

Before I needed to get ready, I slipped away to the bedroom and practiced the parts of the songs that felt the most important. After only a half hour, I stepped out into the living room and there she was—*mi diosa*, looking like the most perfect being I ever laid eyes on. With her hair pulled back, every feature of her face was accentuated, her red lipstick nearly causing my heart to stop. She wore an olive green fitted dress that traced every curve, and her leg peeked out through a high slit. When she looked up and smiled at me, it was impossible not to feel completely captivated.

A stylist knelt in front of her, holding up a black, strappy heel, and an irrational jealousy flared inside me. I strode over, kneeling beside the woman and extending my hand, flashing my most charming smile.

"May I?" I asked.

The woman smiled, handing it over without hesitation.

I looked up at Ana, my perfect, beautiful *diosa*, and she smiled back warmly.

"Can we have a moment, please?" she called out. The room of four or five people stopped in unison, quickly scattering and leaving. The authority in her tone, the confidence in her stance, the gaze she held on me—it was enough to make me hard instantly.

As the door shut behind the last person, I lifted the heel to her foot, waiting for her approval to slip it on.

"I love seeing you on your knees for me, *mi amor*," she murmured softly. "So much so that you need to fuck me quietly, right now, while they all wait outside."

"Yes, *mi diosa*," I replied breathlessly, the heel forgotten as I let it fall to the floor.

She leaned in, her voice a hushed demand. "Find the easiest way to fuck me and make me come without ruining all the work that went into making me look this glamorous."

My gaze swept over her body, taking in the tight, elegant dress that clung to every curve. *Impossible to fuck her in that.*

"I'll need to slip that dress off of you first, *mi diosa*," I whispered, already calculating the quickest way to obey her command.

"Quickly," she demanded.

I rose to my feet as she turned, revealing the zipper of her dress. I carefully slid it down, making sure not to wrinkle the fabric, and she stepped out of it, turning to reveal her beautiful body, bare in only her undergarments.

"Hang it up, baby, and then fuck me," she commanded, her gaze like fucking fire.

I spotted a hanger behind the bathroom door and carefully hooked the dress before turning back to find Ana leaning over the couch. She was completely naked, her back arched and her eyes glancing over her shoulder. The sight—her curves, her plump ass presented perfectly—sent a jolt of need straight to my cock.

I shot over to her, pulling my pants and boxer briefs down hastily, my hands gripping her hips before slamming my cock into her, the intensity of her warmth surrounding me in an instant.

"*Ay*, baby, yes," she moaned quietly, her voice laced with pleasure as I stared, mesmerized, at the way her ass jiggled against me.

"Oh, fuck, Ana… I want to live inside your sweet pussy forever," I groaned, my hips pounding against her in a rhythm that seemed to echo throughout the room.

She exhaled, a satisfied hum. "Mmmm...make me come, and maybe I'll consider it," she teased playfully.

Fueled by her words, I quickened my pace, leaning over to slip my hand around her hips, finding her slick clit beneath my fingers. I rubbed fervently and within seconds, her body tensed, a loud cry escaping her as her pleasure overtook her, forgetting any need to keep quiet.

"Please, *mi diosa*," I pleaded desperately, my voice breaking. "Please let me come in your perfect pussy."

"Yes, baby...come inside me. I want everyone to hear just how good it feels," she whimpered, her words sending me over the edge. I burst, grunting with a primal moan that filled the cottage, her body responding to mine as our breaths began to slow.

I reluctantly pulled out, but the sight of her still bent over, my cum dripping out of her, drew me back. I dropped to my knees, parting her legs and spreading her cheeks. My tongue found her sensitive, slick folds, my taste mixed with hers. I savored every inch until her moans returned, louder and more desperate.

"Charlie," she whispered, her breath hitching as I flicked her clit, refusing to stop until I felt her shuddering climax again.

"Charlie...we need to, we need to—" She gasped, a warning in her voice, but I simply smiled against her, knowing all of her pleasure was because of me, and everyone knew it.

# 17

# Ana

Charlie and I sat together in a sleek black car, inching forward through LA traffic towards the party venue just a couple of miles away. I thought back to the last time I was in a black car like this, waiting to step into the fashion gala where I first met him. So much had changed since then. Now, Miles wasn't the one behind the wheel—Charlie had convinced me to leave him back in New York. I assumed Callan would manage security here, but Charlie had mentioned he didn't want family and work to mix. I wondered if that was his true reason…or if he simply didn't want Callan anywhere near us.

I was a bundle of nerves as we neared the event, a familiar unease about what awaited us inside. Who would be there? Would the relentless bursts of camera flashes follow us like before? Though I knew I'd have to adapt all over again, it wasn't the kind of thing you ever really got used to.

The car finally came to a halt and Charlie turned towards me, gently squeezing my hand. In a dark green suit and T-shirt, paired with dark brown oxfords, he looked effortlessly cool—

the quintessential rock star. His messy hair fell perfectly, and the dimpled smile he gave me set off an inevitable flutter inside me.

"Are you ready, my love?" he asked, his voice soft yet confident. I loved that he knew exactly when to take charge, giving me the confidence I needed most in these moments.

I nodded, taking a steadying breath. "Yes."

The car door swung open and a barrage of flashes erupted, instantly blinding me. Voices shouted my name and Charlie's, blending into a chaotic, almost threatening roar. I watched as Charlie lifted a hand to shield us from the light, his grip on my hand tightening protectively as he led me up the steps to the entrance.

Finally, we slipped into the opulent venue and I released a breath I hadn't realized I'd been holding. The steady thump of music surrounded us, and Charlie's arm slipped securely around my waist, anchoring me to him.

"You alright?" he murmured with concern.

I nodded, holding a calm, composed expression—the same one I wore at most public appearances. But beneath that mask, a prickle of anxiety twisted through me, and my heart raced relentlessly against my chest.

"Are you?" I asked, realizing he probably wasn't used to being asked that in situations like this, or really *any*, with all the time he spent alone.

He looked down, a soft smile on his face. "With you, I'll always be okay."

Anyone else saying those words might have come off as too sweet, even insincere. But coming from Charlie, seeing the earnesty on his face, made my shoulders finally ease with his words.

"Come on. Let's get a drink," he said, taking my hand and leading me further into the venue. The room buzzed with energy, people gathered around the bar and mingling across the space. Overhead, a glass atrium opened up to the night sky, with disco balls scattering light like glistening stars throughout the room. In the center, a stage was set with drums, guitars, and microphones, ready for whatever performances the night held. Long, white couches lined the perimeter where a few guests sat, sipping their drinks and glancing our way as we passed.

"Charlie!" A voice called out from the side.

I turned to see a famous actress approaching us, her arms open for a hug. She was stunning, probably around Charlie's age, and though I knew better, a faint pang of jealousy crept in. But Charlie held my hand firmly, giving her a quick, casual side hug before stepping back to stand close to me.

"Jennifer, this is Ana—my beautiful girlfriend," Charlie introduced us, his gaze lingering on me with a look of pride. His words melted me; it was the first time I heard him call me his girlfriend.

"Oh my God, of course! Ana Martin, it's so nice to meet you! I'm such a huge fan. Not, you know, because of your husband—I mean ex-husband—but I absolutely love–"

"It's Del Rosario," Charlie interjected smoothly. "Ashford someday, I hope." He glanced my way, and while I was grateful he cut off Jennifer's rambling, his casual mention of marriage sent a pang of sadness through me.

Jennifer's face lit up, her blonde curls bouncing as she clapped her hands together. "Oh my God, that's so exciting! You two are the absolute best-looking couple out there," she gushed.

## ANA

"Thanks. Nice to see you, Jennifer. We need to make our rounds," Charlie replied, giving her shoulder a light tap before steering us further into the crowd, his grip still firm around my hand.

He leaned down, speaking softly into my ear, "Sorry about that. She'd go on forever if I didn't stop her." He led me into a sea of familiar and new faces—famous actors, musicians, icons I brushed shoulders with before, others I always wanted to meet, and a few I was glad to only pass by.

Charlie made a point of introducing me as his girlfriend to every single person we spoke to, his pride evident each time he said the words. Most people greeted us warmly, unfazed yet delighted by our presence.

"Let's get you a drink, *mi diosa*," Charlie said in my ear once we circled through a handful of introductions. He ordered me a red wine and a shot of whiskey for himself, which made me raise an eyebrow. It was unusual for him to go straight for a shot; maybe he was nervous about performing tonight? But after a decade on stage, could that still be the case?

"Nervous?" I asked over the beat of the music, leaning closer so he could hear.

He nodded, tossing back the shot and meeting my gaze with wide, vulnerable eyes. "Yes. Not about what *they* think…about what *you* think." His need for my approval was stark, woven into every move he made tonight.

"I know I'll love it, baby. I love everything you do," I replied, offering him a reassuring smile.

A grin spread across his face and he squeezed my hand before leading me back into the crowd. With each introduction, he seemed intent on making it clear: I wasn't just with him—I was *his*. His possessiveness was subtle but clear, at least to me.

Midway through a conversation with a Grammy-nominated singer, someone else approached—a pop icon, easily the biggest star in the world. I felt a flicker of awe just standing there, trying not to let my excitement show too much.

"Excuse me, love. I need to set up. Will you be okay?" Charlie murmured, his lips close to my ear. "Reese will bring you to the stage when we're ready," he added, gesturing to the man I'd heard so much about. Reese was tall, not much older than Charlie, and had a laid-back, hipster vibe that seemed to contrast with the rest of the room.

I nodded, though I was suddenly more anxious than before. Being left alone in a room full of people from an industry I didn't belong to was unsettling. Charlie must have caught the hesitation in my expression, his brows lifting slightly before he nodded and slipped away into the crowd.

"You are so wonderful and elegant, Ana. I've been such a huge fan for years. I love what you did with…" The pop star leaned close enthusiastically, but her words quickly faded into the background. My heart pounded, tension buzzing under my skin as I realized just how much I disliked standing there without Charlie beside me. Somewhere along the way, I became dependent on him in a way I hadn't expected.

The realization unsettled me, yet I couldn't deny how much I wanted him near, how deeply I needed his presence. It was an unfamiliar feeling, but I found myself holding onto it as tightly as I held onto him.

"Check, one, two," Charlie's voice rang out through the speakers, and I barely registered Reese's gentle interruption as he placed his hand on my arm and motioned for me to follow.

"This way," he said, guiding me through the crowd. He led me to a seat just beside the stage, secluded from the rest of the audience but close enough that I was near Charlie. As I sat, I glanced up, catching his eyes as he adjusted the microphone stand. He smiled down at me, a look of nervousness mixed with excitement.

"Hello, everyone. Thanks for having me here," he began, his voice filling the room. An assistant brought out an acoustic guitar and Charlie slipped the strap over his shoulder with the ease of someone born to perform. "I'm so grateful to have been nominated for Album of the Year. It's...truly a dream come true." He placed a hand over his heart and the crowd erupted in cheers, his humble expression making the moment even more endearing.

Then his gaze found mine, his dimpled grin growing as he took a deep breath. "Tonight, I wanted to share a little bit of my world with you," he continued, his eyes still locked on mine. "I've got some new material—stuff you won't hear anywhere else for a while. But tonight, I want to share it with a beautiful, wonderful, amazing woman—Ana Del Rosario." He gestured towards me and as the crowd cheered, heat rose to my cheeks. The attention, the celebration of us, was overwhelming in the best way.

"I've written a few songs for Ana and I want to play a couple for her tonight." His voice softened as he said, "I love you, Ana. More than I ever thought was possible." His gaze held mine, and tears welled in my eyes as he began to strum his guitar.

His voice filled the room, singing about being swept off his feet, caught in an all-consuming love, wanting me more than anything else. Each lyric expressed his desire to worship, adore, and never leave my side, his smooth tone climbing into falsettos and dipping into raspy lows with emotion. Through every verse, his eyes stayed on me, making me feel as though we were the only two people in the room. My heart thundered in my chest, his declaration of love igniting a depth of longing within me I hadn't anticipated from mere words.

As he finished, he transitioned into another ballad, this one about finding me in his darkest moments and how he couldn't imagine breathing without me. His voice caressed each note, and hearing him sing *mi diosa* in the lyrics sent a rush of butterflies swirling in my stomach.

I felt intoxicated, as though his voice had seeped into my bloodstream, leaving me desperate for him. By the time he finished his final song, a wild desire took over me, an urge to pull him into the nearest private space and fuck him senseless.

As applause thundered, Charlie made his way off the stage and took my hand, leading me through the crowd. People reached out to congratulate him, to draw him into conversation, but he didn't stop. Moments later, we slipped into a secluded room and he shut the door, locking it behind us before pressing me hard against the wall. His breathing was rough, his gaze dark and filled with intensity that was only for me.

He captured my mouth in a heated, fervent kiss, his hands roaming my body with urgency. I hitched my dress up, not caring about ruining it now, and wrapped my legs around him, feeling the warmth of his skin pressed firmly to mine. In a swift movement, he tore away my underwear, thrusting into me with a force that made me gasp. I pulled back from our kiss, burying my face in his neck as a moan escaped my lips, biting down to stifle the sound, though the sound of music outside covered any noise.

"I love you, *mi diosa*. I'm all yours. Everything about me is yours," he murmured against my ear.

"Yes, baby. I'm yours, too. I love you," I whispered back, the words spilling out as we clung to each other.

Charlie suddenly sank his teeth into my shoulder, the sharp sensation sending a shockwave through me, mingling pain and desire until they were indistinguishable. A gasp tore from my throat, followed by an unexpected, blinding rush of release.

"Hurt me, *mi diosa*. Make me feel it, make me feel your love, too," he growled, his movements growing rougher, his fierce gaze locked on mine. A faint smear of blood stained his lips, his eyes wild and daring, and I felt a primal need surge within me.

I slid the suit jacket off his shoulders, leaning forward to bite him back hard, my teeth sinking into his skin as that same heat and aggression took over. He groaned deeply, his body responding with a fevered energy that matched my own. As I pulled back to meet his gaze, our bodies tensed and we came together, the intensity of our love-making leaving me breathless and deeply satisfied in a way words couldn't touch.

* * *

We slipped out through a private exit and hurried into the same sleek black car that had brought us to the event. My body was spent, the adrenaline of the night and the intensity of what had happened at the party leaving me drained. Charlie rested his hand on my thigh, a satisfied smile on his lips as he leaned back, his head against the headrest.

"I didn't get to ask you…" he began, his words trailing off, but I knew what he wanted to say. His eyes held a flicker of hesitation, a need for reassurance.

"Charlie," I said, smiling softly. "That was the most amazing thing anyone's ever done for me. I loved it."

He exhaled, his grin widening and his teeth biting his bottom lip. He looked like he was about to say something when my phone vibrated in my hand. I glanced down, my heart dropping when I saw Jake's name on the screen. When I looked up, I caught the shift in Charlie's expression, his gaze flicking from my phone to my eyes, his jealousy and anger unmistakable.

"Why would he be calling you, Ana?" he asked, his voice low, almost accusatory.

I was immediately defensive. "I haven't spoken to him in months, Charlie. It must be important. I'm answering it." Before he could respond, I swiped right and lifted the phone to my ear.

"Jacob," I greeted, not masking the irritation in my voice.

"Ana, hey…" he replied hesitantly. "I'll just get straight to the point. Sarah was murdered in jail."

My mouth dropped open as I turned to Charlie, his eyes widening.

"Are you serious?" I asked, my gaze locked on Charlie, searching his expression.

"Yeah. It happened about an hour ago. A group ganged up on her and…" Jake trailed off, a heavy sigh filling the silence. "I just thought you should know."

A sudden unease crept over me. A thought struck—a suspicion that maybe…*no, I can't think that way*.

I hung up slowly, my heart pounding with disbelief as Jake's words echoed in my mind. Charlie's gaze remained locked on me, his brows lifting slightly as he noticed my expression.

"What happened?" he asked, his voice soft with concern.

I swallowed hard, choosing my words carefully. "Jake just

told me that...Sarah was killed in jail."

For a brief moment, Charlie's eyes widened in surprise, his lips slightly parted. But then, something changed. It was fleeting—a faint, almost imperceptible shift in his expression, a hint of something dark and satisfied that he couldn't entirely hide.

"Wow," he murmured, looking away as if to compose himself. "I mean...I know she did horrible things, but...that's still a bit shocking." His words sounded sincere enough, yet there was a glint in his eye, something cold and almost relieved that set off an uneasy feeling in my chest.

"Yeah, it is," I replied, studying his face, feeling an inexplicable chill. "Jake said it happened an hour ago. She was attacked by a group in her cell."

Charlie nodded slowly, his gaze still a little too intent. "Guess there's some sense of justice in the world then. She can't hurt you or anyone else anymore."

I nodded, though my mind kept circling back to his reaction. His initial surprise had seemed genuine, but now...something felt off.

As silence settled between us, Charlie's fingers brushed along my arm, his touch warm. "You know, you don't have to worry about anyone ever hurting you again," he murmured. "Not while I'm here."

I leaned into him, feeling an unexpected tension build. I wanted to feel comforted, to let myself believe his words, but a tiny voice in the back of my mind kept whispering that maybe Charlie's protective instincts ran deeper and darker than I ever realized.

# 18

# Charlie

I hadn't intended for them to go that far. My plan had been simple: just a scare, something to leave her with bruises and maybe a few broken bones, enough to make her pay for what she did to Sloane, but most of all, to Ana. Jake was untouchable, per Ana's orders, but Sarah...Sarah was exposed and vulnerable. She was the perfect place to start.

Ana hadn't asked me *not* to do anything. She knew how much it tore me apart to see her hurt, to know Jake had caused so much pain. And while I didn't exactly tell her what I planned, it wasn't like I promised to sit idly by.

But death hadn't been my goal.

I replayed Ana's reaction in the car, her expression shifting from shock to cautious, almost suspicious, and that tiny shift bothered me. I didn't want her to know. I didn't want her to guess that my reach extended into darkness she might never approve of. But I needed to act, to make sure no one would ever harm her again, even if it meant doing things she'd struggle to understand.

Now, though...the guilt lingered, heavier than I expected.

## CHARLIE

I overestimated the situation, trusted people to stick to my orders and not take things too far. But there was no undoing it now. And, a dark part of me thought, maybe it was better this way. Ana would never have to worry about Sarah again. Now about Leo...

All night I held her close, but each small move seemed to draw her eyes back to me, her sleepy hazel gaze guarded with a look I couldn't ignore.

I hated seeing that hint of doubt in her eyes. I couldn't bear the thought of her looking at me this way, questioning my intentions, my loyalty. I had to make her believe that I had nothing to do with it. Because if she ever slipped away from me, if she ever doubted what I felt for her, I wouldn't be able to handle it. I couldn't let that happen.

I hadn't slept all night, my mind tangled in the aftermath of what happened with Sarah.

Hours later, Ana and I were meeting Callan and Sloane for brunch. I didn't mind it with Sloane—she'd been warming up to the idea that her mother was in love with me, less bothered by the intensity of our relationship. But Callan...since he ran his mouth last time, I couldn't shake the grudge I held against him.

Of course, we ended up in one of the busiest spots in West Hollywood, a place where eyes trailed our every move. We sat at a small table tucked in a corner of the restaurant, tension lingering in the air between me and Callan.

"I just...I wonder what happened. I obviously didn't like Sarah, but...I never wanted her dead. I'd never wish death upon anyone," Sloane said, her wide, sad eyes shifting between Ana and me.

A fresh wave of guilt hit me. This was never meant to end

in death, but now that it had, would Ana even believe me if I tried to explain?

"I know. It's terrible," Ana replied softly, leaning in toward Sloane.

I felt Callan's gaze shift in my direction, a familiar irritation rising as he studied me.

"I don't know," he said with a shrug, glancing back at Sloane. "Karma's a bitch. What she did to you…I wanted her dead myself," he added bluntly.

"Oh, stop," Sloane said, swatting his shoulder, but I felt a small, involuntary smile tug at my lips. Maybe Callan and I shared more common ground than I thought. But I stayed silent, knowing that anything I added to this conversation would be dissected and could very well twist back on me.

"What do *you* think, Charlie?" Callan asked, his gaze sharp and probing.

"I'm…" I started, lost for words as my mind raced. I wasn't expecting to be put on the spot like this, and for a second, I felt cornered. But before I could find an answer, Ana cut in.

"I don't want to talk about this anymore," she said firmly. "Sloane, baby, did you finalize everything with the wedding cake?"

I leaned back, letting the conversation shift, though I didn't catch a word of Sloane's response. My focus was locked on Callan, his eyes still lingering on me. Had he brought up karma to test me, to see how I'd react? And why was he watching me so closely? Did he have suspicions, or was this just who Callan would always be—someone who didn't fully trust me? I couldn't shake the feeling that, in some way, he'd always be watching, always waiting for a crack in my armor.

I wanted nothing more than to be alone with Ana at our

cottage. I didn't think she even realized it had been one month since we met, but I wanted to make it special. I had thought about giving her the gift later on in the evening, but by the time we returned, I knew I needed to act fast. I could feel her slowly slipping away.

Ana had just kicked off her shoes as I reached into my suitcase, feeling the soft velvet of the small pouch. I chose this gift carefully, still knowing it might surprise her. But it was meant to symbolize everything I felt—my devotion, my trust, and a promise that went deeper than words.

Ana looked at me as I held the pouch out to her, her curiosity clearly sparking as she took it. She opened it slowly, pulling out the synthetic leather collar and matching leash. The collar was simple but elegant, with a single silver ring and her initials etched subtly into the leather. Her eyes widened, a mixture of surprise and intrigue across her face.

"For me to wear?" she asked softly, a hint of teasing in her words.

I shook my head, reaching to take the collar from her. "No. This is for me, Ana. The collar is for me...to wear for you." I paused. "And the leash is for you to lead me however you'd like."

Her smile softened, but I could see the question in her eyes. She touched the leather, tracing the initials with her fingers.

"I wanted to show you a side of myself I've rarely shown anyone," I said quietly. "In the past, I tried to share this...this part of myself. I trusted someone once, told her about my need to surrender, my desire to give up control, to let someone else lead. But she didn't understand." I hesitated, the memory a faint ache, even now. "She made me feel...wrong. She made me question who I was. She said it wasn't attractive, that no one would ever want a man who wanted things like that."

Ana's gaze darkened, her expression filled with a quiet, seemingly protective anger on my behalf.

"She told me that what I wanted was…sick," I continued, the old words still stinging. "For a long time, I believed her. I kept that side of myself locked away, convinced that I couldn't be the man people expected if I wanted…*this*. If I wanted to be completely vulnerable." I took a deep breath. "But with you, I don't feel that way. I feel safe, like I can trust you with every part of who I am."

She stayed silent, her hand wrapping firmly around the leash, her gaze unwavering as she watched me, absorbing every word. When I finished speaking, I could see something suddenly shift in her.

"I want you to know that this collar isn't just a gift. It's my way of saying that I'm yours. Fully. That I trust you to lead, that I'm giving myself over to you with no hesitation or fear."

After a moment, she reached up, her touch soft as she placed the collar around my neck, fastening it with a gentle click. The cool leather pressed against my skin. Her fingers lingered on the clasp, her gaze intent. "Charlie," she began softly. "You don't have to hold anything back with me. I want you just as you are."

Her words were like a balm, easing the tension I was carrying. She lifted the leash, wrapping her fingers around it, and her grip felt possessive, like an anchor pulling me closer. "You're mine," she whispered, her tone now sharper. "And you're not weak. You're real, and I want every part of you."

I leaned into her touch, letting her pull me closer, then I sank onto my knees in front of her. She held the leash firmly, her hazel eyes dark with desire as she looked down at me.

As she tugged gently on the leash, guiding me towards her, I felt a wave of relief and satisfaction, knowing I'd given her a part of myself no one else had. Her focus was entirely on me, her acceptance complete, and any questions or doubts she might have had about Sarah seemed to fade into the background. She was looking at me, truly seeing me, and I knew she wasn't going anywhere.

It felt like I was fully hers, bound to her by something deeper than love—by trust, by devotion, by the promise of this collar around my neck.

She smiled down at me, exuding power, any reservations she had about me seemingly gone. "Come on, baby. Follow me." She tugged on the leash as she turned around and I fell onto my hands, finding myself crawling behind her without hesitation.

"We can have a nice bath together, and I'll make you feel exactly as you deserve."

I crawled after her, following her down the hallway across the cold wooden floor. My gaze was fixed on the sway of her hips, each step making her ass jiggle, and the way she looked back at me with that satisfied, powerful smile lit a fire in my chest.

The bathroom door creaked open as she flicked the light on and reached out to start the tub faucet. I stayed on all fours, my mind blissfully empty except for the desire to let *mi diosa* take control. She tested the water then turned to me, letting the leash fall as she pulled her shirt over her head, unveiling her beautiful body. She leaned down, her bare tits close to my face, and whispered in my ear, "Stand up and get undressed, baby." As she unfastened my collar, she straightened, slowly sliding her jeans down, and I didn't hesitate to follow her command, standing up and shedding my clothes eagerly. My cock pulsed with need, fully captivated by my goddess in control.

Her face lit up as her gaze traveled over me, finally meeting my eyes. She reached out a hand and I took it, steadying her as she stepped into the tub. Letting go, she settled in, turning off the faucet before leaning back and opening her legs in invitation. I could've watched her all day, but her hand extended again, guiding me in. I lowered myself into the water, my back against her chest, feeling her arms wrap around my body, her tits pressing against me.

In the quiet intimacy of that moment, with the water gently moving around us, I felt a whirlwind of emotion that was almost overwhelming. I was so in love with Ana it ached. Wrapped in her arms, our skin warm against each other, I had never felt so complete or so deeply loved.

Goosebumps pricked my skin as her soft lips grazed my neck, each kiss deepening with passion. My hands traced over her soft thighs, settling there as I melted into her. My hard cock jutted out of the water, a bead of precum forming at the tip. I didn't know what Ana had planned; I would have been happy just staying like this, wrapped in her arms, but the way her lips moved against me hinted at something more.

A low moan escaped me as her hands drifted down my abs, finally reaching my cock.

"Relax, baby," she whispered softly in my ear. "Let me take care of you."

I exhaled, closing my eyes as I sank deeper into her embrace, allowing myself to get lost in her touch. Her hands moved slowly, gently pumping my cock, releasing as she reached the tip and beginning again. I inhaled sharply as her lips found my neck once more, her touch so tender it was almost overwhelming.

"I love you, Ana," I murmured.

She chuckled against my neck, her head nodding subtly. "I know, *mi amor*. I love you too," she replied, a smile in her voice. "Now *silencio*," she added, her tone more serious before her lips returned to my skin.

Her lips drifted from my neck to my shoulder, her strokes growing quicker, steadily building in rhythm. The sensation was so sensual, so achingly soft, that it was driving me out of my mind. This was the most erotic and easily the very best handjob I had ever received.

The tension built tight within me; I was seconds from release, but I held back, needing her permission. "Please, *mi diosa*," I pleaded, breathless. "Please, may I come?"

"Yes, *mi amor*," she whispered into my ear. "*Entrégate a mí.* Come for me," she commanded, her hand moving with an intense, insistent pace.

I exhaled sharply as my release crashed over me, pleasure radiating from my core through every inch of my body. My hands gripped her thighs while my heels pressed hard against the porcelain tub. My release spilled over my chest and stomach and she continued to stroke until every last drop was drawn from me. Then, she traced her fingers through my cum-covered skin, lifting them to her perfect, full lips, meeting my gaze as she did so.

"Good boy, Charlie. Now it's your turn to take care of me."

# 19

# Ana

I knew Charlie could tell something was off. The way the hurt spread across his face as I lingered on him too long, unsure if I was able to conceal the concern I felt deep in my chest. But then he surprised me.

I don't know if it was to distract me or if the timing just happened to work that way. The leash and collar—*dios mío*, the control I felt over him overshadowed any power I ever felt, even when I was the First Lady. The way I could control him, his body, the way he reacted to me—it was addicting.

It didn't make me forget, but it certainly helped shift my perspective.

And then came the Grammys, which almost made me forget about it all together.

I had never been to an award show like this. The glitz and chaos were intimidating, and as much as I tried to prepare myself, anxiety lingered in the pit of my stomach. I felt like I didn't belong, like an outsider peeking in on a world I wasn't meant to inhabit. I knew it would be like the party we attended, but multiplied a thousandfold.

## ANA

My team worked their magic, glamming me up to perfection. I chose a gown that was both elegant and sexy: a tight red dress that hugged my curves and featured a plunging neckline that I knew would drive Charlie wild. My lipstick matched the dress, bold and red, while my hair was styled in soft curls that channeled Marilyn Monroe.

Charlie, of course, had his own flair. His '70s style black suit was a perfect mix of retro and modern, complete with bell-bottom pants, a wide-collared shirt unbuttoned just enough to show his tattooed chest, and a red handkerchief tucked into his pocket to match me. His presence was magnetic, as always, his charm amplified by the quiet confidence that had drawn me to him in the first place.

As we slid into a black car, I couldn't stop the nervous shaking of my hands. Charlie noticed; he leaned in close, his breath brushing against my ear.

"You are absolutely stunning, *mi diosa.* I wish I could fuck you in front of everyone tonight to show them that you're mine."

I suppressed a giggle, biting down on my lip as I met his gaze. His green eyes burned with a dark intensity, in a way that only I seemed to be able to ignite. I felt my cheeks flush, but his words worked—my nerves began to fade, replaced by the thrill of being with him, of being *his*.

As the car pulled up to the venue, the roar of the crowd hit us, muffled only slightly by the windows. Flashes of light exploded outside, capturing every movement. I could feel the weight of the attention, the knowledge that every step, every glance, every whispered word between us would be scrutinized.

The door opened and Charlie stepped out first, smoothing

his suit before turning back to offer me his hand. His grip was strong as he helped me out of the car. As I stood, the crowd's energy doubled. Their shouts became louder, more frantic, and I knew that we were the cause.

Charlie wrapped his arm around my waist, pulling me close as we began our walk down the carpet. He whispered low for only me to hear, although the roar of the crowd would drown out most conversation.

"You're fucking stunning. You're mine, Ana. Always."

His words enveloped my body in goosebumps, but I maintained my composure, plastering on a serene smile for the cameras. His hand stayed on my waist, a physical reminder of his claim on me, and I realized that despite everything, I felt safe.

Inside the venue, the air buzzed with excitement. Charlie kept me close, never letting go of my hand as he navigated the sea of celebrities and flashing cameras with the ease of someone who had done this a hundred times before. For me, it was dizzying, overwhelming, but his presence calmed me in the storm.

We took our seats at a table near the front, and the show began. The performances, the speeches, the applause—it all blurred together. I was hyper-aware of Charlie, of the cameras on us, of his hand not once leaving my thigh or hand.

And then, the moment came.

"Album of the Year," the presenter announced, her voice booming through the microphone. The crowd hushed in anticipation. My stomach tightened as the nominees' names were read aloud.

"And the Grammy goes to...Charlie Ashford!"

The crowd erupted into cheers and I felt Charlie's hand tug

me up as he stood, the glow of triumph radiating from him. He turned to me, pulling me into a tight hug, before giving me a quick, gentle kiss. We hadn't talked about the level of PDA we'd show, but I knew with how possessive he felt, he'd show off whenever he could.

"I love you," he murmured after his lips left mine.

Then he was gone, making his way to the stage, shaking hands and exchanging smiles as the applause thundered around us. I sat back down and watched him, pride swelling in my chest, but also something else—anxiety. Charlie was unpredictable and I had no idea what he would say in his speech.

He reached the stage, holding the gold trophy in his hand, and the crowd slowly quieted.

"This is…wow," Charlie began as he leaned into the microphone, his voice steady despite the tears in his eyes. "This award means the world to me and there are so many people I need to thank. My team, my fans…" He began listing names I didn't know of and I was briefly relieved.

He paused, his gaze sweeping over the crowd until it landed squarely on me.

"And Ana."

My heart stopped.

"This woman right here," he continued, his voice growing softer. "She's my inspiration, my anchor, my everything. Ana, I love you. I love you more than I've ever loved anything in my life."

The room fell silent, his words lingering in the air. All eyes turned to me and I felt the heat rise in my cheeks. My chest tightened as I fought to keep my expression neutral, but inside, I was a storm of emotions.

He loved me. On live television. In front of millions.

Charlie smiled, his signature grin lighting up the room. "This is for you. Everything I do is for you."

The applause roared back to life, louder than ever, but I barely heard it. My heart pounded in my ears as Charlie made his way back to our table, trophy in hand, his eyes never leaving mine.

When he sat down, I couldn't speak. My hand reached for his and he held it tightly.

"You didn't have to do that," I whispered, my voice barely audible over the noise.

"I *wanted* to," he replied. "I need the world to know how much you mean to me."

I wanted to be angry at him for putting me on the spot, but the sincerity in his eyes melted any resistance I had. Instead, I leaned in, pressing my lips to his cheek.

"I may have to punish you for this later," I murmured against his skin.

His eyes grew dark as his gaze found mine. "Perhaps that's what I've wanted all along."

\* \* \*

The after-party was a chaotic blur of champagne flutes, flashing cameras, and endless congratulations. Charlie moved through it all with effortless charm, but his hand never left mine. It wasn't just possessive—it felt desperate, like he was holding on too tightly, as though I might slip away if he let go for even a moment.

Meanwhile, I could feel every glance, hear every whispered comment aimed at me. The attention was suffocating, the champagne dulling my nerves but doing nothing to ease the tension curling in my chest. By my third glass, I leaned into Charlie and whispered, "We need to leave. I can't do this anymore."

He didn't hesitate. "Okay. One second," he murmured, brushing a kiss against my temple before excusing himself to say his goodbyes. True to his word, he returned almost immediately, his arm slipping around my waist as he guided me out.

The car ride back to the cottage was quiet except for the throbbing of my heartbeat that was magnified by the alcohol. I stared out the window while Charlie's hand rested on my knee, his thumb drawing slow circles every now and then. Normally, his touch would excite me, but tonight it only amplified the storm building inside me.

When we arrived, the cool night air was a relief against my flushed skin. Inside, I kicked off my heels and sank onto the couch while Charlie disappeared into the kitchen. He returned moments later with a glass of water, crouching in front of me as he pressed it into my hand.

"Drink," he said softly, his green eyes scanning my face. "It'll help."

I took a sip, the cool liquid soothing my throat, but it didn't do much to ease the tension. "Thanks," I murmured, setting the glass on the coffee table.

"You've been quiet tonight," he said, sitting beside me. His arm draped across the back of the couch, his eyes locked onto mine. "What's going on?"

"It's nothing," I said sharply, standing up. The room tilted slightly and I steadied myself against the arm of the couch. "Or maybe it's everything. I don't know."

"Ana." His voice was calm but I could hear the worry in his tone. "Talk to me."

"I said it's nothing," I snapped, the words spilling out too quickly, too angrily. "But fine. You want to know? It's Sarah. It's the fact that she's dead, Charlie. And I can't stop wondering if you had something to do with it."

The air in the room shifted and he stayed eerily still beside me. Slowly he stood, his eyes narrowing as he studied me. "Why would you ask me that?"

"Because it makes sense!" I yelled, my hands trembling. "You had Jake followed, you're always talking about protecting me, about doing whatever it takes. And now Sarah's gone, just like that? What am I supposed to think?"

He stepped closer slowly, his jaw clenched. "You think I killed her?" His voice was too quiet and the calmness of it made me question myself entirely.

"I don't know!" I shouted, my voice cracking. "I don't know what you're capable of anymore! You're so fucking intense, Charlie, and it scares me!"

He froze as his gaze softened, then he took a small step back. "I'm scaring you?" he asked, his voice quieter now.

I nodded, my breath shaky. "Yes. You're scaring me."

For a moment, he didn't move, his eyes searching mine. Then he exhaled slowly, his shoulders relaxing as he stepped closer. "Ana, I'd never hurt you," he said softly. "You have to know that."

"Then tell me the truth," I said, my voice trembling. "Did you have something to do with Sarah's death?"

He clenched his jaw, his gaze dropping for a moment before he looked back at me. "I didn't mean for it to happen," he admitted quietly, and my heart dropped. "I just…I wanted

## ANA

her scared. I wanted her to know that she couldn't hurt you anymore. But it got out of hand. The people in there...they took it too far."

His words hit me like a punch to the chest and I stumbled back a step, my hand gripping the arm of the couch for support. "You...you had people go after her?" I asked, tears falling down my cheeks.

"I didn't tell them to *kill* her," he said quickly, his voice rising slightly. "I swear, Ana, that wasn't the plan. I just wanted her shaken up, enough to back off for good. But...it escalated."

I stared at him, my heart pounding as fear and disbelief collided with something darker—a sick, twisted thrill that I couldn't ignore. He did this for me. He crossed that line for me. And while part of me was horrified, another part felt flattered. Protected. Desired.

"Do you even hear yourself?" I asked loudly, trying to snap myself out of it. "You can't just...send people to scare someone *in jail* and then be surprised when it goes too far!"

"I didn't know they'd take it that far," he said, stepping closer again. "But I don't regret it, Ana. Because now she's gone, and she can't hurt you or anyone else anymore."

"You don't get to make that decision," I snapped, my hands shaking as I pointed at him. "You don't get to decide who lives or dies!"

He stopped in his tracks, his eyes softening as he reached for me. "Ana...I did it because I love you. Because I couldn't stand the thought of her hurting you again."

The room was spinning, my emotions a tangled mess as his words sank in. I wanted to push him away, to scream at him, to tell him he'd gone too far. But when he stepped closer, his hand brushing against my cheek, I didn't move.

"I'll protect you, Ana," he whispered. "Always. No matter what it takes."

I should've pulled away. I should've been disgusted. But instead, I grabbed his shirt, pulling him down to me as my lips crashed against his. The kiss was messy, desperate, charged with anger.

His hands gripped my hips, pulling me flush against him as the tension between us ignited. The fear, the questions, the doubt—they all melted away as his touch consumed me.

I pushed him away quickly, knowing what I wanted to do to him. I needed to take control again. I watched the way his chest heaved with surprise, his green eyes darkening with need.

"Sit." I pointed to the chair behind him and he moved instantly, lowering himself onto it. He spread his legs wide, his arms resting on the sides, but his fingers twitched slightly, as if restraining himself from reaching for me.

I stepped closer. "I want you to behave," I commanded. "No touching. No speaking unless I ask you a question. Do you think you can handle that?"

"Yes, *mi diosa*," he breathed, his voice trembling slightly. I could see the way his body responded to the command, his cock hardening, his breath hitching as he submitted to me without hesitation.

"Good boy," I said with a proud smile.

I could see his effort, the way he was trying to hold back. I pulled his pants down slowly, revealing his hard, aching cock, then lifted my dress. I aligned my body with his and lowered myself onto him, moaning quietly as his cock filled me. I moved deliberately, every shift of my body designed to remind him of the control he didn't have. His chest rose and fell in rapid, shallow breaths, and I could see every fiber of him desperate to touch me but knowing he wouldn't dare.

"Don't ever forget this," I said as I leaned in close, my lips brushing his ear. "I'm the one in control. I decide what happens, when it happens, and how it happens. Not you."

"Yes, *mi diosa*," he rasped, his voice shaking with restrained need as I slowly rolled my hips over him.

I tilted his chin up with one finger, forcing his gaze to meet mine. His green eyes were dark with hunger, his pupils blown wide, but there was something else there—something more dangerous. Devotion. Worship. An unwavering, almost frightening intensity.

"You belong to me," I whispered, running my thumb over his lower lip, my other hand splayed against his chest. "Say it."

"I belong to you," he said desperately.

"Good boy," I murmured, pulling his lip down slightly before letting go.

His breathing continued to pick up speed, his lips parting as if to speak but he caught himself, obeying my rule of silence. A flicker of pride curled in my chest at his restraint but it was quickly overtaken by something else. Even as I said the words, even as I reveled in the power of making him submit, I knew the truth.

I wasn't really in control.

Charlie Ashford was an unshakable force, a man who would do anything—*anything*—for me. He had proven that with Sarah, with the terrifying way he justified what had happened to her. And though he was under my hands, under my commands, I knew the undeniable pull he had over me. It was like standing at the edge of a storm, knowing the winds could sweep me away at any moment but being too captivated to step back.

But I couldn't let him know that.

I dragged my nails down his chest, the red lines standing out starkly against his skin. His body tensed under my touch, a low groan slipping from his lips despite his best efforts to hold it back.

"You're trying so hard, aren't you?" I teased, my voice dripping with mockery as I continued to roll my hips slowly. "Do you want to touch me, Charlie?"

"Yes," he gasped, his head falling back as his body trembled beneath me. "So much."

"Too bad," I said, leaning back slightly, my hands trailing down his arms to where his fingers gripped the chair. "Because tonight, you don't get to. You'll take what I give you, and you'll be grateful for it."

His head snapped up, his eyes locking onto mine. "I *am* grateful. I'll take anything you give me, *mi diosa.*"

"Good boy," I praised, my tone softening. I leaned forward, my hands bracing against his chest as I moved, watching the way his self-control unraveled with every shift of my body.

But even as he submitted, even as he obeyed every command without question, I could feel the storm beneath the surface—the unrelenting power that he held back for my sake. It thrilled me. Terrified me. Consumed me.

"You need to remember this," I started, trying to contain how much I reveled in this. "No matter how much you want to take control, no matter how much you think you can, you'll never be the one in charge. I am. Always."

"Yes, *mi diosa.*" His voice was hoarse, his hands gripping the chair so tightly I thought the wood might break.

But as I looked into his eyes, the unshakable devotion there,

I felt a sliver of doubt. Did he believe me? Or was he simply letting me think I had control, knowing full well that his power over me ran deeper than I was willing to admit?

The thought made my movements falter slightly, but I recovered quickly, leaning down to kiss him, hard and fervently, swallowing the soft groan that escaped his lips. His obedience only fed my need to push him further, to test the limits of his submission and remind myself that, for now, I held the reins.

"You don't come until I say so," I commanded against his lips. "Do you understand?"

"Yes, *mi diosa*," he rasped, his entire body trembling with the effort of holding himself back.

I smirked, rolling my hips harder, faster, savoring the way his head fell back, his chest rising and falling as he struggled to keep control. My hands braced against his chest, feeling the way his heart pounded beneath my touch. He was mine—entirely, completely mine—and the power of it overwhelmed me.

"Look at me," I demanded.

His head snapped forward instantly, his green eyes locking onto mine. The desperation there, the sheer devotion in his gaze, was addicting. My movements quickened, my nails digging into his skin as I felt myself unraveling, the intensity of the moment crashing over me like a wave.

I threw my head back, a sharp cry escaping my lips as my release hit me, my body trembling as I rode out the aftershocks of my orgasm. But I didn't stop there.

I slowed my movements, my breath still uneven, as I leaned down to brush my lips against his ear. "You've done so well, *mi buen chico*," I murmured, my voice soft and teasing. "But I'm not finished with you yet."

I slid off of him, standing in front of him as I let my dress fall, smoothing it back into place. He groaned softly, his body tense and his cock throbbing, his hands still gripping the chair as though it were the only thing anchoring him.

"You've been so good," I said, circling him slowly, my fingers trailing along his shoulders. "So obedient. So patient."

"*Please*," he groaned, his voice strained.

I stopped in front of him, leaning down until our faces were inches apart. "Please what?" I asked, my tone playful as I ran a finger down his chest.

"Please let me come, *mi diosa*," he begged, his voice trembling.

I smirked, leaning in to brush my lips against his, but pulling back just before he could deepen the kiss. "You want to come for me?"

"Yes," he whispered, his eyes pleading.

"Then do it," I said softly, stepping back. "Come for me, Charlie. Now."

The words were barely out of my mouth before he let go, his body shuddering as he finally gave in, a low, guttural moan escaping his lips. His cum shot up, landing over his lap and chest, his head falling back as he surrendered to the release he had been holding back.

I watched him, proud as I took in the sight of him—vulnerable, worshipful, completely mine. When he finally stilled, his breath ragged and uneven, I leaned down and pressed my lips to his.

"Good boy," I whispered, my voice full of praise. "You've earned it."

His green eyes flickered open, still hazy with the remnants of pleasure, and he looked at me with a mix of awe and adoration.

"You're incredible," he murmured, his voice coarse. "I don't deserve you."

I smiled, turning on my heel and heading towards the bedroom.

And as I left him there, still recovering in the chair, I couldn't help but feel the thrill of power coursing through me, even as the quiet truth lingered in the back of my mind.

Control was an illusion. But for tonight, I let myself believe it was mine.

## 20

# Charlie

I told her. At first, she was scared—I could see it in her eyes. But then, something shifted. That fear melted into something else, something I recognized instantly. She was flattered. Tipsy, sure, but I knew my Ana. She was thrilled. And then she teased me so fucking hard I fell in love with her all over again.

I had to turn our phones off as she drifted off to sleep. After my grand display of affection for over fifteen million people, the constant buzzing and lighting up of notifications drained the batteries quickly. My team knew where I was. Hers would know too.

I stared at her olive skin, the faint moonlight seeping through the window as she slept soundly. I couldn't stop thinking about how incredible she was. Tonight had surpassed anything I could have dreamed of. The way she controlled me completely—it was everything I could have ever wanted. I surrendered entirely and she still wanted me, even after what she learned. That was just another sign that she could understand me, love me, despite everything.

And I realized I would do anything to keep what we had. Anything.

I fell asleep at some point, anxiety coursing through me. What if she changed her mind in the morning? What if, sober, she realized how horribly I had behaved?

When she stirred in the morning, my eyes bolted open, bracing for an inevitable argument.

"Good morning, *mi diosa*," I whispered, trailing kisses from her arm to her neck as she stretched lightly, her eyes blinking open.

Her expression was a storm of emotions.

"Good morning, *mi vida*," she murmured, though her face didn't match the gentleness of her voice.

"How did you sleep? How are you feeling?" I asked, the knots in my stomach tightening as I rested on my elbow, watching her.

She sighed heavily. "We need to address last night, Charlie."

*I knew it. She's going to end things.* I nodded, already bracing for whatever she had to say, arguments forming in my head.

"You can't be surprised I declared my love like that." I grinned, trying to distract her. "In fact, I'm sure you expected it, didn't you?"

She blinked, unamused. "It's not that, Charlie. And I think you know that," she said with mild annoyance as she sat up, her bare body exposed as the sheets fell.

My grin disappeared and my heart continued its rapid pace.

"You have to stop this, baby," she said softly. "Trying to protect me from danger that isn't even there. Things are getting ugly and I don't want anyone else to get hurt."

I felt tears well up. "I know," I said, my voice cracking. "Forgive me, Ana. I just…" I shook my head. "I just love you so much. It's making me do crazy things, things I never thought I was capable of."

She gently cupped my cheek and I leaned into her touch, closing my eyes.

"I love you, Charlie. But I'm safe, baby. I'm safe with you." Her words sent a wave of goosebumps over my body and I pressed my lips to her palm.

But then a sudden, loud knock interrupted us.

"Fuck!" I snapped, my head whipping towards the door as I jumped up to look out the window.

The view was blocked by the dense greenery surrounding the cottage. Beside me, Ana sighed, grabbing her robe from the closet.

"Who is it?" she asked, peering outside.

"Mom!" came an angry voice.

*Sloane.*

"*Ay, mierda,*" Ana muttered, tying her robe as she walked into the living room.

I looked down at my nude body and cursed under my breath. This was the downside of being in the same city as her family. I couldn't wait to get back to our bubble in New York.

I slipped on a pair of sweatpants and stayed back, listening as Ana opened the door.

"Mom! I've been trying to reach you since last night. What the hell?" Sloane's voice rang through the small space.

"My phone died, Sloane," Ana replied, exasperation clear in her voice.

"So charge it!" Sloane snapped.

I was about to walk into the living room but stopped myself, wanting to hear as much as I could before they noticed me.

"That's the least of my worries right now," Ana responded

quietly.

Sloane's voice dropped to match hers. "The *least*? You mean after Charlie confessed his love for you in front of the entire world?"

"Why do you say it like that?" Ana asked defensively.

"Because it's so fucking intense, Mom," Sloane bit back. *"He's* intense. I feel like he's…"

"He's *what*?" Ana's tone sharpened.

"He's too much for you. How long has it been since you split from Dad? How long have you actually been on your own? I thought he was just some fun little rebound while you figured things out, but now he's telling anyone who'll listen that he's in love with you."

*What the fuck is wrong with that?*

"So what's wrong with that? Don't I deserve to be loved?" Ana snapped.

"Of course you do, Mom. But I feel like you're losing yourself in him," Sloane said after a pause.

I couldn't take it anymore. I walked out into the hallway and into the kitchen, letting my footsteps creak on the old hardwood floor. They both went silent as I poured myself a glass of water, taking my time before turning to go into the living room.

"Good morning, Sloane," I said with a smile, sliding my arm around Ana's waist.

"Hey, Charlie," she muttered, her gaze flicking to my shirtless chest before returning to Ana. *What would Callan think of that?*

"To what do we owe the pleasure?" I asked, glancing around. "Where's your fiancé?"

Sloane crossed her arms. "In the car. I told him I wouldn't

be long. Just wanted to make sure my mom was still alive after not hearing from her," she said sarcastically, her gaze narrowing on Ana.

Ana sighed heavily, putting a hand on her hip.

"Nothing to worry about when she's with me," I teased, though Sloane didn't crack a smile.

"I'm leaving," she said abruptly, uncrossing her arms and heading for the door. "Call me when you charge your phone, Mom. Bye, Charlie."

The door slammed behind her and Ana sighed heavily again.

"She's just being protective," she said, as if she already knew I'd have something to say.

"Protective?" I repeated. "That's what you call barging in here and basically telling you I'm not good enough? That I'm *too much*?"

"Charlie," Ana said softly, her eyes narrowing just slightly. "She's my daughter. She worries about me. She's allowed to have her opinions."

"Opinions?" I scoffed, shaking my head. "Ana, what she said wasn't just an opinion—it was a warning. She thinks I'm dangerous for you, like I'm some…problem you've decided to take on." My voice was rising and I could feel the anxiety building in my chest. "And you didn't even stand up for me."

Ana furrowed her eyebrows and cocked her head to the side. "Don't put this on me," she snapped. "Sloane has seen me at my worst, Charlie. She's watched me get hurt and she's scared it's going to happen again. That's where this is coming from."

"So I'm just some ticking time bomb in her eyes? Something you need to be careful around?" My voice was sharper than I intended but I couldn't stop myself. "How is she ever going to come around if you don't push back? If you let her think it's okay to—"

"Charlie, stop." Ana's voice cut through my rant like a knife and I froze. "You don't get to tell me how to handle my daughter. She's protective because she loves me. She doesn't know you like I do, and she's scared. But that doesn't mean I love you any less or that I don't defend you in my own way."

I swallowed hard, guilt and frustration clashing in my chest. "I just feel like...she's trying to sabotage us, Ana."

"That's not fair," Ana snapped, her voice trembling. "She's my child, Charlie. Of course she's going to be wary of someone new in my life. It doesn't mean she doesn't want me to be happy. It means she cares. And you pushing me like this is *not* helping."

Her words hit me like a slap. I saw the flicker of hurt in her eyes and my chest tightened with panic. "Ana," I said quickly, stepping forward and grabbing her hands. "I'm sorry. I didn't mean to upset you. I just..." My voice cracked and I shook my head, feeling the weight of my worries crashing down. "I'm so scared of losing you. I can't stand the thought of anything, or anyone, getting in the way of what we have."

She sighed, her shoulders slumping slightly, but she didn't pull her hands away. "You're not losing me, Charlie. But you have to understand that Sloane is my daughter. She's always going to be a part of my life, and if you want to be in it too, you have to find a way to coexist with her."

*I'm pushing her again. I'm making this worse. Stop, Charlie.*

"I will," I said desperately, squeezing her hands. "I swear, I will. I'm sorry, Ana. Please don't be upset with me. Please."

Her gaze softened, though the tension between us didn't seem completely erased. "I'm not mad," she said after a moment, her voice gentler now. "I just need you to trust me.

Sloane will come around. She's stubborn, but she will. I know she will."

I nodded quickly. "I trust you. I do. I just…" I trailed off, my words faltering. "I'm sorry. I'll do better."

Ana exhaled and stepped closer, wrapping her arms around me. I buried my face in her shoulder, holding her tightly as if that could erase the mess I just made.

"I love you," I murmured shakily into her neck.

"I love you too," she replied softly. "We're a package deal, Charlie. You have to remember that."

"I know. I'll remember," I promised, though the knot of doubt in my chest didn't entirely fade.

As she held me, whispering reassurances I didn't deserve, my thoughts turned sour. Sloane wasn't the problem. She was protective and I couldn't fault her for loving her mum enough to worry. But I knew Callan was a different story. I could feel his fingerprints all over this. He probably had been dropping hints, making little comments to Sloane about how I wasn't right for Ana, how I was "too much." He barely hid his disdain for me since Ana and I have been together, so why wouldn't he use Sloane to make his point?

He had no right to weigh in on Ana's life or shape how Sloane saw me.

It made my skin crawl. Callan didn't know me. He didn't see what Ana and I had. All he saw was an opportunity to plant doubt, to play the steady, reliable presence while I got painted as some reckless wildcard. And Sloane probably didn't even realize she was carrying his words when she called me intense, when she told Ana I was too much. She didn't deserve my anger.

I forced myself to push the bitterness down. Ana didn't

## CHARLIE

need to see me tense and wound up. She had already forgiven me for what happened with Sarah, then reassured me after Sloane's visit, and the last thing I wanted was to give her more reasons to doubt me.

But as I held her, burying my face in the curve of her shoulder, I couldn't help the thought: *If it weren't for him, maybe Sloane wouldn't even have these doubts in the first place.*

My need for digging up something on Callan was now my priority. I didn't know what I was looking for yet. Maybe there was nothing at all to find. But I wasn't going to sit back and let him sabotage me in Ana's life. If there was a weakness in his armor, I'd find it.

# 21

# Ana

The media hounded me and Charlie as we left our cottage at the Chateau Marmont, the flashes of cameras relentless against the tinted windows of the black car. With everything that happened at the Grammys, we were in every headline. Every gossip site had an opinion, every talk show dissected our relationship. My team didn't know what to do with it. My publicist had been clear: *Ignore it. Don't address it.*

I agreed. What could I possibly say that hadn't already been shown? The message was clear: Charlie and I were together, in love.

But my chest felt tight, the pressure of the past few days mounting. The chaos didn't seem to touch Charlie; he embraced it with ease, his confidence unwavering. But for me, it was like a storm I couldn't escape, the winds whipping faster with every headline and whispered judgment.

"You okay?" Charlie asked softly, his hand resting on mine as the car sped towards Sloane and Callan's house.

We planned to have lunch before Charlie and I headed back

to New York, but Charlie suddenly claimed he had a "meeting." I didn't question him; he was still tense about the conversation Sloane and I had the other day, and I didn't even want to know what he was thinking about Callan anymore.

"I'm fine," I said, forcing a small smile. "Are you?"

"I'm great," he replied, his grin wide and genuine. "As long as you are."

I nodded, though my stomach churned. I couldn't shake the anxiety lingering from my last conversation with Sloane. The way we had left things didn't sit right with me and I wasn't sure how today would unfold.

When we arrived, Charlie leaned over, pressing a soft kiss to my lips. "Text me when you're ready, okay? I'll be close."

"Okay, baby," I replied, feigning confidence as anxiety swarmed in my chest. "I'll see you in a bit."

I entered the gate code at the private entrance to Callan and Sloane's Spanish-style 1920s renovated home in Hancock Park. Sloane stood waiting for me at the door, her smile warm but tinged with hesitation. The unease between us lingered, faint but present. I hated when things were like this—thankfully, it wasn't often.

"Hi, mama," she said, pulling me into a tight hug.

"*Hola, mi niña*," I said, squeezing her back.

She held on a little longer. "I hate how we left things last time. I'm sorry for coming at you like that," she said as she let go.

I took her hands, shaking my head gently. "Don't be sorry, baby," I said, though I could sense the conversation wasn't over.

We walked into the bright living room, sunlight streaming through the windows. Sloane's green thumb was clearly apparent in her space, with plants hanging and potted in every corner.

"You said *I* had a lot of plants," I teased, glancing around. "Look at you—you've doubled the number since the last time I was here."

Sloane laughed, her tension softening for a moment. "There's a great nursery down the street. I can't help myself," she replied.

Callan appeared from the dining room beside the kitchen, giving me a cautious smile. "Hey, Ana."

"Hey. Food smells great. *You're* cooking?" I teased, trying to lighten the mood.

"Trying to," Callan replied with a laugh, glancing at Sloane as he wrapped his arm around her. "I mean, we kinda did it together."

"It's all ready," Sloane said, glancing towards the kitchen. "We can eat in there," she suggested to Callan.

He nodded. "Yeah, sure."

I followed them into the kitchen and to the small round table beside the island, where bowls of sautéed vegetables, avocado, tortillas, and tofu scramble were laid out.

"Tofu tacos," Sloane announced brightly as she sat down. "A staple around here."

I smiled but I sighed as I took my seat, the weight of the inevitable conversation pressing against my chest. The small talk was light; we talked about the nursery Sloane mentioned, her classes, little projects around the house, wedding planning. But I could feel the lingering tension beneath it all.

When there was a momentary pause between conversation, Callan broke the silence. "How's Charlie?" he asked, his tone casual but tainted with bitterness.

"He's good," I said, nodding as I avoided his gaze. "He's at a meeting right now. He's sorry he couldn't make it."

Callan gave a stifled laugh. "Yeah, sure."

"What?" I snapped.

Sloane and Callan exchanged a look before Sloane finally spoke. "We're just a little worried, Mom. Like I said…he's really intense."

"Intense?" Callan interjected. "That's one way to describe him."

My irritation flared. "I don't understand why you two are having such a hard time accepting this. Shouldn't you be happy that I'm with someone who clearly loves me and isn't afraid to show it? Shouldn't my happiness matter?" My voice grew louder. "So what if he's intense? So what if he's passionate and has made mistakes in his past? I think you know a thing or two about that, Callan," I snapped, the words cutting before I could stop them.

Callan's jaw tightened as he looked down at his plate, his silence heavy.

"Mom," Sloane said, her tone sharp, almost scolding.

I exhaled heavily. "I'm sorry, Callan. I just…"

I trailed off, the regret settling in my chest. Deep down, I knew they were right to be worried. I had seen the red flags since the beginning and had chosen to ignore them. I *continued* to ignore them because I loved him. I truly was happy with Charlie, even if it felt like I was losing a part of myself—someone I wasn't sure I liked but was learning to live with.

"You're right, Mom," Sloane said softly. "We've all made our mistakes. Maybe this isn't such a bad thing, but…" She hesitated. "Just be careful. I don't want to see you get hurt."

"That's not going to happen, Sloane," I replied firmly, though even I knew it wasn't true. Hurt seemed inevitable for both Charlie and me, but it didn't matter—not right now.

Callan pushed his chair back abruptly, standing. "I need to use the restroom," he said quietly before he left the room.

I tilted my head toward Sloane, exasperated. "*¿Qué coño?*" I asked under my breath.

Sloane shook her head with a small sigh, her expression tired. "I can't change his mind about him, Mom. I'm sure he'll come around, though," she said with a shrug.

I bit my lower lip, nodding. The conversation was pressing too heavily on me and I desperately wanted to move past it. "Show me all your new plants."

Sloane's face lit up at the change in subject and she led me to the living room, pointing out her latest additions with enthusiasm. Thirty minutes later, after discussing plant care tips and laughing about her growing "jungle," Callan still hadn't returned. His absence hung in the back of my mind but I decided not to press it.

When it was time to leave, Charlie texted that he was waiting in the car. I gave Sloane a tight squeeze at the door. "*Te amo*, baby," I said softly.

"I love you too, Mom," she replied warmly.

In the car, I found Charlie scrolling through his phone. He glanced up with a grin. "Ready?"

I nodded, settling into the seat as the car pulled away.

We didn't talk much during the drive to LAX. Charlie held onto my leg possessively, as if he needed to declare me as his, even when no one was looking. I stared out the window, letting the city blur past while my thoughts churned. There was no escaping the weight of the conversation with Sloane and Callan or the lingering doubts it stirred. But for now, I pushed it aside. All that mattered was getting back to New York and holding onto the fragile calm Charlie and I had managed to find amidst the chaos. The chaos *we* created.

\* \* \*

Getting on our flight, and the actual journey itself, was uneventful. But once we landed at JFK, the atmosphere shifted. My team had hired extra security detail in response to the heightened media attention. As we exited through a side door to the waiting car, paparazzi swarmed us, cameras flashing relentlessly. Charlie held onto me tightly as he led me into the car.

Miles was already in the driver's seat with another guard in the passenger seat. I caught the flicker of irritation in Charlie's expression when he saw Miles, though he didn't say anything. I knew he wasn't thrilled about the added security, but our safety came first.

The car ride was quiet, Charlie holding onto my thigh as always, and I avoided my phone as I stared out at the beautiful New York City skyline. Once we arrived at my building, the elevator ride felt even more stifling. Miles and the extra guard stood silently beside us, their presence heavy in the small space. Charlie didn't say a word to either of them, but his body language spoke volumes—the way his fingers tightened around mine, the subtle clench of his jaw.

When the elevator dinged to signal our floor, Charlie finally broke his silence.

"See you boys later. I've got it from here, thanks," he said cheerfully, but the sarcasm in his tone was unmistakable.

Miles' eyes flicked to mine, questioning, and I nodded softly in response. Charlie tugged on my hand, pulling me out of the elevator before they could say anything else.

As the doors slid shut behind us, I glanced at him. His jaw was still tight, his grip on my hand unyielding. "They're just doing their job," I said gently, though I knew it wouldn't change how he felt.

He exhaled sharply. "I know," he muttered, but the tension in his body didn't ease.

I paused in front of the door, keys in hand, tilting my head at him. "What's bothering you, baby?" I asked softly, keeping my tone gentle; I knew he needed that from me right now.

He hesitated, his eyes flicking away for a moment before meeting mine again. "You're quiet," he admitted quietly. "You barely spoke on the plane. I feel like…like you're going to leave, and I'm just…I'm upset. I'm upset at myself for everything I've done." His voice broke slightly and I saw tears forming in his eyes.

My chest tightened, guilt washing over me. I shook my head slowly, hating the way his insecurities took hold of him. I could feel the weight of Sloane and Callan's disapproval pressing on both of us and I knew it was getting to him. But the truth was, no matter my own doubts, I'd never walk away from him. I was sure of that, even if he couldn't see it.

I reached up, placing my hand on his cheek, my thumb brushing softly over his lower lip. His eyes stayed on me, filled with pain that made my heart ache.

A thought flickered through my mind briefly, without warning. His vulnerability had a way of disarming me, stripping away my frustrations with him—frustrations I hadn't fully let go of since Sarah, since even before that. Was this raw honesty a perfectly planned distraction, or was it entirely genuine? Maybe it was both.

But as I looked at him, I knew it didn't matter. Whatever his reasons, his pain was real and I couldn't stand to see it.

"Charlie," I said softly. "I'm not going anywhere. You have to believe that."

His lips trembled slightly as he closed his eyes, leaning into my hand. "I don't want to lose you," he whispered, pulling me close to him.

"You won't," I promised. "I'm here. I'm always here."

His eyes opened and he smiled at me, my words of reassurance seeming to ease him. "I just want to lay in bed and hold you. Can we do that?"

I exhaled, a smile creeping on my lips. "That sounds perfect."

After stripping down and pressing our naked bodies together, Charlie slipped his hand between my legs, his touch igniting a fire in me.

"I really did just want to hold you," he huffed into my neck, swirling his finger against my clit. "But I can't resist you, *mi diosa.*"

I moaned as my fingers tangled in his hair as his mouth found my nipple.

"Please," he breathed. "Please just let me explore every part of you."

I smiled, tugging his hair harder. "You don't always have to ask, baby. Take me any way you want me."

His lips moved to my other nipple, his finger circling faster. "*Any* way?" he murmured, his tone deepening.

I hesitated for just a moment as he teased my nipple with his teeth, a flicker of curiosity and anticipation coursing through me. When I looked down, his eyes met mine through his lashes, his sly smile accentuated by the dimples that never failed to make my heart leap.

"Any way," I repeated, out of breath from my building orgasm.

"Fuck, Ana…I don't know if you want to unleash that part of me," he warned.

Between the biting and the intensity of his need to mark me, my curiosity outweighed any hesitation.

"Show me what you've got, my good boy," I murmured. "Take what you need from me, and I'll give you more. I'll fuck you the way I know you've been dying to get fucked."

His lips curved into a mischievous grin against my skin, his eyebrows raising in playful defiance. "Just stop me if it's too much."

In one swift motion, Charlie grabbed my hips and pulled me towards him as he knelt on the bed. The sight of his tattooed, muscular arms flexing as he positioned my body made my heart race. I couldn't tear my gaze away as he took his hard cock in his hand, stroking it slowly.

"I'm going to pull out my knife again, Ana. Don't be afraid."

The darkness in his eyes and the low, gravelly tone of his voice sent a spark of fear through me. But I realized that I craved it. I wanted it all, everything he had to give, because it was from *him*.

He slid off the bed, retrieving his pocket knife and retracting the blade with ease. My heart furiously pounded as I watched him, the mix of thrill and fear blurring together.

He gripped my thighs, spreading me open as he slid down to bury his face between them. His tongue flicked over my clit, his movements overwhelming my already sensitive nerves. Two fingers slipped inside me while his hand with the blade rested firmly on my thigh. Just as my orgasm built to a breaking point, I felt the blade press into my skin. The sharp sting made me wince, but the pain bled into pleasure and I moaned his name loudly.

Charlie's tongue didn't falter. Even as the warm trickle of blood slipped down my thigh, he kept working me unrelentingly. I looked down to see his hand slick with my blood, gripping the blade as another orgasm shattered through me. My fingers tangled in his hair, pulling him closer as I rode the waves of pleasure, my body trembling with the aftershocks.

When he finally lifted his mouth from me, he proudly grinned. Without a word, he dragged the blade across my thigh again, this time deeper. I screamed, my cry a mix of pain and ecstasy as I stared down at him. His grin deepened and he smeared the blood with his hand, painting a streak over his chest above his heart.

"I have so many dark thoughts, *mi diosa*," he murmured, his voice soft and pained. "But I'm not afraid of them with you. You let me be myself. You love me, flaws and all. Maybe even because of them." His hand returned to my thigh, squeezing firmly, sending another jolt through me.

I couldn't explain why the sight of him marked with my blood sent a terrifying, dark desire within me.

"Yes, baby. I love you," I whispered, leaning up on my elbows. "All of you."

He leaned down, his fingers pressing hard against my thigh as the blood trickled down. "I want to take you in ways no one else ever has," he said, brushing his lips over mine, his cock teasing at my entrance. "And I want you to take from me what no one else ever could."

"Yes, Charlie," I breathed, lifting my hips to meet him. "Take everything. Give me everything."

He pushed into me slowly, his blood-slicked hand rising to his lips as he tasted it. Goosebumps flooded my skin, the thrill of his every move consuming me.

"Taste me, *mi diosa*," he growled, lifting his body slightly. He brought the blade to the side of his forearm, slicing down in a clean line. Blood pooled and trickled as he pressed the wound to my lips. Without hesitation, I darted my tongue out, desperate to take him in.

"Fuck," he groaned, his hips snapping forward, thrusting harder and faster as the metallic taste filled my mouth. "Ana, you're so fucking beautiful," he moaned into my neck, his tongue tracing my skin before his teeth grazed my shoulder. "I want to crawl inside you. I want to be a part of you."

As his teeth sank into my shoulder, my orgasm tore through me and I cried out, my vision blurring with tears as pleasure overwhelmed me.

"Fuck!" Charlie's pace quickened, his moans turning guttural as he pounded into me, his movements slowing only when he finally shuddered with release. His weight collapsed over me, his breath ragged and uneven.

The only sound in the room was our shaky breaths. As the pleasure faded, tears streamed down my cheeks as I grappled with so many overwhelming emotions. I loved him so deeply it scared me. His obsession, our shared obsession, burned too brightly, too dangerously. What lengths would he go to for me? What was he capable of? What was *I* capable of?

"Ana," he whispered, lifting his head to meet my gaze.

I stared down at him, his lips still stained with my blood. "Charlie," I said softly.

"Do you still love me?" he asked hesitantly, the vulnerability clear in his eyes.

I let the tears flow freely and nodded. "More than ever."

# 22

# Charlie

My desperation, my obsession with Ana seemed to grow stronger with each passing day.

I knew it was illogical to be jealous of everyone, of *anyone,* who had her attention. But I couldn't stop it. Miles, the new bodyguard, Sloane, Callan, even her fucking publicist calling her—it all drove me insane. This relentless need to consume her, to keep her entirely to myself, plagued my every thought.

Even when I was inside her, it wasn't enough. Even when I tasted her blood and she tasted mine, it only dulled the edge momentarily. But the anxiety bubbling in my stomach refused to subside. The fear that she'd leave, that she'd finally see too much of my darkness, gnawed at me. My perverted fantasies. My need to be controlled. The extreme lengths I'd gone to keep her safe.

She may have been right—there wasn't any actual danger. But knowing that didn't ease the growing anxiety inside me.

We hadn't left the apartment in days, still recovering from the intensity of that night together. I was waiting, restless, for her to fulfill her promise to fuck me the way she said she would. I was ready to beg for it, to drop to my knees if that's what it took.

And yet, the world outside was pulling at me. The tour loomed closer. It was just weeks until the first show at Madison Square Garden. Everyone was ready except for me. I didn't want it. I didn't want *any* of it. All I wanted was to stay here, in this apartment, keeping Ana close, filling her with every inch of me, drowning in her.

I could feel her walls breaking down, see her giving up all her preconceived hesitations. And while that pulled me closer, it also fed my obsession. I needed more. I needed to prove to her that I was the only one who could make her happy.

So I hired the guy who stalked Jake to stalk Callan. That wanker tried to rip us apart and I wasn't going to let him get away with it. He was in Sloane's ear, filling her head with shit that spilled over to Ana. I had to put a stop to it.

At first, there was nothing. Callan was clean, annoyingly so. Days passed with no results.

And then, finally...something.

I was sitting on the couch, mindlessly scrolling through my phone while Ana got ready for a Zoom meeting when the text came through.

**Got something. Corner Chevron on La Brea and Beverly, near their house. Callan stops there every so often. Clerk remembers him. Said he bought a small bottle of vodka a few days ago. Paid cash.**

*Holy shit. A recovering alcoholic buying vodka?* It wasn't enough proof, but now we had somewhere to dig.

"I'll just be an hour or so, baby," Ana said, startling me as she appeared in the living room.

I looked up, locking my phone quickly, and gave her a smile as I stood, taking her hands in mine.

"You sure you don't want me on my knees in front of you, pleasuring you while you try to keep your composure?" I teased, flashing the grin I knew she couldn't resist.

She smiled, shaking her head with a soft laugh. "No, Charlie. I need to get things done. I haven't worked in what feels like weeks," she said, almost apologetically.

But my mind was already racing. *Who would be on that Zoom meeting? Who would be talking to her when I wasn't there to watch?*

"Okay," I said, keeping my voice light, though I wasn't sure how well I hid the jealousy that began to simmer. "I'll be here waiting."

Her expression softened as she placed her hand on my cheek, her touch lingering. I turned into it, kissing her palm.

She hesitated before finally letting go and walking to the other room.

As she disappeared into her office, I sat back on the couch, my thoughts spinning between Callan's secret and the idea of Ana on that Zoom call, laughing, talking, giving someone else her attention.

I was about to check my phone again when it buzzed in my hand. *Reese*.

I let out a sigh and answered. "What?"

"Good to hear your voice, too," Reese said dryly. "Listen, we need to talk about the tour. You're cutting it close, man. You've barely been responding to anything and the team's starting to freak out."

"I told you, I'm handling it," I snapped, walking out to the terrace where the cool breeze bit my cheeks.

"Are you, though?" Reese pressed. "We're weeks away

from Madison Square Garden, Charlie. *Weeks*. You haven't approved the final setlist, the lighting cues are still a mess, wardrobe is freaking out, and don't even fucking get me started on the promo shoots you've skipped. People are noticing."

"Reese, I said I'll handle it," I growled, though anxiety burst through my chest.

"Look, I know you've got...whatever's going on," Reese continued, hesitating. "But this is the biggest tour of your career. You can't just ignore it because—"

"Because what?" I cut in sharply.

Reese sighed. "Because you're holed up with Ana. I get it, man, but you've got responsibilities. People are counting on you. Just—try to keep your head in the game, okay?"

I clenched my jaw, ready to hurl my phone off the terrace. "I'll call you later."

"Charlie—"

I ended the call, walking back inside and tossing my phone onto the couch.

The irritation continued to grow. I knew Reese was right; I couldn't ignore the tour forever.

I glanced towards her office door, the faint sound of her voice drifting through. My world had narrowed to her, and the idea of stepping outside of it, of focusing on anything else, sent a spike of dread through me. She was going with me, but it wouldn't be just the two of us anymore.

I knew Reese wouldn't let up, and the clock was ticking. I had to figure this out, because Ana was now my only priority.

\* \* \*

I managed to get Ana and myself out of the apartment the next day for a meeting about the tour. The media hadn't let up on our whirlwind romance, and there was always a camera or five waiting to catch a glimpse of us.

As we stepped onto the concrete, heading to the waiting car that Miles drove, someone snapped a picture. The click of the shutter sent a spike of irritation through me and I snapped.

"Get the fuck out of her face!" I barked as Ana slid into the backseat.

"Hey, man, I'm just doing my job!" the paparazzo shot back, unfazed.

"Yeah, fuck off," I muttered under my breath, getting into the seat beside her and slamming the door harder than necessary.

"You're so tense, baby," Ana said softly, reaching over to take my hand.

"I'm just not looking forward to any of this," I admitted, turning to meet her gaze.

"I know," she said with a nod. She understood—I shared my anxiety about stepping outside our bubble. Though I knew she felt the same, she was the one pushing us along, being the more responsible of us two. "But I have a surprise for you when we get back home."

She gave me a slow, teasing smile. I knew exactly what she meant.

"What is it?" I asked, trying to keep my voice steady, though my heart pounded wildly in my chest.

"You'll have to wait and see," she teased.

*She's going to fuck me. Fuck. Yes.*

"Well, now I don't want to go," I said, grinning as I took her hand and pressed it against my instantly hard cock. "Let's go back and you can show me."

## CHARLIE

She laughed, shaking her head. "No. You have to get through your meeting and then you'll be rewarded," she said, her voice sultry and confident.

I let out an exaggerated groan, leaning back in the seat. "I've been waiting so long for this, *mi diosa*. And I've been so good," I added with a grin.

"I know you have, *mi vida*. That's what's going to make it even better," she replied, her smile promising everything I had been craving.

I could barely concentrate during the meeting. My thoughts were divided, torn between the anticipation of what awaited us back at the apartment and the simmering jealousy that flared when Ana left with Miles for "errands." He was a tall, good-looking chap, and I didn't want her seen with anyone but me.

The conference room buzzed with energy that felt stifling to me. A projector displayed a timeline for the tour—weeks of relentless shows, press, and travel—and yet, I could barely focus. My knee bounced under the table, my hands trembling as I counted the minutes until I could leave and get back to Ana.

"We'll need to finalize the press strategy before rehearsals ramp up," Reese said, glancing around the table. "There's already a lot of media attention on the two of you, Charlie. We need to decide how much of that narrative we're leaning into."

I tensed, my gaze snapping to Reese. "What the fuck does that mean?"

"It means…" Reese continued carefully. "It means your relationship with Ana is dominating headlines. It's not a bad thing—it's keeping you relevant. But we need to control the story. Maybe let a photographer in for a staged shoot? A few well-timed comments in interviews?"

"No," I said flatly.

Reese sighed. "Look, I'm not saying we exploit it, but the fans are eating this up. It's good for ticket sales, for merch—"

"I said no." My voice came out sharper and louder, making heads turn.

"Alright," Reese relented, raising his hands defensively. "But that brings us to the next point: rehearsals. We've only got a couple of weeks before Madison Square Garden and we're behind schedule. We need to hit the ground running, and that means full-day rehearsals starting tomorrow."

"I'll be there," I muttered, already deciding Ana would be with me the entire time, even if it meant she just sat at the side of the stage—as long as she was there.

"Will you?" someone piped up from across the table. It was Trevor, one of the members of the band I had known for years but never truly liked. "Because you're not very reliable lately."

My eyes narrowed. "What the fuck is that supposed to mean?"

Trevor leaned back in his chair. "It means we've all been picking up the slack while you've been playing house with your hot cougar. We're busting our asses to get ready for this tour and you're too busy chasing Ana around to care."

The room went silent, and I suddenly saw red.

"You don't get to talk about her," I growled, my voice low, feeling a burning rage.

Trevor shrugged, unfazed. "Just saying what everyone's thinking."

I shot up from my chair, the scrape of the legs against the floor echoing in the room. "Say one more word about her, and I swear to God—"

"Charlie," Reese interrupted loudly. "Sit down, man."

I stood there, chest heaving, ready to fight. My mind was already racing—Trevor's words, the endless schedule, the thought of Ana with Miles somewhere outside this building. It was too much.

"Fine," I spat, grabbing my phone off the table and heading for the door. "You want me at rehearsals? I'll be there. But don't anyone of you ever fucking bring her up again."

Without waiting for a response, I stormed out of the room and immediately dialed Ana.

"Hi, baby. That was quick. I thought you'd be gone for a few hours," she answered, her tone bubbly and light, a stark contrast to the anger brewing in me.

"I got out early. I need you, Ana. Where are you?" I muttered, the frustration still clear in my voice.

"I'm just out with Miles, running errands. We're grabbing a few things for the apartment. Why? What's wrong?" Her tone shifted, the concern creeping in.

I clenched my jaw. The thought of her with Miles only fueled the anger still pulsing from the meeting. "I don't like that you're with him," I said, the words sharper than I meant them to be.

"Charlie…" she sighed softly, and I knew her patience was wearing thin. "We've talked about this. Miles is just doing his job. You trust me, don't you?"

"It's not you I don't trust," I shot back, pacing the floor outside the meeting. "It's everyone else."

"Baby," she said gently, her voice soothing my nerves. "You have to stop this. You know I'm coming right back to you."

"I know," I muttered, exhaling a shaky breath. "It's just…the meeting was shit. They're all riding me about the tour."

"Okay," she said gently. "Meet me at the apartment? Or should we pick you up?"

The thought of her spending another second alone with Miles made my stomach churn. "Pick me up," I said quickly.

"On our way," she promised, and we hung up.

I shoved my phone into my pocket, trying to steady my breathing, but the sound of hurried footsteps snapped my attention back. Reese stormed out of the meeting room, his face full of frustration as he came down the hall towards me.

"Charlie!" he barked, his voice echoing in the hall. "What the fuck was that back there? You can't keep walking out like this!"

I turned to face him, shaking my head. "I'm not doing this right now, Reese."

"No, you *are* doing this right now," he shot back sharply. "Do you even care about this tour? Because if you don't, there are a hell of a lot of people wasting their time trying to make it happen."

"I said, not now," I growled, stepping closer, every nerve in my body on edge.

Reese didn't even flinch. His arms crossed, his eyes full of disdain. "You think you can just coast on your name and your headlines with Ana? You've got a team depending on you. Grow *up*, man."

The blood rushed to my ears, a low roar drowning out reason. I stalked forward, my voice dropping to a low rasp. "I told you to keep her name out of your fucking mouth."

Reese smirked, taunting me. "God damn, Charlie. She's got you so fucking whipped you can't even focus on your career."

My vision blurred with rage as I grabbed the front of his

shirt, shoving him back against the wall. He was taller than me by a couple of inches, probably just as built, but I'd take the fucker on if he kept going.

"Don't fucking test me, Reese!" I shouted, my voice echoing down the hallway.

Reese's eyes widened briefly before he composed himself. "What are you gonna do, huh? Hit me? Fire me? Go ahead, Charlie. Burn it all down because you can't keep it together."

My grip tightened. "You think you can talk to me like this because we're friends? Because I let you in? I'm the reason you have this fucking job, Reese. I can take it away just as easily."

"You've lost it, man," he said, his voice calmer now, more calculating. "You're unraveling. You're fucking unhinged and everyone sees it. You're not even fighting for your music anymore. You're just fighting for her, and it's pathetic."

I shoved him harder against the wall, my mind racing. "You don't know shit. Don't *ever* talk about her again. You got that?"

Reese's expression was cold now. "Fine," he muttered. "But you're gonna wake up one day and realize you've got nothing left except that obsession of yours. And by then, it'll be too late."

I released him, stepping back as he straightened his shirt and glared at me. He didn't say another word; he just shook his head and turned away, disappearing back into the meeting room.

My chest heaved as I ran a trembling hand through my hair. My phone buzzed in my pocket and I fumbled to pull it out, seeing Ana's message.

**We're here.**

I stormed towards the exit, the anger still boiling inside me. I was clinging onto the only thing keeping me from snapping entirely. *Her*.

\* \* \*

I sat in the car, staring out the window, trying to calm the storm raging inside me. The tension in my chest wouldn't ease, but I stayed quiet, afraid I'd burst if I let anything out.

By the time we walked into the apartment, the pressure had built to a breaking point. I walked in first, then turned around to face Ana, ready to unload everything—the meeting, Reese, my spiraling thoughts—but the words suddenly erased from my mind.

She stood by the door, her movements slow as her fingers were already undoing the buttons of her blouse.

"Stop thinking," she said softly. Her blouse slid off her shoulders, pooling at her feet, exposing her full tits in a lacy push-up bra. "Turn off your brain, take off your clothes, and do as I say."

The weight in my chest shifted, the frustration melting into pure desire. My heart raced as I stared at her, my thoughts colliding in a chaotic swirl. She knew exactly how to pull me out of the darkness and center my focus entirely on her.

Without a word, I reached for the bottom of my shirt, pulling it over my head. I quickly unbuttoned my jeans and thumbed them along with my boxer briefs, pulling them down in a rush, my hard cock bobbing out.

She eyed me up and down with a satisfied smile. "On your knees."

I knelt in front of her as she started walking towards me, her presence commanding the room without a word. Her hand cupped my cheek as she gave me a small smile.

"You're everything to me, Charlie Ashford. Do you know that?" she asked, her voice softer than I expected, momentarily pausing our play to check on me.

"Yes, *mi diosa*. You're everything to me," I breathed, staring up at her, lost in the confidence of her hazel eyes.

Her smile widened and her hand slid away from my face as she moved past me. The clink of her heeled boots echoed in the silence until her sultry voice filled the air. "Stay."

I remained on my knees, straining to hear what she was doing behind me down the hall. The anticipation was unbearable, every second stretching longer than the last. My heartbeat hammered in my chest as I sat back on my heels, my hands twitching with the urge to touch myself, though I wouldn't dare without her permission. My eyes landed on a framed picture on the shelf. It was a selfie I had taken of us on the terrace just a couple of weeks ago. She looked radiant in the photo, the very embodiment of everything beautiful and good.

With that thought, the dark spiral began. *I don't deserve her. When is she going to see that?*

The sound of her boots returning pulled me back to the present and desire pulsed through me as I caught sight of her from the corner of my eye. My goddess stood there in a black harness, a strap-on dildo hanging in place. She held my collar and leash in her hands, her confidence radiating.

"Oh, fuck," I murmured, my cock throbbing, my body aching for her.

I looked up into Ana's eyes, catching the faint smile on her lips before my gaze trailed downward, lingering on her perfect tits spilling out of her bra. This was it—this moment I had fantasized about for years but never thought I'd be brave enough to ask for.

"Are you ready, baby? Are you ready for *tu diosa* to fuck you like you deserve?" she asked, her voice low and teasing.

"Yes, *mi diosa*. Please," I begged, my voice almost shaking.

"Tell me what you want," she demanded.

"I want you to fuck me," I replied quickly, the words tumbling out in my desperation.

"How?" she pressed, her brow arching.

I hesitated. She knew exactly what I wanted, but saying it out loud felt like jumping off a cliff, thrilling and terrifying all at once.

"Speak, Charlie," she repeated, her tone commanding yet still soft.

"I—I want you to fuck my ass, *mi diosa*. Please," I said, my voice faltering.

She tilted her head, her brows pulling together, unsatisfied. My heart leapt into my stomach as I panicked, my need to please her overwhelming.

"I want you to fuck my ass, *mi diosa*," I repeated, this time with a tone lower and more certain. "Please."

She crouched down, setting the leash and collar aside, her hand reaching for my cheek. "You can tell me to stop if you don't want this, Charlie," she said softly. "If it's not the right time, just say the word. I won't be upset."

Her confidence wavered for the briefest moment and I shook my head quickly.

"No, please. I want this, Ana. More than anything," I admitted, my breath shaky. "But I'm scared. I'm scared you won't like it. I'm scared you'll think less of me if I do."

Her hazel eyes softened as she leaned in closer, both of her hands now softly cupping my cheeks. "Baby, you don't have to hide that part of yourself. I want this too. Do you have any idea how fucking hot this all is?" she asked, a smirk tugging at her lips.

She was pulling me back out of my darkness and back into that deep desire. "Fuck, I do, Ana. Seeing you like this…" My gaze scanned over her body. "Please."

Her smile widened as she stood gracefully, clasping the collar around my neck and attaching the leash. With a gentle tug, she guided me to crawl after her into our bedroom. The view of her perfect ass, swaying with each confident step, was something I'd never tire of.

Inside the room, she had prepared everything: a towel neatly laid out on the bed, lube, a butt plug, and a smaller dildo arranged meticulously. My heart raced at the sight, my body trembling with anticipation.

Ana turned to me, the leash wrapped loosely in her hand. She gave a soft pull, bringing me to the edge of the bed.

"On the bed, baby. All fours," she commanded, her voice a perfect balance of softness and authority.

I obeyed without hesitation, positioning myself on my hands and knees. My heart pounded in my chest, my muscles taut as she circled me, her gaze heavy, inspecting me like I was her prized possession.

She stopped behind me and kneeled down, her warm hands trailing up the backs of my thighs, over my ass, and along my lower back. "You look so good like this," she murmured. "So fucking good, Charlie."

Her words alone nearly unraveled me, my cock throbbing painfully as I lowered myself onto my elbows, pressing my forehead against the bed. My body tensed when her hands spread me open, leaving me completely vulnerable.

"Relax, baby," she whispered. "We'll go slow."

I nodded, too breathless to speak. I heard the sound of the lube bottle clicking open in the quiet room, and I imagined her spreading it across her fingers. My body tensed instinctively, but her hands returned as she began to massage the tight ring of muscle.

"Breathe, Charlie," she whispered. "Let me in."

I exhaled shakily, focusing on the warmth of her touch, on the trust I felt in every word she said. Slowly, I relaxed as she worked me open, one finger sliding inside. She paused, letting me adjust, before adding another. The initial discomfort eased, replaced by a slow, growing pleasure.

"That's it," she murmured. "You're doing so well for me, *mi amor*."

Her praise melted me, a groan escaping me as my body surrendered completely. Pleasure began to coil in my stomach, my cock twitching beneath me.

"Ana, fuck," I breathed, my voice strained. "That feels…"

"Good?" she asked, her fingers pressing against a spot that made my whole body jerk. "Like this?"

"Yes," I gasped. "Just like that."

She chuckled softly, her free hand trailing up my spine. "I knew you'd love this. You just needed to trust yourself. And me."

"I do," I whispered. "I trust you with everything."

Her fingers withdrew, leaving me achingly empty. My breath hitched as I heard the faint sound of her adjusting the harness, the slick of more lube, and then the warm press of the dildo against me.

"Do you want this, Charlie?" she asked gently.

"Yes, *mi diosa.* Please," I begged, pushing back slightly, desperate for more.

She took her time, easing the tip inside. I sucked in a sharp breath at the stretch, but her hands on my hips steadied me.

"Good boy," she praised, her voice like velvet. "You're doing so well."

Her words sent a flood of pleasure through me, overwhelming any discomfort. I moaned, pushing back to take more of her, needing to feel her completely.

"That's it," she encouraged, sliding deeper. "Take all of me, Charlie."

I obeyed, trembling as she filled me, her hands stroking my back and sides. She paused to let me adjust. "Ready for more, baby?"

"Yes," I whispered.

She began to move, her thrusts slow, her hands never leaving me. Each movement sent waves of pleasure through my body, building into something I couldn't control. She began a rhythm that left me gasping, moaning, completely at her mercy.

"You're mine," she growled, her tone turning possessive. "Say it."

"I'm yours," I choked out. "Completely yours, *mi diosa.*"

Her pace quickened, each thrust driving me closer to the edge. I moaned, raw and guttural, unable to hold back. She was perfect. *This* was perfect.

"*Such* a good fucking boy, Charlie," she purred.

"Fuck, Ana," I gasped. "I can't—I need to come."

"Not yet," she ordered, pulling out slowly. I groaned at the loss, but she guided me to lie on my back. "I want to see your face when you come."

I followed her command, spreading my legs wide as she repositioned herself. The sight of her, the way her tits bounced as she thrust into me, her lips parted in concentration, pushed me even closer.

"*Ay, dios mío,*" she moaned. "You look so fucking good, baby." Her pace quickened and she moaned as if she were going to come soon. "Now, Charlie. Come for me *now*."

Her command sent me over the edge. My release surged through me, intense and overwhelming, spilling onto my chest as Ana slowed her movements. Her own deep moans filled the room as she gripped my thighs tightly.

There was no fear, no shame. Only trust, satisfaction, and deep fucking pleasure.

"Good boy," she murmured, leaning down to lick the cum off my chest, making my cock instantly hard again. "I'm going to take this off, and you're going to fuck *my* ass now."

*Holy fucking shit.*

"Yes, *mi diosa.*"

\* \* \*

As I lay content, holding my perfect, sleeping goddess after fucking her ass like a wild animal, the buzz of my phone pulled me out of the moment. I glanced at the screen and saw the number from the private investigator. Careful not to wake Ana, I reached for my phone.

**Callan purchased a large bottle of whiskey with cash at 10:45 a.m. Witnessed drinking alone in his parked car at 1:15 p.m. in a parking garage. Photos attached for confirmation.**

## CHARLIE

I couldn't help but feel a rush of victory. *I got you, fucker.*

# 23

# Ana

I hadn't expected Charlie to insist I come to his rehearsal, especially when I knew he needed to focus. But, as usual, he got his way. "I can't be away from you right now," he said, his voice so sweetly vulnerable that I didn't have the heart to argue. Not just that, but I didn't *want* to be away from him either. So here I was, standing just inside the doors of a huge rehearsal studio.

The room buzzed with energy. Soundproofed walls muted the outside world, while the faint hum of amplifiers and the occasional strum of a guitar filled the air. A sleek, makeshift stage dominated the center of the space, taped-off sections marking where equipment would eventually go. Technicians adjusted cables, bandmates chatted in clusters, and assistants scurried around with tablets and headsets, all seamlessly coordinated like the gears of a finely tuned machine.

This was Charlie's world.

He was already on the stage, adjusting the mic stand to his height, his inked arms showcased perfectly. His easy confidence drew every eye in the room. His dark T-shirt clung to his back as he moved, the casual way he carried himself so different from one I'd seen so many times before. Unsure of himself. Needing approval. *My* approval.

I couldn't stop thinking about last night. I fucked Charlie. *Fue asombroso. Mejor de lo que podría haber imaginado.* Perfect.

I had to stop thinking about it; heat would rise throughout my body, and watching Charlie in his element made it even harder to ignore.

His team moved like clockwork around him, but he wasn't watching them—he was watching me.

"Stop staring," I mouthed at him, unable to stop the smile that crept onto my face.

He grinned, unapologetic, his dimples flashing as he continued to adjust the mic stand. That smile was for me and no one else, and I could feel my cheeks warm under his gaze. He was supposed to be focused, but instead his attention kept drifting towards where I stood.

"Charlie," a sharp voice called from across the room. "We need to go over the transitions again before the lighting team gets here."

I turned to see a tall, striking woman walking towards him with a tablet in hand. Her body language and tone screamed authority, and the way she spoke to Charlie, direct and confident, made it clear she was used to running the show. Her name was Kate, the tour manager. Charlie had mentioned her before, but he didn't talk much about work with me. And now that I was in his element, out of our bubble, it all seemed surreal. I had almost forgotten that he was one of the biggest rockstars in the world.

I watched as Charlie did his thing—testing the mics, singing a certain verse or two—but even as he did, he would keep stealing glances at me, his dimpled grin making my heart flutter each time.

"Charlie," Kate called him again, this time from the edge of the stage, her voice sharp. "We need to go over the second chorus again. The tempo's off, and you're dragging the transition."

"Got it," Charlie replied without looking at her. Instead, his eyes drifted towards me and he gave me another one of his disarming grins.

I sighed, the heat rising between thighs as he openly stared at me. I waved him off, mouthing, "Focus!"

Kate frowned, following his gaze. Her expression narrowed as she looked back at her tablet, clearly annoyed. She stepped closer to him, saying something quietly, but even with her standing directly in front of him, Charlie's attention kept slipping my way.

"You know," a voice said beside me, cutting through my thoughts. I turned to see Reese standing there, his tablet tucked under his arm and an unmistakable annoyance in his tone. Up close, in this lighting, he was insanely attractive, with dark brown hair and piercing blue eyes, standing at least six inches taller than me. "If you weren't here, he might actually get something done."

I blinked, caught off guard. "*¿Perdón?*" I asked sharply.

"You're clearly a distraction," he said dryly. "Kate's been trying to get him to focus for twenty minutes but he's too busy vying for your attention."

I stiffened, anger rising within me. His attractiveness instantly evaporated. "I didn't exactly ask to come, Reese. You know how Charlie is. I had to be here," I shot back.

He raised an eyebrow. "*Had* to?"

## ANA

I rolled my eyes, exasperated. "¡*Lárgate*! I don't need to explain myself or Charlie, to you—to anyone."

With that, I turned and walked away, seething. How dare he call me a distraction, as if I were ruining everything. I marched towards the other side of the studio, trying to keep my composure. My presence already felt like too much and Reese's comments only made it worse.

"Charlie, come on!" Kate's voice boomed through the studio, but when I turned my head, Charlie wasn't on the stage. He was heading straight for me, anger radiating off him.

His eyes flicked over my face, softening slightly when he saw my expression. "What happened?"

"Charlie, get back up there," I said quickly, trying to redirect him. "You need to focus. Maybe I'll step outside, get some work done—"

"What was that with Reese?" he cut me off, not giving up.

"It was nothing," I said, trying to wave it off.

"Nothing?" His eyebrows shot up, disbelief and anger flashing in his eyes. "I saw him with his fucking attitude and then you stormed off. What did he say to you?"

I hesitated, glancing around at the growing number of eyes on us. "He just...pointed out that you were distracted," I said, offering the half-truth. I didn't want to escalate things further, not when the studio already felt like a pressure cooker.

Charlie's jaw clenched and without another word, he turned and stormed towards Reese, fury all over his face.

"Reese!" he barked, his voice cutting through the chatter of the room. Everyone froze, the studio falling into silence.

Reese turned, pulling off the headset he had on one ear, his expression a mix of annoyance and confusion. "What now?"

"You're fired," Charlie growled, his voice low and seething

with anger. "Get the fuck out."

Reese's eyebrows shot up. "You're fucking kidding me," he said, disbelief turning to anger. "Over what? Over talking to Ana?"

"You upset her, so you're done," Charlie snapped. His voice rose as he turned to address the room. "In fact, let me make this clear: if anyone else has anything to say about me and Ana, you can get the fuck out and not come back. Ana is here with *me* from now on. She's *part of me*. So I suggest everyone get the fuck over it and do your jobs."

The room stayed silent and tense. Reese, however, wasn't finished.

"You should do *your* fucking job, Charlie," he shot back. "Not a single thing has been done since you walked in here. You've wasted hours, days, weeks, because you're too busy obsessing over her to get ready for this tour."

Charlie took a step closer but Reese wasn't backing down. "You know what? I'm happy to go," Reese spat. "Clean this fucking mess up yourself."

Without waiting for a response, Reese threw his headset onto a table and stormed out, the slam of the studio door echoing through the room.

Charlie stood there, his chest heaving, his face a mask of fury. Slowly, he came back to me, his eyes softening as his shoulders dropped. "You okay?" he asked quietly.

I nodded, though my stomach churned. The room was still silent, everyone pretending to busy themselves, their eyes flicking our way when they thought we wouldn't notice.

"Maybe I shouldn't have come," I whispered.

Charlie shook his head firmly, his gaze intense. "No. You're exactly where you're supposed to be."

His words should have reassured me, but as the silence stretched on, Reese's accusations echoed in my mind. *Am I too much of a distraction? Am I dragging Charlie down, hurting his career?* The doubt lingered, clawing at me as I tried to push it away.

We stayed for another few hours, the rehearsals resuming as before, as if nothing happened. I found a quiet corner and opened my laptop, determined to take up as little space as possible. I didn't want to give anyone a reason to whisper about me.

But he didn't make it easy. Charlie checked on me more often than necessary, his strides purposeful as he crossed the room to where I sat. Each time, I felt the weight of every pair of eyes following him. Yet, instead of feeling annoyed or embarrassed by the attention, an unexpected swell of pride filled my chest.

He wasn't hiding me, like I was trying to hide myself. If anything, his actions were a declaration. I wasn't just someone tagging along; I was someone who mattered to him. I mattered to him more than anything: his career, his friends, his staff.

That should have worried me, troubled me…but instead, I let myself bask in the satisfaction it gave me. No one had ever felt this way about me before, and it was intoxicating and thrilling, in the way that only Charlie could make me feel.

It was thrilling and absolutely, completely destructive.

\* \* \*

The next few days were almost identical: hours at the studio where I'd melt every time I heard Charlie's voice, followed by his constant check-ins, as if I might disappear the moment he looked away. We'd return to the apartment only to obsess over one another, as though we hadn't just spent the entire day together.

Even after all of this time, my love for him wasn't waning. If anything, it was growing stronger with each passing day, consuming me in ways I hadn't known were possible.

But being outside of our bubble every day brought something new into focus. I had to watch Charlie interact with more people—beautiful people, women who smiled too easily or laughed too loudly at his jokes. He paid no attention to them. And yet, the jealousy ignited in me like a spark every time.

I hated the way it made me feel, hated the tightness in my chest, the irrational anger that flared inside of me. I hated who I was in those moments. But at the same time, I couldn't imagine living any other way.

Loving Charlie was all-consuming, thrilling, and maddening in equal measure.

And I was losing myself. I was acting in ways I didn't know I was capable of.

We were finally in Madison Square Garden, everything coming into place for the tour. The venue was buzzing with technicians, crew, people scattered about, putting everything into place. Charlie stood near the stage, talking to a woman I didn't recognize, but the earpiece she had on hinted that she worked for the crew. And she was stunning. She leaned towards him, brushing her hand over his arm as she spoke. He wasn't flirting but he wasn't shutting it down either. He looked over at me, oblivious as he gave me a warm smile.

*If he's going to act oblivious, I'll remind him what he has to lose.*

I turned, scanning around until my eyes landed on Trevor.

## ANA

He stood near the other side of the stage, guitar slung over his shoulder, concentrating on tuning it. Charlie hated Trevor for some reason.

*Perfect.*

I marched over, letting my feet hit the ground hard, knowing what this kind of walk did to men. My breasts bounced, my hips swayed, and I instantly drew Trevor's attention. He looked up, a grin widening when he saw me. "Ana," he said with a hint of smugness. "To what do I owe the pleasure?"

I smiled, tilting my head. "Just checking in with everyone who's important."

Trevor chuckled, clearly eating it up. "You're too kind," he said, leaning against the wall. "What can I do for you?"

"Oh, I don't know," I said, running my fingers lightly over the strap of his guitar. "Maybe you can tell me how you make it all look so effortless, playing this. It's impressive, really."

Trevor's grin widened and he leaned closer, lowering his voice. "Maybe I'll show you sometime."

I laughed softly, but before I could respond, I felt it—Charlie's gaze from across the room. I glanced over, meeting his eyes. His jaw was clenched, his smile gone, replaced by a look that was dark and unmistakably jealous.

It didn't take long. He strode towards us, his energy radiating pure anger and frustration. Without a word, he grabbed my arm—rough, firm, enough to make a point.

"Excuse us," Charlie said coldly to Trevor.

Charlie guided us into the backstage area, down the hall, and into his dressing room. The door slammed shut behind us, the energy from the venue fading into the background.

"What the hell was that?" Charlie demanded sharply.

I put my hand on my hip, glaring at him. "What was *what*?"

"Don't fucking do that, Ana," he snapped. "Flirting with Trevor? Really?"

I scoffed. "Oh, you mean the way you were flirting with that woman? Laughing at everything she said, letting her touch you like she had any right to?"

His brows furrowed, confusion crossing his face before he slightly raised his voice. "I wasn't flirting, and you know it."

"And I wasn't either." I shot back, my tone mocking.

His jaw clenched and he stepped closer, his eyes narrowing. "What are you *doing*?"

I closed the distance between us. "What am I doing? What are *you* doing? Standing there like some clueless *idiota* while another woman throws herself at you. Did you even notice me watching? Or were you too busy enjoying the attention?"

He swallowed hard, his gaze flickering with frustration. "I didn't enjoy it," he said, his voice quieter now. "I only care about you, *mi diosa*." He was turning into the needy, desperate Charlie that I knew so well.

"Do you?" I whispered, stepping even closer until our bodies nearly touched. "Because right now, it doesn't feel like it."

I grabbed the front of his shirt, shoving him back against the wall. He let out a small gasp, his hands instinctively gripping my hips, but I slapped them away. "No," I said firmly. "You don't get to touch me. Not until I say so."

His eyes widened, his breathing uneven. "Ana—"

"*Cállate*," I snapped, my hand sliding down his chest to the waist of his jeans. "You need to remember your place. Do you know what that is, Charlie?"

He shook his head slightly, his lips parting as he struggled for words.

I smirked, my fingers grazing his hard cock beneath his

## ANA

jeans. "Your place is wherever I tell you to be. And right now, it's beneath me. *¿Entiendes?* Do you understand?"

"Yes, *mi diosa*" he whispered, his eyes blazing with desire.

I tugged his jeans open. "Good boy. You're so eager, aren't you? So desperate to prove yourself."

His groan was low and rough, his head falling back against the wall as I gripped his cock firmly. "You're pathetic," I murmured, my lips brushing his ear. "But at least you know who you belong to."

"I belong to you," he rasped, his body trembling beneath my touch.

"*Es cierto*," I said, pushing him down onto the couch beside the wall. "And I'm going to make sure you never forget it."

His desperation fueled my control. I peeled off my jeans and underwear and straddled him, sliding onto his hard cock with a sharp gasp as goosebumps pricked my skin. His hands instinctively reached for my thighs but I grabbed his wrists, pulling them away and pressing his arms firmly to his sides.

"You don't get to touch me," I said, my voice commanding. "I'm taking what's mine, Charlie. I'm going to fuck you until I come, and if you're a good boy for the rest of the day, maybe I'll let you come tonight."

Charlie gasped my name, his body trembling beneath me as he surrendered completely. I rolled my hips, chasing my own pleasure, teasing my breasts just inches from his face, knowing it was driving him insane.

Every sound he made, every shudder, only pushed me further. I didn't know what exactly I was doing. I wanted to test him—test his loyalty, his devotion. I wanted to see how far he'd go for me, to know what he'd endure just to please me. It was reckless, maybe even cruel, and I knew it. But I couldn't stop myself.

I wasn't Ana Del Rosario anymore. I was Ana, Charlie's *diosa*, the queen of his world.

And I knew neither of us wanted it any other way.

\* \* \*

After Charlie reluctantly returned to the main floor without me, I took a moment to clean up, assuring him I'd only be a few minutes. The room felt quieter without him, but the hum of activity outside still lingered faintly in the background.

My phone vibrated on the end table and I assumed it was Charlie already checking in, asking where I was. But when I picked it up, the screen displayed an unknown number. Beneath it, a text message appeared:

**You're too smart to let this go on. He's going to ruin you.**

# 24

# Charlie

I was drained by the relentless demands of tour rehearsals. All I wanted, all I could think about, was being with Ana. Just the two of us. I knew it was selfish. I had a crew counting on me, sponsors to satisfy, a management team relying on me, and fans I couldn't afford to let down. But none of that mattered. All I wanted was to make Ana happy.

She was becoming everything I didn't know I needed—jealous, possessive, degrading. And fuck, the anger and authority in her eyes when she took me backstage had me instantly hard. It was so insanely hot I thought I'd lose control right then and there. I'd never felt anything like it before. She owned me completely.

But even afterwards, as she rode the last wave of her orgasm, she made sure I was okay.

"*¿Estás bien?* Was that too much, baby?" she murmured, her voice soft but still carrying that commanding undertone.

I lifted my hips slightly, savoring the warmth of her perfect pussy wrapped around me. "No, *mi diosa*. It was perfect."

\*\*\*

I sat on the texts from the PI with proof of Callan's relapse. Part of me itched to call him, to tell him to back the fuck off of me and Ana. But another part hesitated. I felt bad for the poor sod. I understood secrets and vices—addiction was no joke. Still, I'd do anything to protect what Ana and I had. If he made another move to fuck with us, I wouldn't hesitate to use it against him. No matter how much guilt it stirred, Ana was my priority now.

But this fucking tour.

It was taking too much of my time with her and I could feel her silently pulling away. No matter how much I demanded we spend time together—between lighting setups, rehearsals, meetings, photo shoots—it never seemed like enough.

At home, she sat quietly scrolling on her phone. Every glance at the screen was like a stab to the gut. Was she talking to someone? Hiding something? I hated that my mind went there, but the silence between us was worse than any argument.

I was one second away from calling off the entire tour, dragging her to some deserted island where it would just be the two of us. Forever. Away from the noise, the pressure, the distractions. Because if I lost her…I didn't know what the fuck I'd do.

"I'm calling off the tour," I said abruptly one night, only nine days before it started.

We had just gotten under the covers, well after one in the morning. It was another night of her pulling away. She had locked herself in the bathroom earlier, sitting in the bath so long it must have gone cold. I sat outside the door, listening.

## CHARLIE

I wasn't certain, but I thought I heard her crying.

She came out eventually, red-eyed, her face pale. I'd tried to ask her what was wrong, but she'd just kissed my cheek and climbed into bed, silent as ever.

"No, no…Charlie. Don't do that," she said softly now, turning towards me. Her voice was calm, but her hand shook as it reached for mine. Her eyes, wide and panicked, gave her away.

"Then tell me what to do to make this better, *mi diosa*. I can't stand this anymore. What's going on? What did I do? It's the tour, isn't it?" I began, not even bothering to hold back tears.

Now that the floodgates had opened, there was no turning back. The panic had risen in my chest and I stood up, pacing.

"No, baby. It's not that," she answered back quickly, her voice cracking.

"Then what is it?" I snapped, my anger and frustration and fear mingling into one.

She only shook her head, tears spilling over, like she was afraid to say the words.

"Tell me, Ana! I'm dying each day you pull further away from me. Is it because you don't love me anymore? Just say it. Just tell me," I said, dropping to my knees beside the bed, gripping her hand.

She shook her head harder now, her breathing uneven. "I do love you, Charlie. More than anything."

Her voice broke, and her sobs came fast and heavy. I stood up, my chest tightening, and grabbed the pocket knife off the dresser. Without thinking, I pressed it to my forearm, the sharp edge cold against my skin.

"Stop!" she demanded, jumping off the bed towards me, her voice trembling with panic.

"Then tell me why you're being so distant, Ana. I can't take it. If you leave me, it will kill me. Don't you know that?" I yelled, the knife biting into my skin just enough to sting.

"I'm trying to protect you, Charlie! Please. Just trust me. I'm not leaving you!"

Her words didn't make sense, but the desperation in her voice made me freeze. Slowly, I lowered the blade. Her hands came up to wrap around my wrist, gently pulling it from my grip and setting it back on the dresser. She didn't let go of me, her fingers trembling as they pressed against my skin.

"You're my everything," I whispered, my voice breaking. "Don't hide from me, Ana. Whatever this is, we can get through it together."

She nodded quickly, too quickly, but her silence lingered. Her eyes darted to the side, just for a second, before she whispered, "I love you. I'm not going anywhere. You have to believe me."

I wanted to believe her. I wanted to feel the certainty in her voice wrap around my chest and pull the panic out of me. But there was something in her eyes, something she wasn't saying.

Her phone vibrated softly on the nightstand. She flinched, pulling back just slightly, like she didn't want me to notice.

"You're hiding something," I said quietly.

Her breath hitched, but she didn't look at me. "You have to trust me, Charlie. Please."

Her phone vibrated again, the faint sound pulling my attention like a magnet. She glanced at it nervously, her jaw clenching. We both looked back at each other, almost like a stand off to who would get to it first.

"Ana," I said sharply, my heart racing. "Who's texting you at this hour?"

## CHARLIE

Her shoulders tensed, and she didn't answer.

"Ana," I said again, stepping closer, my voice dropping to a low whisper. "What aren't you telling me?"

The look on her face, fear and resignation all at once, was enough to send dread through me.

"Charlie, please...you just have to trust me," she whispered, her voice cracking.

"No." My voice came out harder than I meant it to. "This—whatever *this* is—it's eating you alive, Ana. And it's eating me alive, too. You're crying in locked bathrooms. You're pulling away from me. And now someone's texting you in the middle of the fucking night?"

Her breathing hitched as she looked down at her hands. "It's nothing. It's just...work stuff," she said weakly, her tone so unconvincing it made me angrier.

I grabbed her phone off the nightstand before she could stop me, my thumb already pressing on the screen.

"Charlie, no!" she gasped, lunging for it.

But it was too late. The message was right there, burning into my brain:

**Why haven't you left him yet? Time's running out.**

I stared at the text, my heart pounding. "Who the fuck sent this?"

"Charlie, give it back!" she pleaded, tears spilling over as she reached for the phone.

I stepped back, holding it out of reach. "No. You're going to tell me right now who sent this. Is it Callan? Someone else? Ana, who?"

Her lips trembled, but she didn't answer.

"Is someone threatening you?" I demanded, shouting.

"Charlie..." She shook her head, and then quietly, she spoke.

"It's Jake."

I froze. The name hit me like a slap, and for a second, I thought I'd heard her wrong.

"Jake?" I repeated, my mind racing. "What the fuck does he want?"

She covered her face with her hands, her sobs muffled by her palms. "He knows," she choked out.

"Knows what?" My voice was trembling now, barely controlled.

"About Sarah," she whispered.

I staggered back a step, staring at her. "What the fuck does that mean?"

Ana wiped her eyes, her face pale. "*He's* the one who had her killed, Charlie. And he knows you hired someone, too. And now he's threatening to expose you, hurt you, or worse…if I don't end this."

My blood turned to ice. "Hurt me? Why? What does he want from you?"

"He wants *me*, Charlie." Her voice was flat, cold. "He knows about you hiring someone to watch him, about hiring someone to rough Sarah up, about your past with your ex. He's said things about Callan, threatening to use it so Sloane will leave him. He's using it all to twist the knife. He says if I don't comply, if I don't go back to him, he'll expose everything."

I stared at her, anger and fear tight in my chest. "And you were just going to let him get away with this?"

"What choice do I have?" she snapped, her voice rising. "He knows too much. He's dangerous, Charlie, and powerful. And he's watching us. If he thinks I'm not playing along, he'll…" She couldn't finish the sentence.

I shook my head, barely able to think, just react. "We need

to do something, Ana. He can't do this to us. Let's just...let's fucking kill him."

Ana inhaled sharply, an audible gasp filling the room. Her eyes widened, a mix of fear and disbelief flickering in her eyes. "Charlie, you can't just—"

"I know, I'm just thinking out loud," I interrupted, shaking my head as my thoughts spun. "But we can't just sit back and let him destroy everything. There's got to be a way to stop him."

Ana looked away from me, shaking her head. She was quiet for a moment, her head down, her thoughts clearly racing. When she finally looked up at me, her expression was guarded, but her voice carried her usual confidence.

"There's one thing I could do," she said carefully, almost hesitantly. "But you're not going to like it."

My stomach dropped. "What?"

She took a deep breath, her eyes locking onto mine. "I could pretend to leave you, Charlie. Go to Jake. Make him think he's won. Pretend I...wanted him all along."

Her words hit me like a punch to the gut. "No, Ana." My voice was trembling with disbelief. "You're not serious."

"I am," she replied firmly, stepping closer. "It's the only way to throw him off. He's obsessed with control. If I give him what he wants, if I make him think I'm playing by his rules, it could buy us time. Time to figure out how to stop him."

"No," I said immediately, my voice rising. "Absolutely not. You think I'm just going to sit here while you pretend to crawl back to that psychopath? Do you even hear yourself?"

Her expression softened, but her determination didn't waver. "Charlie, listen to me. This isn't about pride or feelings. This is about survival. Jake has all the power right now, and the only way to tip the scales is to make him feel secure. If I go to him, act like I'm done with you, he'll let his guard down. And that's when we strike."

My jaw clenched so hard it hurt. "You don't understand how dangerous this is, Ana. You're putting yourself in his hands, giving him every opportunity to hurt you—or worse."

"I know the risks," she said quietly, her gaze steady. "But he won't hurt me. Not if he thinks he's getting what he wants. He's too arrogant for that. And I'll make sure I'm always in control."

"Ana, no," I said again, my voice breaking. I reached for her hands, gripping them tightly. "There has to be another way. I can't let you do this."

Her eyes glistened, but she didn't look away. "There isn't another way, Charlie. I've thought about this for days. He's too smart, too calculated. The only way to beat him is to play his game better than he does."

I shook my head, desperation clawing at my chest. "You don't know what he's capable of."

"And you don't know what I'm capable of," she shot back, her voice rising. "I've survived worse than Jake. I can handle this."

I stared at her, my heart pounding, every instinct screaming at me to protect her. "What if he sees through it? What if he figures out it's an act?"

"He won't," she said with quiet certainty. "Not if we plan it right. Not if I play the part perfectly."

My throat tightened as I considered her words. The idea of her being anywhere near Jake, much less pretending to want him, made me sick. But she was right—Jake was holding all the cards. And this...this could give us the upper hand we desperately needed.

"Fuck," I said through gritted teeth. "You're right. I can't fucking believe this."

I pulled her into my arms, holding her tightly, as if I could shield her from the nightmare we were about to walk into. "If he touches you, Ana—"

"He won't," she whispered, cutting me off. "Because I won't let him."

Her confidence was both reassuring and terrifying. I just hoped we weren't making a mistake we couldn't come back from.

And if he fucking touched her, I vowed that I'd kill him myself.

# 25

# Ana

I ignored the text, hoping it was the wrong number, something that wasn't meant for me.

But a call came the next morning as I sat in Charlie's dressing room in the backstage of Madison Square Garden. The same number flashed across my screen and I hesitated before answering.

"Ana." His voice was low, the same tone I knew so well when he was at his breaking point.

"Jake," I whispered, and it suddenly all made sense.

"I'm glad you picked up. I didn't want to leave this in a message."

"What do you want?" I asked as I stood up, trying to calm the panic rising in my chest.

He chuckled softly, the sound as familiar as it was infuriating. "Still so defensive. Relax, Ana. I'm just here to offer you a little advice. You might want to keep a closer eye on your boyfriend."

My stomach churned. "What are you talking about?"

"Charlie," he said, dragging the word out with disgust. "Do

you really think you can stay with someone like him? With his track record? He's a fucking trainwreck, Ana."

"Don't," I snapped. "You don't know him."

"Oh, but I do," Jake said smoothly. "And I know what he's capable of. For example, I know he paid someone to intimidate Sarah in jail. Did he tell you that? Or did he conveniently forget?"

I froze, a lump forming in my throat. *How did he know that?* "I don't know what you're talking about."

"So you did know," he said casually. "But perhaps what you didn't know ws that I handled it for him. I had them just do the fucking deed, something that should have been done a long time ago."

A wave of nausea crashed over me. "You...*you* did that?"

"You're welcome," he said, his tone light, almost playful. "And don't worry. I've made sure Charlie's involvement won't come back to haunt him. For now."

"For now?" I choked out, dread swirling in my chest.

"Here's the thing," he said, his voice going low. "Charlie's... messy. His obvious obsession with you. The impulsiveness. The carelessness. I'm surprised you've stayed this long, actually. He's one step away from ruining you, Ana. And when he does, I won't be able to clean up the mess. In fact, I might be forced to make sure the mess sticks—to him, not me."

"Why are you doing this?" I whispered, tears stinging my eyes.

"Because I'm the only one who knows how to protect you, to make you happy," he said coldly. "You've let him into your life, into Sloane's life, and he's going to destroy everything. Look at Callan. Look at the damage already done."

I froze. "What *about* Callan?"

There was a pause before he spoke. "You mean he hasn't told you? That's interesting. I thought you'd know by now." He paused again. "Callan's been drinking. And it's not just a little relapse. We're talking full-on spiral. I have proof, of course. Video evidence, photos. Do you think Sloane knows? Do you think she'd stick around if she did?"

"You're lying," I said weakly, though a sinking feeling in my gut told me he wasn't.

"You know I'm not," Jake said smoothly. "He's reckless, Ana, and dangerous. Just like Charlie. And when it all comes crashing down, you'll be the one picking up the pieces. Unless you do something now."

My chest tightened with anxiety and I struggled to find my voice. "What do you want from me?"

"Simple," he said casually, like we were discussing the weather. "End it with Charlie. Make it clear that it's over. Come back to me. Otherwise, I'll make sure the truth about Charlie comes out. And trust me, Ana, once the media gets ahold of it, *and* the police, there won't be anything left to salvage."

I scoffed. "What the fuck are you doing, Jacob? Haven't you taken enough from me already?" I asked bitterly.

There was a pause before he answered. "And haven't you taken enough from *me*? If you would've just stood by me, like the good fucking wife you were supposed to be, we would have made it through everything! And now you're playing house with this twenty-something, immature rockstar who worships you, when you're supposed to be *mine*!"

The muffled sound from the music on the stage stopped and I panicked, knowing Charlie would be in to check on me at any moment. "You're crazy if you think I'll come back to you," I muttered coldly.

"And you're crazy if you don't think I'll ruin Charlie like a drop of the hat," he bit back. "You don't have any other choice, Ana. Leave him. Figure it out, or he's gone."

The call ended.

*What the fuck am I going to do?*

Charlie burst through the door, sweat clinging to his shirt, his eyes hungry for me. But he must have noticed something was off because his expression quickly shifted to worry.

"What's wrong, *mi diosa*?" he asked quietly, pulling me close to him.

There was no way I could leave Charlie. There was no way I could put him through that. He wouldn't survive it.

"I just missed you," I said, forcing a small smile, though I could feel tears pricking at my eyes.

He studied my face, the worry etched across his face. "I'll call it a day," he said softly. "Let's go home."

\* \* \*

The days that followed were torture. I checked on Sloane constantly, making sure she and Callan were okay. If Jake was telling the truth about Callan's relapse, Sloane didn't seem to know.

When I called her, she sounded cheerful, blissfully unaware. "We just did a walkthrough of the wedding venue today, Mom. It's gonna be perfect."

My heart ached. "And I was thinking," she added hesitantly. "Maybe you could walk me down the aisle. I know Dad won't. I don't think he'll even come."

I swallowed the lump in my throat. "Don't worry about your father. I would love to walk you down the aisle, *mi pequeña*."

As the days dragged on, my mind kept circling back to Jake. He kept sending messages, continuing the threats:

**Do you remember the day we fucked for hours under the stars at the lake house? I'll bet the kid you're with now has no idea how to fuck a woman like you.**

**Ana, you're running out of time. You need to leave him. I can do more than just expose him. Look what happened to Sarah. Don't test me.**

**Do it soon. I can't wait much longer.**

A thought kept circling back to me: If Jake wanted me to leave Charlie, maybe I could pretend. Play along, lower his guard, and buy us some time. But the thought of deceiving Charlie felt like a knife twisting in my chest.

I kept wracking my brain, desperate for a way to gain the upper hand with Jake. What could I use against him? He'd been clean as a whistle during his presidency. Callan once joked he was a boy scout, the kind who always played by the rules. So how did he end up like this? Was it the forced resignation? Our divorce? Losing Sloane? Had all of it driven him to this obsessive, vengeful asshole?

The questions plagued my mind and yet the answer seemed painfully clear. What if I did go back to him—but not really? What if I pretended to leave Charlie, make Jake believe I had given in? Maybe it would buy me enough time to figure out how to stop him for good.

But the thought sent a wave of nausea through me. Charlie would die if I left him—emotionally, perhaps even physically. I could see the devastation in his eyes, the way it would break him. *How do I do this?*

## ANA

*I have to tell him. He deserves the truth, doesn't he?* But if I did, he'd do something reckless, something impulsive, something that would destroy everything and put him at even greater risk. *I can't tell him. But I have to. There's no other way.*

The cycle of my thoughts was suffocating, my chest tightening with the outcome of the impossible decision. Every option led to ruin, every path riddled with danger. And yet, somehow, I had to choose one. For Charlie. For Sloane. For all of us.

\* \* \*

It was only a week before Charlie's tour started. We made love for hours, each touch and kiss more desperate than the last, as if we both knew we were running out of time. The intensity grew with every moment, our emotions spilling out in a tangle of passion and grief. When it was over, he lay beside me, his face buried in my neck like he couldn't bear to let go.

But eventually, he had to. With trembling hands, Charlie packed a bag, his movements slow, as if each item he placed inside was a piece of his heart he was leaving behind. I stood by the door, watching helplessly as he zipped it closed and slung it over his shoulder.

"I'm coming back to you, Charlie," I whispered, my voice cracking as I clutched his face in my hands. "Please don't do anything stupid while I'm gone. Please."

His eyes glistened with unshed tears, his jaw tightening as he nodded. "I'll be waiting, *mi diosa*."

The elevator doors opened and he stepped inside. He turned to look at me one last time, his composure barely holding, before the doors slid shut, cutting us off.

I stood frozen, staring at the closed elevator, my chest heaving. *I'm sorry, Charlie. I'm so sorry.*

I knew Jake had to be watching. Or if not him, then one of his people. He would want proof that I had done as he demanded. Every moment I had shared with Charlie had likely been under their surveillance. The thought made my stomach turn, but I forced myself to stay calm. I waited ten minutes, pacing the length of my apartment as my heart raced, before finally picking up my phone and dialing Jake's number.

He answered on the first ring. "Ana," he said smoothly, his voice oozing triumph.

I swallowed hard. "I did it," I said, my tone flat. "He's gone, Jake. You won."

There was a pause and I could almost hear the smirk in his voice when he replied. "Good girl, Ana. I'll send a car over for you."

I ended the call without another word, my hand trembling as I lowered the phone. The weight of what I'd just done settled heavily on my chest, but I couldn't break down—not now. Not yet.

*One step closer,* I told myself, though the thought offered little comfort.

An hour later, a sleek black SUV was idling at the curb. I hesitated before getting in, clutching a small travel bag like it was the last piece of stability I had. The driver was someone new, silent and professional, his eyes fixed on the road ahead. I didn't bother making small talk. My thoughts were too scattered, my chest too tight as the lights of the city faded behind me.

We headed south towards the lake house in Maryland. The same house I once tried to escape to when I learned of Jake's betrayal. Now, it felt cruelly fitting that I was heading there again, this time to betray Charlie.

*No. You're not betraying him. You're saving him.*

But the mantra did little to soothe the gnawing guilt. I promised Charlie I wouldn't let Jake touch me, that I would hold firm. But deep down, I knew it wasn't that simple. Jake's texts had been laced with reminders of our past, of the passion we once shared, and I wasn't naive enough to think he wouldn't push for more.

My phone vibrated relentlessly in my bag, pulling me from my thoughts. Charlie's name flashed across the screen over and over, and each time I saw it, my chest tightened.

*Stop, Charlie. Please stop.*

I typed out a quick reply, my fingers shaking. **You have to trust me. I'll call you when it's safe.** I deleted his messages to erase any evidence Jake might look for.

When the car finally pulled up to the lakefront property, I felt a wave of bittersweet nostalgia. The house was as beautiful as I remembered—large, bright, with its glass windows glowing warmly in the night. It was a place of so many good memories, now irreversibly tainted.

Jake was already waiting. His shadow moved towards the door as we pulled in, tall and confident as ever. His salt-and-pepper hair was neatly styled, his sleeves rolled up casually, and his hands rested just inside the front pockets of his jeans. His light eyes, once so familiar, almost betrayed a softness, though I knew better.

"Ana," he greeted warmly, a smug smile on his lips.

"Jacob," I replied curtly, my tone sharper than I intended. *Careful, Ana.* I couldn't afford to be this defensive yet.

His eyes swept over me, lingering in ways that made my

skin crawl. "It's been a while, hasn't it? You look better than ever," he said with a hint of self-satisfaction.

I swallowed hard, biting back the retort that sprang to my tongue. *It's because I got rid of you.* Instead, I forced a tight smile, letting him believe he had power over me.

"Come in," he said smoothly, gesturing towards the open door. "I've just opened a bottle of wine. Your favorite."

I hesitated briefly, my hands tightening around my coat. Then, with a deep breath, I walked past him and into the house. The familiar scent hit me immediately—clean wood, faint cologne, and the past I tried to leave behind.

I shrugged off my peacoat, hanging it on the coat rack, and made my way to the kitchen. I needed the wine—anything to steady my nerves. The dark hardwood floors of the hall creaked slightly as I made my way further into the house. I walked through the living room, everything looking exactly as it was the last time we were here; the built-in bookshelves lining the walls, books overflowing throughout. The couches nestled atop a cozy rug, one I had picked out with Sloane when she was little. My heart ached. *I need to focus.*

I was finally in the kitchen and rested my palms against the black marble countertop, bracing myself as I heard Jake's footsteps approaching behind me.

He circled around me, moving to the counter to pour two glasses. His movements were smooth, confident, the smirk I used to love tugging at his lips as he slid a glass towards me. I took a large sip, the wine burning slightly as it went down, and carefully set the glass back on the counter.

"So," I said, keeping my tone calm, even though I felt anything but. "Now what? You've got me here. What's the plan?"

## ANA

"Straight to the point, as always." Jake took a small sip of his wine, studying me with that infuriating smirk. "Now, we reconnect. Catch up. I've missed you, Ana." His voice was soft, almost tender, as if this were some kind of romantic reunion.

I let out a bitter laugh. "And we just ignore the fact that you've blackmailed and threatened people I love to bring me here?"

His expression darkened briefly before he regained his composure. "You just needed a little push. I couldn't let twenty years go down the drain because of one mistake."

"One mistake?" My voice rose, my anger bubbling instantly. "That's what you're calling it? Sleeping with Sarah—someone who put Callan through hell, who you *knew* was unstable? You risked everything. For what?"

Jake's jaw tightened as he gripped the edge of the counter. "You don't need to keep reminding me," he said sharply. "I've paid the price. I lost Sloane. I lost you. But I'm trying to make things right."

I scoffed, my laugh bitter. "Right? You're doing a great job of that, Jake. Threatening people? Manipulating? Who even are you anymore?"

His eyes flashed with anger and he stepped closer. "Don't act like you're some saint, Ana. Letting that narcissist parade you around like a trophy. You used to be strong, independent. Now you're just his…toy."

The words struck like a slap, but I recovered quickly, glaring at him. "You have no idea what our relationship is like. Charlie loves me, and he's not afraid to show it. You never did that, Jake. You never fought for me the way he does."

Jake's anger flared and he closed the distance between us in one swift movement. His hands gripped my hips, pulling me against him. "You want passion? You want me desperate and reckless? Well, you've got it, Ana," he growled, his face inches from mine.

I tried to push him away, my fists weakly pressing against his chest. "Stop," I whispered, the guilt and fear swirling in my chest.

But Jake didn't stop. His grip tightened and his voice dropped to a low, menacing whisper. "You missed me. You missed *this*." He pressed his erection into my stomach. "Say it, Ana."

My voice trembled as I whispered, "I missed you."

His smirk returned, wicked and triumphant. He believed he won. That was exactly what I needed him to think.

He turned me around, pressing my body firmly against the counter. He pulled my jeans down in one quick motion, sliding his fingers between my thighs, feeling the inevitable heat.

"See?" he whispered into my neck. "So wet for papa, just like always. Like the fucking whore you've always been, just for me," he continued, sticking a finger deep into me while another rubbed my clit.

"Stop, Jake. Wait," I whispered, using every last ounce of my pride to reluctantly protest, tears stinging my eyes as the guilt gnawed deep within me.

"I'm not waiting any longer, Ana," he groaned into my ear, then as he swiftly removed his fingers, his cock thrust deep into me, making my wince and shudder, the pleasure and guilt hitting me like a block to my chest.

His nails dug into my hips as he held onto me, thrusting wildly against me, his grunts loud and erratic.

"I'm taking back what's mine, Ana," he said between breaths.

"This pussy. This body. It's always been mine," he growled.

I gripped the counter, pushing against him, coaxing reactions I desperately tried to suppress, the pleasure igniting in my core like a wildfire.

"No," I protested under my breath, as if that could dim the guilt that clawed at my chest.

Jake didn't hear me, or if he did, he ignored it.

"Come on, Ana. Come on my cock like a good girl," he said breathlessly, his fingers finding their way back to my clit.

My pussy instantly seized and I let out a sob, the guilt overwhelming me. Jake grunted loudly, his hips slapping hard against mine, spilling himself into me.

*Charlie, I'm so sorry. Please forgive me.*

# 26

# Charlie

**You have to trust me. I'll call you when it's safe.**

Her message sat on my screen, feeling like hope and a curse, pulling me in opposite directions. My fingers hovered over my phone, desperate to respond, to keep some sort of connection. But I couldn't. Not without putting her at greater risk.

Ana had given me the address of the lake house but she made it clear: Jake was always one step ahead. If I acted impulsively, it wouldn't just put her in danger…it would unravel everything.

And I hated to admit it, but I needed help.

The thought twisted in my stomach like a blade. I hated admitting I couldn't handle this on my own, hated the vulnerability of reaching out. But there was no other option. I wasn't going to jeopardize Ana's safety because of my pride.

I scrolled to his name and hit *call*.

He picked up after two rings.

"Charlie," Callan's voice came through, sharp and cautious. "What do you want?"

"It's Ana," I said quickly. "She's in trouble. I need your help."

Callan's tone shifted immediately, the caution replaced by urgency. "What kind of trouble? Where is she?"

"She's at the lake house in Maryland. With Jake," I said, forcing the words out. "He's blackmailing her, threatening her. But it's more complicated than that. I need to tell you everything, and it's not going to be easy to hear."

"Then start fucking talking," he snapped.

I hesitated, my throat tightening. "I've been watching you," I admitted, the words heavy with guilt and embarrassment.

"What do you mean, 'watching me'?" Callan asked, his voice hardening.

"I was keeping tabs on you," I said quickly. "Trying to find dirt, something I could use to make you back off. I thought if I had leverage, I could stop you from interfering in my relationship with Ana."

The silence stretched, and I looked at my phone to make sure he was still on the line.

"You've got to be fucking kidding me," Callan said finally, his voice low and cold. "You were spying on me?"

"Yes," I answered quickly. "I know it was wrong, but I was desperate. Every time you questioned me, it felt like you were trying to turn Ana against me. I thought if I could get you to stop—"

"Fucking unbelievable," he interrupted.

"There's more," I said quickly. "I…I know about your relapse."

His silence was deafening.

"Jesus fucking Christ, Charlie," he said finally, his tone like ice. "So, you've been sitting on this? Spying on me, digging into my life, knowing I was struggling? What the fuck were you doing, laughing about it until you could throw me under the bus?"

"I didn't know what I was going to do with it," I admitted. "But Jake knows too. He's using it against Ana, threatening to tell Sloane."

There was a sharp breath on the other end, but Callan didn't interrupt, so I forced myself to continue. "And Sarah," I added, my stomach churning. "I hired someone to scare her in jail. I just wanted to make sure she couldn't hurt Ana, or Sloane, again. But Jake somehow knew. He escalated it. He's the one that had her killed, Callan. And now he's using that, too."

More silence. When Callan finally spoke, his voice was calm but laced with fury.

"So, let me get this straight," he said. "You spied on me, hired someone to intimidate Sarah, which got her killed, and now you're coming to me for help?"

"Yes," I said, the admission heavy on my chest. "I fucked up, Callan. I know I did. But Ana's in danger, and…I can't fix this on my own."

There was another pause, and then his tone softened, though I could still hear the frustration. "Where are you?"

"My loft," I said quickly.

"I'll catch the next flight out. Meet me in D.C—it's closer to the lake house. We'll need to go over everything before we make a move."

"Thank you," I whispered, relief washing over me.

"I'm not doing this for you," he said sharply. "I'm doing this for Ana."

I hesitated. "Are you telling Sloane?"

Callan let out a heavy sigh. "Not yet. She doesn't need this weighing on her right now. But if Jake so much as hints at her,

## CHARLIE

I'll handle it. Just keep me updated and I'll be in D.C. tonight."

"Okay," I said, nodding as if he could see me.

"And Charlie?" His tone dropped, colder and sharper. "If you ever pull this kind of shit again—spying, lying, dragging Ana into your mess—I won't just sit back and let it slide. I'll make sure you feel every ounce of the damage you've caused. Personally. Do you understand me?"

I bit my tongue. Now wasn't the time to argue with him, especially after asking for his help.

"Fair enough," I said quietly.

As the call ended, I stared at my phone, my heart pounding. *What the fuck are we going to do?*

* * *

I sat alone in a hotel room in D.C., perched on the end chair near the window, staring at a photo of Ana and me on my phone. We were both smiling, my arm wrapped around her, caught in one of those perfect days when it felt like the rest of the world didn't exist. I'd give anything for another day like that.

This was the longest I'd been without Ana since the night I came to her apartment to make dinner, and it was killing me. My heart physically ached.

I told my team I needed the next day off. I had no idea what the plan was yet, but I knew we'd need time to figure it out. They weren't happy about it, but the show couldn't go on without me. They'd have to make do. I'd been busting my ass prepping for the tour, making up lost time, sacrificing precious time with Ana. I couldn't keep doing that—not anymore, not without her by my side.

A sharp knock at the door broke through my thoughts. Startled, I pocketed my phone and stood.

I opened the door to find Callan standing there, and to my surprise, Sloane was with him.

"Sloane," I said, taken aback. Her scowl told me everything. "Callan," I added with a nod before stepping aside to let them in.

Sloane marched past me, her presence electric with frustration. Callan followed, his disdain barely masked as his eyes lingered on me.

"I can't believe my mom is in this mess," Sloane said, hands on her hips as she glared out the window. Then she turned, her eyebrows shooting up. "Charlie. What the fuck?"

I sighed, shutting the door behind me. "I know. This is my fault. But I'll do anything for your mum, Sloane. I'd fucking die for her if I had to. I didn't know things would get so…so fucked up," I said, my voice cracking, feeling like the guilt was eating away at my chest.

Her expression softened slightly as I wrung my hands, pacing the room.

"Alright, Charlie. You fucked up. Now let's fix this," Callan said, his arms crossed as he stood next to Sloane by the window. "What exactly does Jake know, and what's he threatening Ana with?"

I hesitated, sinking back into the chair. "Like I said…I hired someone to watch him. The same guy I used to hire you. But Jake knew all along. He knows about Sarah. He knows about…" I glanced at Sloane, then back at Callan. "About what you're going through."

Callan's jaw tightened. "Sloane knows, Charlie," he muttered.

Sloane shifted uncomfortably, her eyes dropping to the floor before meeting mine. "What were you gonna do with all this, Charlie? Why were you watching my dad?"

"I don't know!" I snapped, the words spilling out louder than I intended. "I wanted to take down anyone who hurt Ana. I didn't have a plan."

"And you wanted to take me down because you thought I was threatening your relationship," Callan interjected coldly. "Because I was suspicious of you, Charlie. Turns out I had every fucking reason to be. Now look at this. Look at this fucking mess."

"Okay, stop," Sloane said, raising her hands. "Let's stop blaming Charlie. It's clear he didn't mean any harm," she said, pausing briefly. "At least…not to my mom."

Callan huffed but didn't argue. "So Jake's threatening to expose you," he said, his tone still sharp but less cutting. "He's threatening to tell Sloane about my relapse, which is fucking cruel. What else?"

I exhaled shakily. "He said he could do to me what he did to Sarah."

Callan sat on the edge of the bed, rubbing his face with his hands. "We need to figure out how he's staying a step ahead. Who did you go to about the shit with Sarah in jail?"

"I, uh…" I stared at my hands, the weight of the admission sinking in. "I had my assistant, my friend Reese, find someone."

Callan nodded slowly. "Alright. We start there."

"The thing is…" I hesitated. "I fired Reese. I don't know if he'll help us or not."

"Jesus fucking Christ," Callan muttered, dragging his hands down his face. "Fine. I'll get it out of him. Give me his number."

I pulled out my phone, found Reese's contact information, and handed it to Callan. Without a word, he disappeared into the hallway, leaving Sloane and me alone in the tense silence that filled the room.

She sank onto the edge of the bed where Callan had been, her shoulders heavy with a sigh.

"My dad wasn't always like this, you know," she said softly, staring down at her hands. "He was a good dad. A good guy. And then he just threw it all away." She glanced up at me, her voice sharper now. "You didn't make this mess, Charlie. My dad did the day he decided to ruin our family."

Her words took the edge off the guilt gnawing at me. She didn't hate me, after all. She might have been angry, but now her anger had shifted, redirected to her father.

"Do you still speak with him?" I asked carefully, trying to piece together a plan. Maybe she could help in ways no one else could. An idea began forming in the back of my mind.

She shrugged. "Sometimes. He calls every so often. I only answer maybe half the time. Our relationship is…strained, to say the least. It's hard to look past everything he did. Now I don't think I ever want to speak to him again. My mom doesn't deserve any of this."

I let out a slow breath. "Do you think you'd speak to him again if it would help your mum?"

Her brow furrowed in confusion. "Of course I would. Why? What are you thinking?"

"Maybe you could call your mum and tell her you've found out about Callan," I said, leaning forward as the plan began to solidify. "Say you're upset, that you're having an argument and need to get away. If Jake overhears, he might try to play hero and invite you to the house."

Sloane's eyebrows shot up as her mind churned through the idea. Before she could respond, Callan burst through the cracked door. He closed the door behind him, leaning against the dresser as he let out a heavy sigh.

"Well?" I asked impatiently, standing from my chair.

"He talked," Callan said, his voice clipped. "Not much, but enough."

"What did you say to him?" Sloane asked as she leaned forward on the bed.

"I told him I'd take what I knew about his involvement with Sarah to the authorities if he didn't cooperate," Callan said, his eyes narrowing. "That scared him enough to spill."

"What did he say?" I asked, dreading the answer.

"He admitted to hiring someone for you—a freelancer named Kenneth Bart," Callan explained. "I know of him. Bart is one of the best: discreet, thorough, and expensive. You paid him a fortune to watch me and Jake, didn't you?"

I nodded, guilt pressing hard against my chest. "I wanted someone who could get the job done. I didn't want to take any chances."

"Well, congratulations," Callan said dryly. "Bart might've flipped."

Sloane straightened. "What do you mean?"

"Bart works for whoever pays him the most," Callan continued. "If Jake figured out someone was watching him, it wouldn't take much to offer Bart more money. If that's the case, Jake's had access to everything you've been doing, Charlie. That's how he's been staying one step ahead."

The room fell silent.

"So, what do we do?" I finally asked.

"We find Bart," Callan said firmly. "If he's double-dipping, we'll find out. And if he's been working for Jake, we might be able to use that to our advantage."

Sloane, who had been sitting quietly, suddenly perked up. "I think I should call my mom." She was testing our plan with him.

Callan frowned, his head snapping towards her. "What? No. Absolutely not."

"Just hear me out," Sloane said, holding up her hands. "If I tell her I found out about you, that I'm upset and don't know what to do, my dad might overhear. He'd want to swoop in and play the hero. That could be our opening."

"It's too risky," Callan shot back. "If Jake catches on that it's a setup, you'll put her, and yourself, in even more danger."

"I'm not saying we tell her everything," Sloane argued. "Just enough to make her believe I'm upset. She won't question it."

Callan crossed his arms, shaking his head. "And if Jake doesn't take the bait?"

"He will," Sloane said confidently. "You said so yourself—he's been watching. He'll think it's the perfect chance to drive a wedge between us. It's exactly the kind of move he'd make. He *hates* us together, Cal."

Callan's jaw tightened and for a moment, it seemed like he might shut the idea down. But then he sighed, shaking his head. "Fine. But you need to be convincing, Sloane. If this goes sideways—"

"It won't," she interrupted. "We don't have time to second-guess everything. We need to move…soon."

Callan nodded reluctantly, his gaze still wary. "Alright. But we stay close. If anything feels off, we pull the plug."

"Deal," Sloane said, pulling her phone from her pocket.

## CHARLIE

"Not yet," Callan said, resting his hand lightly on hers. "Tomorrow. If you call tonight, it'll look too obvious. Jake's probably paranoid and he'll see through it."

Sloane hesitated, then nodded. "Okay, yeah. You're right."

I let out a heavy sigh, sinking back into the chair. Tomorrow felt like an eternity away. My thoughts spiraled, twisting into dark places I didn't want to go. *What was she enduring right now? What sick games was he playing?*

The questions burned, flashing unwelcome images in my mind. Him touching her. Him fucking her. Whispering things in her ear. *Did she like it?*

I gritted my teeth, biting my lower lip so hard it started to bleed.

"Charlie," Callan said sharply, snapping me out of my spiraling thoughts. "Stop panicking. You're no good to her if you're losing it."

I blinked, forcing a shaky exhale as I dragged my focus back to the room. "I know," I muttered, though my voice lacked conviction. Even I didn't believe it.

"She's strong," Sloane said quietly, her voice softer than I expected. "She's been through worse than this. If anyone can hold her own, it's my mom."

I nodded stiffly, the words meant to comfort me falling flat. She *shouldn't* have to hold her own. That was on me. *I* should've kept her safe.

But my thoughts betrayed me, circling back to the darkest places. She'd told me she wouldn't let him touch her. She'd said it with such conviction, and I wanted to believe her. But what lengths would she go to if it meant protecting me? Protecting Sloane?

The questions tore at me, leaving no room for rest. I didn't sleep. Instead, I spent the night pacing the images of my mind, replaying every possibility, every horrible scenario. Each one only made my decision clearer.

I didn't care what it would take.

*I'm going to kill him.*

# 27

# Ana

I couldn't sleep. What Jake had done—what *I* had done—haunted every corner of my mind. The images wouldn't stop. I could see Charlie's face, the betrayal that would carve through him when he found out. *He can't find out.*

I kept going back and forth, the weight of each possibility crushing me a little more every time. My chest ached, my head spun, and no matter which way I turned, the pain only deepened.

*What am I going to do now?*

Jake wouldn't let me go without a fight; that much was clear. I'd never seen him like this—so menacing, so cunning. The Jake I once knew, the one who could fake charm and wield influence like a weapon, was gone. Something had snapped in him and there was no coming back.

I lay next to him in the dark room that we once shared as a happy couple. I could only taste the bitterness of what our current reality was. *Think. There has to be a way out of this.*

And then, it hit me—a spark of an idea so risky that I almost dismissed it completely.

*What if I turn the tables on him?*

Charlie had awakened something in me, something I'd always known I had but had let slide for too long. With Jake, I was only submissive in the bedroom. During his presidency, I was the one who made things work behind the scenes. I kept us on track, handled the fallout from his missteps, and ensured the image he projected to the world stayed intact.

He thrived on being in control, but the truth was, that control only extended as far as I allowed it. Everywhere else, I had the reins, guiding us through every storm, every crisis, every carefully orchestrated appearance.

That's why he needed to have power in the bedroom. Because everywhere else, it was mine. He craved that dominance, that feeling of control I didn't give him in the rest of our lives. So, I let him have it there. I gave it to him, convincing myself it was a small sacrifice to keep the balance.

But now, I could see how much it had fed him. It had become the foundation of his arrogance, his need to dominate, and his ability to manipulate. And now, stripped of his title, his influence, and the adoration he once commanded, he clung to that control with a new, dangerous intensity.

This wasn't the Jake I knew before. This was someone else—unhinged, menacing, desperate. His newfound madness made him reckless, but it also made him vulnerable.

*So what if I twisted it?*

Jake had always been sure of himself, convinced of his power over me. But this need to prove he was still in control was something I could exploit.

If I challenged him in ways he wouldn't expect, I could unravel him. I could use his desperation against him. Make him question the very power he thought he still held.

## ANA

This time, I wouldn't give him what he wanted. This time, I'd take the control I'd once given away—and use it to make him fall apart.

I sat up slowly, watching Jake's chest rise and fall as he slept. My hands trembled, though I clenched them tightly to still the shaking. This had to work. I had to find a way to regain control.

*You've done this before. You've taken control with Charlie. You can do it again.*

I took a deep breath and crawled onto him, straddling him. The mattress shifted under my weight, and Jake stirred slightly, his brow furrowing as his eyes fluttered open.

His lips curled into a slow, lazy smirk as he took in the sight of me. "What's this?" he murmured.

I leaned forward, resting my hands on his chest to keep him pinned down. "This is me taking the lead," I said, my voice steady despite the flutter of nerves in my chest. "Things are going to be different now, Jake. If we're going to make this work, you're going to give me what *I* want."

His smirk faltered, replaced by a flicker of confusion. "What are you talking about?"

"I've always let you have control," I continued. "I gave you that because it's what you needed. But now it's my turn. You're going to let *me* take control."

For a moment, he didn't move, his expression a mix of surprise and disbelief. I could see the wheels turning in his head, his usual arrogance faltering as he processed my words.

"And what makes you think I'll do that?" he asked with skepticism.

I leaned closer, letting my lips hover just above his. "Because you don't have a choice."

Jake's smirk returned, but it was weaker now, less certain. "You're serious."

"Dead serious," I said, my voice unwavering.

I pressed my weight into him, holding him in place. "Stay," I commanded softly, and to my surprise, he obeyed.

For a moment, I thought I had him. His breathing quickened and his pupils dilated as he stared up at me. I felt his cock hardening beneath me and I slightly swayed my hips, urging him on.

"See?" I murmured, letting my lips graze his jaw. "It's not so bad, is it? Letting someone else take control."

He swallowed hard, his body relaxing beneath me. I could feel the tension melting away, the cracks in his arrogance widening.

*I've got him.* A flicker of triumph sparked in my chest.

But then his hands shot up, gripping my hips tightly as he flipped us over in one sharp motion.

I gasped as my back hit the mattress, Jake looming over me now, his smirk back in full force. "You really thought that would work?" he asked, his tone full of mockery.

"Jake—" I started, but he cut me off, grabbing my wrists and pinning them above my head.

"You think you can just flip the script?" he continued, his grip on me tightening. "That's not how this works, Ana. That's *never* how this worked."

Panic bubbled in my chest as I struggled against him, but he held me firm, his weight pressing me into the mattress.

"You almost had me," he admitted, his voice quieter now, more menacing. "For a second there, I thought you had changed. That maybe you figured out how to take control."

His lips curled into a cruel smile. "But you haven't. You're still the same, Ana. Still mine. And now, I'm going to remind you exactly where you belong."

He reached for something in the drawer of the bedside table. I knew exactly what it was. This was something he loved doing—tying me up, having me completely at his mercy.

Jake's smirk widened as he tied silk fabric tightly around my wrists, the knot digging into my skin as he secured me to the headboard.

"Perfect," he murmured, sitting back to admire his work. "Now you can't try that again, can you?"

"Jake, stop," I said, my voice trembling as I tugged futilely at the restraints. "This isn't right. You need my consent, and I haven't given it to you yet," I said, trying to reason with him, trying to fuel guilt into his mind, to explain exactly what he was doing.

His laugh was sharp and cold. "This isn't right?" he echoed, leaning over me again. "You think you get to decide what's right here? You lost that privilege the moment you started playing games with me. I didn't give my consent to that either."

"I'm not playing games," I whispered, tears stinging my eyes.

"Oh, but you are," he said, trailing his hand down my body, hovering over me as his other hand forced my legs apart. "You think you can tease me? Act like you're in control? You don't know who you're dealing with, Ana. I'm a changed man."

I turned my head away, bile rising in my throat as his hand slid lower, his fingers grazing the edge of my underwear. My body tensed, every instinct screaming at me to fight, but I forced myself to stay still, knowing it would only make him angrier if I struggled.

"See? There it is," he said smugly, his fingers slipping beneath the fabric and down to my pussy that betrayed me, wet and ready. "You're so predictable, Ana."

"Jake, please," I said, my voice cracking.

"Please?" he mocked, his smirk deepening. "Oh, I always loved how you begged."

I clenched my jaw, my breath hitching as his fingers circled my clit, knowing exactly how to work me.

"I felt it last night," he continued, his tone cruel and taunting. "The way your body responded. Coming all over my cock. You can't fake that, Ana. No matter what you say, I know the truth. You wanted it. You missed me."

Tears spilled down my cheeks as I stared at the ceiling, refusing to meet his gaze. My body betrayed me again, the unwanted sensations building in my core despite the revulsion and hatred twisting in my chest.

"Look at you," Jake said, his voice dripping with mockery. "Trying so hard to act like you're above this. But your body doesn't lie, does it?"

I bit down on my lip, trying to suppress the sounds threatening to escape, but he didn't stop. His fingers moved with cruel precision, exploiting every weakness, every reaction.

"You think you're so strong," he murmured, his breath against my ear. "But here you are, completely at my mercy. And you love it. Don't you?"

"No," I whispered, my voice shaking.

"Liar," he hissed, pressing harder, faster, until my body arched involuntarily against him. "Say it, Ana. Say you love it. Say you love me."

I clenched my fists, the silk digging into my skin as my body reached the edge, unwilling and unstoppable. My breaths came in shallow gasps as the pressure built, and I hated myself for not being able to stop it, for letting him take this from me.

When it finally broke, a reluctant, choking cry escaped my lips, and Jake laughed triumphantly.

"There it is," he said, his tone smug and satisfied. "I told you. You can't fight it. You'll always be mine."

I turned my face away, tears streaming down my cheeks as he leaned back, his hand leaving me like I was a possession he'd just proven he owned.

"See? You're so much better when you stop pretending. When you remember your place."

I didn't respond, my body trembling with the aftershocks of the betrayal it had just endured.

And then he was on top of me again, his boxers lowered and revealing his hard cock before he began teasing my entrance.

"This is how it's going to work from now on, Ana. The more you resist, the harder I'll make this for you," he said into my ear before thrusting into me hard and unrelentingly.

"Oh, fuck, Ana," he growled, lifting my shirt to reveal my breasts, then gripped them tight. "I bet he doesn't fuck you like this, does he? I bet he lets you pretend you're the little dominatrix he wants. But that's not you, baby. Not at all," he went on breathlessly. "You're such a good little slut, taking it hard for papa."

He reached down, thumbing my clit as tears spilled down the sides of my cheeks. He was going to make me come again, whether I wanted it or not.

"Come on, Ana. Let me feel your pussy squeeze my cock. Let me see that pretty face come for me, just like you always do."

The pressure built in my core once again, and I squeezed my eyes shut tight, turning my face to not give him the satisfaction.

"Look at me, Ana!" he yelled, twisting the fear in my chest, but I refused. "Look at me, or I'm fucking killing Charlie myself," he snapped.

I turned my head sharply, forcing myself to meet his gaze. Jake was now someone desperate—desperate to reclaim what little control he could, no matter the cost.

"Now come like a good fucking girl, Ana," he demanded, furiously rubbing my clit as he pounded into me hard.

I let go, my release crashing over me, tainted by a flood of guilt and seething hatred. His smirk widened as he laughed triumphantly, reveling in my humiliation.

He pulled out abruptly, roughly flipping me onto my stomach, my restraints twisting and tightening further. Gripping my hips, he forced himself back into me, wild and relentless. I clenched my teeth, silently begging for him to come quickly, for the torture to be over.

Then, with a loud, guttural grunt, he pulled out, his cum spilling across my back. The sensation turned my stomach, a wave of nausea rolling through me, but I stayed perfectly still, swallowing the sobs threatening to escape.

I lay there, my eyes squeezed shut, every muscle in my body tense. My wrists throbbed from the strain, my skin stung where the restraints had bitten into me, but none of it compared to the fire raging inside—an all-consuming hatred that burned brighter with every passing second.

*You think you've won, Jake. But this isn't over. I'll make sure you pay for every second of this. Every single one.*

\*\*\*

I sat in the bath, hugging my body tightly, my arms wrapped around my knees pulled to my chest. My mind raced, circling

## ANA

the same questions with no answers. *How am I going to get out of this?* I needed to know how Jake had found out about Charlie, about Sarah—about everything. Revenge simmered in my body, but it was eclipsed by a heavier ache: my longing for Charlie.

He hadn't tried to contact me during the night, and though it was a relief since Jake checked my phone every time it buzzed, I now found myself wishing he would. Anything to break the suffocating silence. Anything to make me feel less hopeless.

The bathroom door swung open, making me flinch. Jake stood there, holding my phone, his expression urgent.

"Sloane is calling you," he said, his tone clipped. "Pick it up."

*Why does he care?* But I didn't question him; I quickly stood, drying my hands on a towel hanging nearby. Before I could reach for the phone, Jake answered it himself and put it on speaker.

"Hi, baby," I said, forcing warmth into my voice despite the cold dread gripping me. I had to be strong for her.

On the other end, I heard crying. My heart plummeted. I glanced at Jake, and for the first time, worry mirrored on both our faces.

"*¿Qué tienes, estás bien?*" I asked, stepping out of the tub and wrapping the towel around me.

"Callan…Callan and I got into a fight, Mom," Sloane sobbed, her voice trembling. "He's been drinking again. He was hiding it from me."

The pain in her voice was gut-wrenching. I looked back at Jake, only to find a cruel smirk creeping across his face. *¡Hijo de puta!*

"*Ay, mi amor, pobrecita,*" I said gently, taking the phone from Jake's hand. "Are you okay?"

"No," she cried. "I need you, Mom. I can't stay here right now. He's just…he's not himself right now. It's like he doesn't even care."

I glanced at Jake nervously, unsure of what to say. *Do I tell her I'm here with him? Do I lie?*

"I understand, baby," I said softly. "I know it's really hard right now. But…" I trailed off, searching for words.

Jake's voice broke through, uncharacteristically soft and warm. "Hey, honey."

There was a pause. "Dad?" she asked, disbelief clear in her tone.

"Yeah, it's me," he said, his voice oozing pride. "Your mom and I are at the lake house. We're…we're trying to reconcile." He looked at me, smirking like a predator who'd cornered his prey.

*I hate you.*

"Really? Mom?" Sloane asked, clearly confused.

I swallowed hard. "Yeah," I murmured. "It's…it's complicated, baby. But your dad and I—" I hesitated, looking away. "We have twenty years of history. That's a lot to just throw away."

The words felt like poison on my tongue, but I knew it was what Jake wanted me to say.

"What about…what about Charlie?" she asked hesitantly.

Shame and embarrassment burned through me, even though none of this was my fault. "He was too much, baby," I said quietly, each word stabbing at my heart. "I think we all knew that."

Sloane sighed, as if disappointed. "Well…I mean—"

"You're welcome to come stay with us here at the lake house, honey," Jake interrupted, his tone feigning kindness. "Get

## ANA

away for a bit. We can be like a family again."

I rolled my eyes, my face hot with anger and humiliation. But the idea of having Sloane here gave me a glimmer of hope. At least I wouldn't be alone with him anymore. I only hoped he wouldn't turn on her. *But he wouldn't do that to his own daughter...*

"Um..." Sloane hesitated. "I don't know."

"I think it would be nice, baby," I chimed in. "It's a chance for us to reconnect as a family."

Jake shot me a cautious look, but my words seemed to seal the deal. Sloane sighed again before finally giving in.

"Okay. Alright, yeah. I'll take the next flight out," she said.

*Thank God.*

"Let me know your flight details, honey," Jake said smoothly. "If you need me to, I'll have someone pick you up from the airport and bring you home."

The word *home* sliced through me like a dagger, but I bit back my response, forcing myself to stay quiet. Instead, I focused on the only thing that mattered: silently forming a plan to get us out of this.

\* \* \*

The lake house was eerily quiet as I stood by the window that night, watching the driveway for Sloane's arrival. Jake was in the kitchen, pouring drinks, his earlier threat still echoing in my mind.

"If you even *think* about telling her, Charlie will be dead in an instant," he had said, his voice low and venomous. "She doesn't need to know anything. Do you understand me?"

I nodded stiffly, my stomach churning as his words settled

over me like a dark cloud.

Now, as the black SUV pulled up and Sloane stepped out, a flood of relief and fear rushed through me. I had to be careful for her sake.

She spotted me in the window and waved, her face lighting up with a hesitant smile. I forced myself to smile back, though it felt like my face might crack from the effort.

The front door opened and she was in my arms within seconds, hugging me tightly.

"Mom," she murmured, her voice trembling.

"I'm so glad you're here, baby," I said, my arms wrapping around her as if I could shield her from everything going on.

Jake appeared in the doorway, his smile wide and disarmingly warm. "Sloane! Hi honey. You've grown so much since I've last seen you."

She pulled back from me, her expression guarded as she looked at him. "Hi, Dad," she said, her tone polite but distant.

"Come on, let's get your bags inside," Jake said excitedly. "We'll have dinner and catch up."

The table was set with candles and an assortment of dishes Jake had ordered in, his attempt at playing the doting husband and father. Sloane sat across from me, her eyes darting between me and Jake, as though trying to figure us out.

Jake was all charm, asking Sloane about school, her life—carefully avoiding anything that might spark tension. She answered politely, but her tone was clipped, her smile forced.

I barely spoke, focusing on my plate and nodding along to their conversation, though my mind was elsewhere. Every now and then, Jake's hand brushed my arm or rested on my shoulder, a silent reminder of his control.

When we finished eating, Jake stood and stretched. "Let

me fill your glass of wine, sweetheart," he said to me, his tone dripping with false affection.

I nodded, forcing a smile. "Thank you."

As he disappeared into the kitchen, Sloane pulled out her phone, her fingers moving quickly over the screen. She hesitated, then slid it across the table towards me.

I glanced down at the screen, her notes app open with a message written.

**I know what's going on. We're gonna get you out of this.**

My breath caught in my throat and I quickly lifted my eyes to hers. She gave me a subtle nod, her expression calm but her eyes blazing with determination.

I swallowed hard, my fingers trembling as I reached out to slide the phone back to her. Before I could respond, Jake's footsteps echoed down the hall.

Sloane slipped the phone back into her lap, her face a perfect mask of casual indifference just as Jake walked in with a glass of wine in hand.

"Here you go," he said, placing the glass in front of me.

"Thank you," I murmured, quickly taking a sip.

Sloane smiled politely at Jake, but the tension was still there. I could feel her gaze on me, her silent promise hanging in the air.

*We're gonna get you out of this.*

# 28

# Charlie

I crouched near the window, staring out at the faint glow of the lights in the lake house in the distance. We were in the vacant lake house next door, though it was about 100 meters away. Every second we waited felt like torture. My jaw was clenched tight, my palms sweaty despite the biting cold of Maryland.

Behind me, Callan leaned against the wall, arms crossed like he had all the time in the world. His calm demeanor irritated me, but I knew it wasn't indifference—it was experience. He'd been here before, maybe not in this exact situation, but close enough.

"It's been hours," I muttered, the words escaping before I could stop them. "Still nothing."

"That's a good thing," Callan replied, his voice maddeningly composed.

I turned to face him. "How the fuck is that good? They're in there with him and we're sitting here doing nothing."

He pushed off the wall, meeting my glare head-on. "We're not doing nothing," he said sharply. "We're waiting. Bart did his job. Jake doesn't know we're here. That's what matters."

I let out a sharp breath, trying to keep the frustration hidden. "We're putting all this on a guy who's been working for Jake. How do we know he won't just double back and sell us out?"

Callan's eyes narrowed, his voice dropping to a sharper edge. "Because we paid him more than Jake ever did. Bart doesn't have loyalty, he has a price. And we made sure ours was higher."

It made sense, but it didn't feel like enough. I ran a hand through my hair, pacing near the window. "And you think that's all it takes?"

"Yep," Callan said simply. "He told us everything. And now he's been feeding Jake bullshit to keep him off our backs. Right now, Jake thinks you're still in New York, and that's why we're here, waiting for our time to strike."

I stopped pacing, staring out at the lake house. My chest ached with the unknown.

"What about Sloane?" I asked, my voice quieter now. "Have you heard anymore from her?"

Callan stepped closer, his expression softening just slightly. "She's keeping an eye on them. Says they both went up to their room, but she's lingering around, trying to catch him off guard."

I nodded, swallowing hard. The thought of Ana in there with him made my stomach churn. And Sloane…fuck, if I dragged her into this, if either of them got hurt, I'd never forgive myself.

"They're both tough," Callan added, as if reading my mind. "And fucking smart. They'll be okay."

I let out a shaky breath, gripping the window frame as I stared into the night. "I hate this," I muttered. "I hate waiting.

I hate knowing they're in there with him."

"I know," Callan said. "But we have to do this right. Jake's dangerous, and if we rush in blind, we'll just give him more power. Bart gave us this chance. Jake has no idea we're here. We use it."

I nodded stiffly. The waiting was killing me, but Callan was right. Bart had flipped for the money, and now we had to trust that he'd done his part.

A moment later, Callan's phone vibrated loudly in his pocket. He answered, putting the call on speaker. There was no greeting, just faint, muffled sounds. I realized Sloane called and hid the phone, likely in her pocket.

"Get your phone out. Record this," Callan whispered, gesturing to his phone.

I nodded, pulling my phone out.

Through the static came Jake's voice, sharp and angry.

"You think you're clever, don't you, Ana?" he snapped. "Sneaking around, thinking you can manipulate me?"

"I'm not doing anything," Ana replied, her voice wavering but still steady.

Jake laughed coldly. "You really think I believe that? You always were a terrible liar. You think I don't know what you've been up to? That Charlie hasn't been sniffing around?"

My blood boiled at the sound of my name on his lips, but I stayed silent.

"You're paranoid," Ana said, her tone sharper now. "No one's coming for me, Jake. You've made sure of that."

"Paranoid?" he shouted, and then there was a crashing sound, like a chair had been turned over. "You don't get to call me paranoid. Not after what your pathetic little boyfriend did, trying to get into my business."

"Leave him out of this," Ana shot back loudly.

"Why should I?" Jake snarled. "You think he's going to protect you? He's nothing. And if he shows his face here, he's dead. Do you hear me? Dead."

Callan's jaw tightened beside me but he stayed silent.

Then, Sloane's voice cut through, muffled but clear. "What are you talking about? Why are you threatening Charlie?"

There was a pause, the kind that made my chest fill with dread.

"Sloane," Jake said, his voice cold. "How long have you been standing there?"

More muffled shuffling came through the line, and then Sloane spoke again, her tone firmer. "Long enough. What are you doing? Why are you threatening Mom and Charlie?"

Jake let out a low, humorless laugh. "Oh, sweetheart. You really don't understand how the world works, do you?"

"Then explain it to me," Sloane pressed.

"You want the truth?" Jake said, his voice hardening. "Fine. *I'm* the reason Sarah's gone. *You're welcome.* She thought she could play me, just like your mother does. But no one crosses me and gets away with it. And your mother is only here because she's protecting her precious boyfriend since *he's* the one who started all of this."

My stomach dropped. Callan stiffened beside me as he processed Jake's words.

"Wait. You had Sarah *killed*?" Sloane asked, her voice full of disbelief. I was impressed with how well she was feigning ignorance.

Jake scoffed. "She was a liability. Just like Charlie will be if he comes anywhere near this house."

"You're insane," Sloane said, her voice stronger now.

Jake's tone turned icy. "Careful, Sloane. You don't want to push me."

"You're threatening Mom, threatening Charlie, and you think I'm just going to stand here and let you?" she snapped.

The silence that followed was suffocating.

Then Jake spoke, his voice low and menacing. "You keep pushing, and Callan's next. Do you hear me? You keep your mouth shut, or I'll make sure he's gone too."

My eyes widened with horror. Was he going to turn on his own daughter?

"Stop it!" Ana said in the background, her voice filled with anger. "You're scaring her."

"She should be scared," Jake shot back. "You both should be."

"Mom!"

The call ended abruptly, leaving a deafening silence in its wake.

Callan and I glanced at each other with an unspoken understanding.

"This isn't good," he said, already moving. "He's escalated too quickly. Let's move. Now."

We were out the door before I could even think.

"What's the plan?" I asked Callan, eyeing the .45 he packed in his waistband.

"This is for the worst case scenario, Charlie. We go in and tell him we have this shit on him, threaten him, and go on our merry way with Ana and Sloane," he explained calmly, our shoes crunching on the leaves as we stepped outside, the cold air biting my cheeks.

I felt for the pocket knife in my jeans. It was there, just as always.

"You don't think he's gonna fight it?" I asked cautiously.

"I don't fucking know, Charlie. He might. Be prepared for anything."

My heart raced as we glided towards the house, but the sheer anticipation I felt kept my adrenaline high.

"We go through the back door. Follow my lead. Got it?" he asked, stopping as we took in a perfect view of the house just ahead.

I nodded. "Got it."

We began for the house again, pacing quickly ahead, and I knew I'd do whatever it took to keep Ana, even Sloane, safe.

There was a sudden commotion inside as we approached it; there was some muffled yelling and a loud clunk, like something—or someone—dropping to the floor. Callan ran ahead and I followed, and as he swung the back door open, there was Jake getting up from the floor. There was blood dripping down his temple, his hand held firmly against it. Sloane and Ana were gone. I looked down to find a ceramic vase and plant shattered on the floor.

"Callan," he said as he turned around, noticing him first, then locked eyes with me. "Charlie," he spit out, his voice low and venomous. "What the fuck are you doing here?"

"Where's Sloane and Ana?" Callan asked, leaving no room for me to answer.

He pointed to the front door that was wide open, headlights pulling out of the driveway. "Ana hit me then took off with Sloane. Which was stupid of them, really. Now they've just sealed both of your fates."

Callan let out a bitter laugh. "Tough guy now, huh, Jake? It doesn't fit you," he retorted.

"I've always been like this. I've just been good at hiding it,"

Jake shot back, then turned to me with a glare.

My anger was simmering with each passing second.

"Well, that's gonna serve you well in prison, bud, 'cause we got your confession on Sarah," Callan said, causing Jake to break our eye contact as he turned back to him.

"That's rich," Jake said with a bitter laugh. "That's all you've got? What is it, an audio recording? That'll never hold up in court."

"Yeah, so maybe we should just fucking kill him, Callan," I said through gritted teeth.

Jake turned back to me, his eyebrows shooting up. "And so he speaks!" he said mockingly. "And *you*? Kill *me*?" His mocking laugh returned.

"No one's killing anyone," Callan quickly interjected.

"He might want to once he knows what Ana and I did…" Jake said, holding onto the couch now, the blood from his wound drying on his hand.

My blood began to boil. "What the fuck did you do to her?"

Jake smiled, crossing his arms as he leaned against the couch. "Nothing she didn't already want," he said smugly.

I inched forward, discreetly grabbing my pocket knife. "She didn't want you. She was here to protect *me*," I said through gritted teeth.

His eyebrows shot up. "And whose fault is that?" he asked mockingly as he adjusted his stance confidently. "Sure seemed like she wanted to be here when I felt her perfect pussy clench around my fingers—"

I snapped, my vision red, and without another thought, I lunged towards him as I flipped the blade out from my knife. I fisted Jake's shirt while I held the knife up high and plunged it deep in his chest with all my strength. Callan's hands were on my arms, pulling me back, but he was too late. Jake's eyes widened as he looked down at the knife, collapsing to his feet.

My heart raced, and I was breathless as I watched him fall to the ground with a thud, his eyes fluttering shut, blood flooding from his body.

"Charlie! Fuck!" Callan yelled, but it sounded like he was a million miles away as I watched the life drain from Jake's eyes. "You just turned this into a fucking murder scene, you idiot. We had him. We had the recording—"

"And it wouldn't have been enough," I shot back, my voice rising. "He would've found a way. He would've hurt them."

Callan cursed under his breath, kneeling beside Jake. He pressed two fingers to his neck, checking for a pulse.

"He's still alive," Callan muttered, his voice grim. "But not for long."

He stood abruptly, grabbing my shoulder and forcing me to look at him. "We don't have time for this. We need to clean this up before anyone else shows up."

Just as he said it, my phone vibrated in my pocket. I snatched it out, Ana's name flashing on the screen.

I answered immediately, putting it on speaker. "Ana?"

"We're out," she said, her voice shaky but full of relief. "I'm driving, heading to town. I hit him, Charlie. I hit him hard, and we ran. I don't think he's following us."

Her voice rooted me back to reality, her beautiful voice like music to my ears. "Ana, fuck, I've missed you. You did so good, *mi diosa*. You took him down and we got to him. He's not going anywhere."

I looked up at Callan and he shook his head, as if urging me not to tell them.

"Sloane said you guys planned all of this. Baby," she choked up. "Where is Jake now?" she asked, composing herself.

"He's restrained. We're talking to him. We'll take care of it. You two head back to the hotel in D.C. We'll meet you there," Callan answered before I could even think.

"Please be careful," Sloane's voice rang through. "I've never seen him like this. He's fucking lost it," she said, her voice shaking.

"We will, baby. I love you," he said softly, and I glanced up at him, his face a look of determination.

"I love you too," she said back.

"Charlie," Ana cut in again. "I love you."

I smiled, forgetting where I was as I turned and found Jake's lifeless body on the ground. "I love you too. More than anything."

The call ended and I looked up at Callan. "What now?"

Callan moved quickly. "Don't touch anything. We're gonna wrap him in that rug and get him out of here. I'll come back and make sure we've cleaned up without a trace."

I stared at him, the weight of what I'd done finally starting to sink in. "What are we gonna do with him?"

"We're gonna dump him out in the bay. If no one finds him, no one knows," he explained, moving the couch that covered the rug.

I blinked before moving to the rug to help him, wiping the blood off my hand on my jeans. "You've done this before."

Callan didn't respond at first, carefully moving Jake's body to line him up with the rug. He eyed me carefully as I began to help. "Let's just say I've cleaned up messes like this. Now stop wasting time yapping and help me get this done."

# 29

# Ana

Jake could hurt me, threaten me, all he wanted. But when he brought Sloane into this, when he threatened her, something inside me snapped. The rage surged so quickly, so fiercely, that I didn't even think. Swinging the heavy ceramic vase at his head with all my strength, with all that adrenaline built up, was easy. He went down fast, and we had a chance to run.

I didn't know if it would kill him, and in that moment, I didn't care. All that mattered was getting Sloane out, away from him. Now we were on the highway, heading towards D.C., the lights of passing cars flickering through the windows.

"Charlie and Callan are next door. They heard what was happening. They should be there by now," Sloane had explained as we sped off. Relief had flooded through me.

But now, my mind was racing again, replaying everything. "How did this all happen?" I asked, breaking the silence. "How did you know? Did Charlie come to you?"

Sloane shook her head. "No," she said simply. "He went to Callan."

I blinked, stunned. Charlie had put aside his ego to ask Callan for help. It made sense—if anyone could help him, it was Callan—but it still surprised me. Charlie hated him. The fact that they worked together for me made my chest ache in a way I couldn't describe.

"And…did you already know about Callan?" I asked hesitantly, piecing everything together.

She hesitated, her voice quieter when she spoke. "Yeah. I found out when I came home one day and he was passed out. I could smell the booze all over him." She paused, exhaling slowly. "It's been hard, but he's getting help. Slowly, but surely."

My heart ached for them both. "Callan's a good man, baby," I said softly. "He's strong. And so are you. You'll get through it."

"I know," she said, and the quiet confidence in her voice made me smile.

The highway stretched endlessly ahead, the hum of the engine filling the silence between us. We were in the car I used back in the day, back when we still lived in New York as a family. It was a reliable little Jetta, and it felt odd speeding down the highway after all these years.

"*Mi diosa*, huh?" Sloane teased suddenly, and my cheeks burned hot.

I shook my head with a soft laugh. "Yeah. So what?"

She giggled, the sound light and warm. "It makes all the sense in the world."

The silence returned, but this time it wasn't heavy.

"What do you think they're doing to him?" I asked quietly after a while. "Do you think they're really only talking to him?"

Sloane sighed deeply, staring ahead. "I don't want to know.

## ANA

And, honestly...Dad deserves whatever's coming to him."

I swallowed hard, staring out at the darkness beyond the window. "Yeah," I said softly. "He does."

But even as I said it, my mind turned back to Charlie. To what might be happening right now. And no matter how much I tried to push the thoughts away, I couldn't help but wonder just how far he'd go to make sure I was safe.

\* \* \*

We waited hours at the hotel in D.C. I stared out the window and could see faint morning light as the sun got ready to rise. Sloane had fallen asleep, drifting off as I held her close to me, cuddling like we used to when she was little. But my mind couldn't stop running, couldn't stop wondering where they were and what they were doing.

I jumped when I heard the sound of the key card unlocking the door, but it only opened slightly ajar since I had flipped on the security lock. I hurried over to the door, peeking out at Callan and Charlie, their faces withdrawn and exhausted. I unlocked the door and flung it open, wrapping Charlie in my arms, the sobs that I held back for hours finally escaping as he held me tight.

"Ana," he whispered into my neck. "My love."

"Where have you been?" I asked, slightly letting go to reach my gaze to his.

He blinked, hesitation in his eyes. "Just making sure Jake wouldn't talk," he said simply.

I only nodded. I turned to see Callan and Sloane reuniting, then turned back to see Charlie holding up a key card in his hand. "We have the adjoining room. Let's go."

Charlie started a hot shower, undressing alongside me. I noticed a faint dark spot on his jeans and he looked down as he realized where my gaze pointed to.

"I would throw those clothes away, Charlie," I said, then opened the glass shower door, not waiting for a response.

I let the warm water wash over me, the sensation spreading goosebumps all over me. Charlie's hands were suddenly on my arms as he pressed his body against my back, jutting his hard cock between my ass cheeks.

Between the heat rising throughout my body, already aroused for him, a gnawing guilt ached deep in my chest.

"Charlie," I whispered, turning my head so he could hear me.

"Ana," he said, grazing his hands under my arms, up my stomach, and then squeezing my breasts.

"I have to tell you something," I said breathlessly as one hand trailed down to the front, his fingers finding my wet spot.

"No," he said into my neck. "Don't tell me."

My heart dropped. "Why?" I said after stifling a moan.

"Did you want it?" he asked, his hands stopping, grazing back up to my arms.

I hesitated. "No," I whispered, tears streaming down my cheeks, mixing in with the warm water.

"Then don't tell me," he responded quietly. "Unless you want to. Unless you need to," he added.

"No," I echoed.

His hands returned to my breasts, trailing back down my stomach. "If you're not ready for this, Ana, tell me now," he whispered.

"I'm always ready for you, Charlie," I whimpered as his fingers circled my clit.

## ANA

"Take back your power, *mi diosa*. Use me exactly how you need to. Please," he begged. "I *need* you."

I smiled, reaching back to graze my fingers over his cock, patiently waiting for me.

"I just want my good boy, Charlie. *Tu diosa* needs her good boy to do exactly as she says. You think you can handle that, baby?"

"Yes, *mi diosa*," he whispered in my ear. "Please."

I steadily turned around without letting go of him, gripping him tighter as I faced him, his face contorted with pleasure as he eyed me with need.

"Good. Get on your knees then," I said, turning the shower head above me so it faced the wall, giving us room to play.

Charlie immediately knelt down, getting on both knees, looking up at me with his hands on his thighs. I smiled as I lifted my leg and rested my thigh on his shoulder, then clutched his hair in my hand and pulled him close, burying his face into my pussy.

"Eat my pussy, baby. Don't stop until I say so," I demanded, lifting my hips as his tongue began to move.

My body reacted instantly, my hips arching to meet the rhythm of his mouth. My release was close, my back pressing against the shower wall as Charlie gripped my thighs to hold me steady, his tongue flicking my clit with determination.

"Fuck, Charlie, yes," I gasped, the tension in my core bursting, my orgasm ripping through my body.

I greedily let him continue as he worked his mouth on me, igniting wave after wave of pleasure until my legs trembled uncontrollably. Finally, I pushed him away, sliding down the slick wall to face him as I tried to catch my breath.

He gave me a faint smile, his eyes filled with awe and desire, the very look that had drawn me to him from the start.

"Is *mi diosa* satisfied?" he asked softly, sitting in front of me and resting his hand on my thigh.

My head leaned back against the wall as I nodded, my gaze dropping to his hard cock, patiently waiting for my touch.

"What about you, baby?" I asked quietly as I met his eyes. "Does my control satisfy you?"

The years I spent being so compliant with Jake, sacrificing my own wants and needs just to keep him happy, were beginning to weigh on me heavily. When we met, I was hopelessly in love with him. He was older, confident, so sweet and loving. At just twenty years old, I was still finding my voice, and though I grew into it over time, our sex life never seemed to evolve with me.

I didn't want Charlie to ever feel that way.

His brows twitched together briefly, as if my question had confused him.

"Of course I am," he said, interlocking his fingers through mine. "Everything you do to me, *for* me, is perfect."

"You enjoy my dominance?" I asked hesitantly, my confidence faltering for a moment.

Charlie studied my face, as if he'd caught the flicker of uncertainty.

"I enjoy your dominance. I enjoy your sweetness. I enjoy the way you let me share my deepest, darkest fantasies. I enjoy every part of you, Ana. Everything we do together is fucking perfection," he said with unwavering conviction.

His confidence in me built me back up, motivating me to take the lead again.

"Grab your knife. I want to try something," I said, getting onto my knees.

Charlie's eyes widened slightly, darting towards the shower glass door. "I've, uh…I've lost it," he said quietly.

"You lost it? You take that thing everywhere," I teased, but as the words left my mouth, a sudden realization hit me.

*Did he use the knife on Jake?*

Charlie glanced back at me, not saying a word.

"You know what…I don't need it," I said quickly, shoving the thought aside. I took his arms and gently pulled them behind his back. "All I need is for you to put your hands here and keep them there."

I rose to my feet, aligning my body above his. He looked up at me, his eyes filled with desire and anticipation, fully submitting to me.

I lowered myself back onto my knees, positioning his body between my thighs. Arching my back, I leaned forward, letting my breasts hover close to Charlie's face. His eyes burned with desire as he tried to press his mouth against me, but I pulled back with a playful laugh, keeping him wanting more.

"I didn't say you could touch me, Charlie," I teased.

He groaned softly, the desperation in his eyes nearly making me give in.

"You drive me so fucking crazy, *mi diosa*," he said breathlessly, his gaze flicking between my eyes and my breasts, unable to resist.

I smiled and leaned in, my lips brushing his ear. "I know I do, baby," I whispered, sliding my legs open as I settled onto his lap, my pussy hovering just in front of his cock.

"Oh, fuck," he moaned as I gripped his length firmly, teasing him by letting my slick folds glide along the length of him. I swayed my hips slowly, driving him wild.

"Please," he begged, his voice breaking.

I couldn't help but bask in the sound of him begging. Smirking, I positioned the tip of his cock at my entrance, pushing in just enough to make him gasp before pulling back.

"No!" he groaned, frustrated. "Please, *mi diosa!*"

"I just love the sounds you make when you're desperate," I said, feeling a mischievous smirk on my lips. "Almost as much as I love feeling your cock stretch me." I teased him again, just the tip, before pulling away once more.

He whimpered, his hips lifting instinctively in search of me.

"How long do you think you'll last like this, baby?" I asked mockingly, arching my brows.

"I won't," he whined. "Please."

Stifling a giggle, I tilted my head. "Do you think it would be harder if I let you suck on my breasts?"

He bit down on his lip, his restraint slipping. "It would," he admitted, his voice low.

I leaned closer, letting my breasts brush against his face, and he didn't waste a second. His lips latched onto my nipple, sucking with a hunger that made my pussy twitch.

"You're getting me so fucking wet, Charlie," I moaned, stroking his cock with both hands as his mouth worked me.

He groaned into my breast, his desperate eyes meeting mine, silently begging for release.

"You better not come yet, baby. I'm not done with you," I warned, quickening my strokes before suddenly slapping his length and pulling my chest away.

"No!" he groaned, his frustration growing.

I smiled and stood, turning and lifting a leg to position myself so he was behind me, my ass in full view. Teasing him again, I slid his length against my entrance, my movements slow and steady. His moans grew louder, more desperate.

## ANA

"Please, *mi diosa*," he begged, his voice trembling. "Please, fuck me!"

"I'm going to need more begging, baby," I said playfully as I picked up my pace.

"Please, *mi diosa*, I need your pussy. I'm gonna fucking burst," he whimpered.

"Yeah? And whose cock is this?" I asked, glancing over my shoulder into his desperate, pleading eyes.

"Yours!" he gasped, his voice cracking.

"That's right," I said, finally positioning him at my entrance. With one swift motion, I pushed him deep inside of me, my hips moving quickly as I slid along his length.

"Oh, fuck, Ana," he groaned, his breaths uneven. "I'm gonna come."

I stopped abruptly, pulling him out. "Not yet, Charlie," I said with a laugh, enjoying his groan of frustration.

I continued to torment him, alternating between teasing and letting him inside me for only a few seconds at a time, until the tension built to an unbearable point—for both of us.

"Okay, baby," I finally said, shifting to face him, straddling his lap. My hands rested on his shoulders as I leaned in close. "You've been such a good boy. I'm going to fuck you until I come, and you may come when I say so."

With that, I sank onto his cock, his thickness filling me completely. I moved my hips quickly, chasing my release, the pleasure crashing over me in waves almost instantly.

"Come inside me, Charlie. Now," I demanded breathlessly, still trembling as the aftershocks of my orgasm coursed through me.

He let out a guttural moan, his hips lifting as he spilled into me, his face contorting with relief and pleasure.

As our bodies stilled, I tugged his hair gently, both of us catching our breaths.

"Thank you, *mi diosa*," he said softly.

I leaned forward, pressing my lips to his in a tender kiss, feeling completely recharged, like I was fully myself again.

\* \* \*

Charlie and I headed back to the apartment with Callan and Sloane after a few hours of restless sleep. The weight of what we'd all endured lingered in the air, but the quiet wasn't heavy or tense—it was the quiet of exhaustion, of survival.

Stepping into the apartment felt like walking into a sanctuary, leaving the horrors of the lake house behind us. The familiar space wrapped around me like a shield, offering a reprieve from the chaos of the last few days.

Sloane and Callan drifted towards the guest room without a word, their steps slow and heavy. I sat onto the couch with a deep sigh, my body sinking into the cushions as if they could absorb the tension still clinging to my muscles.

Charlie joined me, settling beside me and grabbing my hand. I leaned my head against his shoulder, his warmth everything I needed at that moment.

"Everything feels lighter now," I said quietly, closing my eyes.

"That's because it is," he murmured, his voice carrying a soft smile.

I tilted my head slightly to look at him. "Is it, though?"

He nodded, squeezing my hand. "You know...you didn't need me to rescue you. You got away from Jake on your own. Callan and I just...we stopped him before he got worse."

## ANA

I sat up straighter, searching his face for doubt. "Did you think I couldn't handle it on my own?" I asked, a flicker of uncertainty passing through me.

His dimpled smile melted the tension from my chest. "I never doubted you. I just hope you know it, too," he said, his voice low and full of reassurance.

I felt my breath catch as his words sank in.

"You've not only saved yourself, Ana," he continued, his fingers brushing over mine. "You've saved me. I was so fucking lost until I found you. This life—the fans, the music, all of it—it's nothing without you. I was so alone before, and now..." He paused, his eyes locking with mine. "Now I know I'll never be lonely again."

His words settled over me like a blanket, heavy and warm. I held his gaze, seeing the vulnerability there, the truth in every syllable he had spoken.

As I leaned back into the cushions, my thoughts began to spin, pulling me into the depths of everything that had brought us to this moment. Everything we'd done together, *for* each other, weighed against my chest, each memory surfacing like a ghost. The lies we told, the fights we endured, the manipulation and the desperate choices made in moments of panic, jealousy, and desire.

It wasn't a soft, gentle love story we had. It burned, bright and all-consuming. A fire that we couldn't escape, even if we wanted to.

And I'd known that from the beginning. I'd known we'd get burned.

I'd told myself when it all started, when his obsession first started pulling me in: I was playing with fire. And I was right. We'd both been scorched by this, scarred by it.

But as I sat there, his hand in mine and his eyes locked on me like I was the only thing that mattered, I realized something else.

I liked the burn.

I pressed my lips to his, the kiss slow but full of the fire that had always burned between us. When we pulled away, I smiled.

"I love you," I said.

"And I love you, *mi diosa*," he said, his grin matching mine.

As the moment stretched on, I knew one thing for certain: we'd gone to the edge and back for each other. We bled for each other. Lied for each other. Burned for each other.

And I'd do it all again.

Not because it was right, but because his love made me feel untouchable. And mine brought him to his knees.

Together, we weren't just in love. We were lethal, a force that devoured everything in its path…including ourselves.

# 30

# Charlie

Callan drove the boat deep into the Eastern Bay, seemingly miles from civilization, until the lights from town were just faint twinkles, like the stars above us. In the silence, I had too much time to think. I couldn't stop replaying the fact that I had just killed a man. Not just any man—the former President of the United States.

Callan had assured me we'd cover everything up perfectly, but I was still anxious with the unknown. What if Callan turned on me? What if he threw me under the bus, just as I had planned to do with him?

But then it hit me—he was just as deep in this as I was. He was the one who came up with the plan to wrap Jake's body in plastic, anchor it with bricks, and drive out into the sea. Like a real-life fucking *Dexter*.

The boat suddenly came to a stop, and Callan shot up, moving to the front of the small vessel. He turned back to me. "You helping me or what?"

I stood, grabbing Jake's feet as Callan stepped over the body, gripping beneath Jake's arms. Together, we lifted him and hurled him overboard. The body disappeared into the black water below, swallowed whole by the night.

Callan sat back into the driver's seat, starting the engine again. "I'll go back to the house to clean up. You head back to D.C.," he instructed.

I sat in the passenger seat beside him as we began to move. "I can help, you know. Clean up the fucking mess I made," I offered, though the exhaustion in my voice betrayed me, and even though I wanted to get back to Ana as soon as possible, I knew I needed to help.

Callan glanced at me, his tone softening. "You know, I would've done the same. If someone said that shit about my girl."

My eyebrows shot up. "So you and I are more alike than I thought," I said with a smirk.

"Nah," Callan said, shaking his head. "We're just men who'd do anything for the women we love. I guess it's not so bad that you're fucking crazy. Otherwise, you're right...the audio wouldn't have been enough." His gaze stayed fixed ahead, a small smirk rising on his lips.

I followed his line of sight. "You're sure you can cover this up?" I asked hesitantly.

Callan shot me a sidelong glance, a small, almost amused smile breaking through. "Yeah, Charlie. I'm sure. You're gonna have to trust me now. And I guess I'm gonna have to trust you."

I let out a dry laugh. "Yeah. Fuck."

The tension between us seemed to dissolve in that moment. Turns out killing someone and dumping their body together had a way of forging a connection that defied logic. Or maybe it was just that we both knew we were stuck with each other now.

He wasn't going anywhere, and neither was I.

After a few moments of silence, Callan spoke again, his voice casual. "You know, Leo's still rotting in jail." He slowed the engine slightly, glancing at me. "What are the chances of him getting away with the shit he pulled?"

A slow grin spread across my face. "I don't know, mate. Are you thinking what I'm thinking?"

Callan nodded. "You're gonna have to help me rack up more cash for Bart," he said with a laugh.

I grinned back at him, shaking my head. "See? I told you we're alike, my friend."

\* \* \*

Ana and I were backstage in my dressing room before the first show of the tour. I had just finished rehearsing, and Ana was sitting in front of the vanity, applying her red lipstick. She was so fucking stunning, and I couldn't stop thinking about how much my life had changed since she showed up.

She had filled the void in my life that I was desperately seeking for years. She showed me that it was okay to be vulnerable, that even if I was too much, I still deserved love. And she loved me despite my flaws, despite my growing need for her; in fact, she reveled in it.

She could see the darkness in me and match it, as if she wasn't afraid to step into the shadows I tried so hard to hide for years. She didn't flinch from the parts of me that felt too broken. She embraced them, made them her own. It was as though she understood the storm raging inside me because she carried one of her own.

She could take everything from me—my fears, my doubts, my control—and strip me bare, leaving me vulnerable in a way I never dreamed of letting anyone see. Yet in the very next moment, she'd give it all back. With just one kiss, she'd rebuild me, stronger, steadier, more whole than I ever thought I could be.

Her lips held power, not just over my body but over my entire being. In her kiss, there was fire and tenderness, chaos and calm. It was the perfect contradiction, just like us.

She didn't just meet my darkness; she challenged it, tamed it, turned it into something beautiful. And in doing so, she showed me that even the deepest shadows could hold light.

Ana wasn't afraid of me, of the unfiltered, unhinged version of who I was. She matched me step for step, holding her own while letting me fall apart in her hands.

She could see me in a way no one else ever had. She could shatter me and put me back together in a way that made me feel whole.

And she was mine. My salvation. My obsession. *Mi diosa*.

And no matter what it took, I would make sure she stayed that way.

Forever.

As I walked to the stage, her red lips on my cheek, claiming me for the world to see, the crowd's deafening cheers filled the air. But all I could think about was her. The fire we had created was eternal—and it burned brighter than ever.

# 31

# Epilogue

The tour bus rolled down the highway, the faint vibration running beneath my feet. The soft glow of the TV screen flickered above me, and nearby, a handful of bandmates lounged, chatting and laughing.

I sat in the corner, my knees tucked up against my chest, scrolling through my phone, my attention focusing between that and the TV. That's when a sudden news report filled the screen, the anchor's urgent voice coming through.

**Breaking News: Former President Jacob Martin Reported Missing.**

My chest tightened as the anchor continued.

"Authorities confirm that Jacob Martin, the 48th President of the United States, has been reported missing. Martin was last seen at his lake house in Maryland earlier this week. While investigators have not released further details, sources suggest foul play has not been ruled out."

The image on the screen shifted to a photo of Jake, smiling in that polished, practiced way that once captivated a nation. My stomach twisted, but not with fear. It was something far more thrilling.

Across the room, Charlie leaned against the kitchenette counter, laughing at something a bandmate had said. His ease was mesmerizing, his charm effortless, as if nothing in the world could touch him.

Then, the anchor's words must have reached him; his eyes flicked to the screen, catching the headline. He lingered there for just a moment before his gaze shifted to me.

A slow grin spread across his face. It wasn't the easy, charming smile he flashed for cameras or fans. It was darker, sharper, full of a knowledge we didn't need to speak of aloud.

My heart pounded as adrenaline shot through me, spreading like fire.

He knew it.

Now I knew it.

And that unspoken understanding passed between us in the space of a single glance.

Charlie looked back to his bandmate, his laugh returning, casual and unbothered, like he hadn't just confirmed what I had suspected all along.

I leaned back in my seat, my fingers resting lightly against my lips as I tried to calm my racing heart. The anchor's voice droned on, speculating on Jake's disappearance, but the words faded into the background.

I should have felt guilt. I should have felt fear or regret.

All I felt was exhilaration. *Pride.*

I glanced at Charlie again, watching the way his shoulders shook with laughter, the relaxed stance of his body, turning to glance at me every few moments, as if he was unable to help himself.

He did this—for me.

## EPILOGUE

I let a small smile curl at the corner of my lips, a quiet acknowledgment of what we'd done and where it had brought us.

This was who we were now. This was who *I* was now.

And I wouldn't change a thing.

# Acknowledgments

Thank you to Hollie and Lexy for being my hype ladies and alpha reading the first drafts of this book. You gave me all the confidence I needed to keep going and I appreciate you two from the bottom of my heart!

I would like to thank my beta readers for all of your input, encouragement, and kind words as always!

Thank you to my ARC readers for reading, reviewing, and helping to spread the word!

My family and friends who blindly support me—thank you for not reading my work and sparing us both the awkward conversation about some very detailed sex scenes. Your support (from a safe distance) is truly appreciated.

My husband—thank you for always believing in me and encouraging me to follow my dreams. I love you!

And thank *you* for reading this. I appreciate you and you make this all worth it!

# About the Author

Cassandra lives in Southern California. In her free time she enjoys tending to her house plants, reading, playing video games with her daughter, and laughing at cat videos with her husband.

**You can connect with me on:**
- https://authorcassandravega.com
- https://www.facebook.com/groups/372402495511960

www.ingramcontent.com/pod-product-compliance
Lightning Source LLC
LaVergne TN
LVHW011946060526
838201LV00061B/4219